Logan stood ~~beside her~~
The evening air continued its rush, chilling her skin. Violet waited for his answer.

She tried to ignore that her heart was recognizing the man—announcing so with its rapid beats. Her foolish heart mistook them for the kids that had clung to each other in the moonlight all those years ago. That was not who they were any more. Yet her heart—her source of life—did not care about that. It knew no calendar. Time had no effect on its memory. Violet's heart knew only that *this was Logan*.

He tilted his head and let one side of his mouth turn up into a smile. His dimple appeared like a pinch in his cheek. When she saw that dimple her heart reacted to it like a bold hussy—bumping and grinding against her ribcage. She touched her hand to her chest to steady the beat, to coax the pulsing traitor to *knock it off.*

From a review of M. Kate Quinn's **SUMMER IRIS**, first book of The Perennials series:

"A remarkable talent for creating realistic characters, secondary characters are as well developed as the main characters. One thing is for sure, M. Kate Quinn is definitely an author to keep your eye on!"
~*Detra Fitch, Huntress Reviews*

MOONLIGHT AND VIOLET

"An intriguing look at love the second time around. ...Quinn tugs at your heartstrings with her tale of love lost and found again. ...Family, love and honor meld together perfectly in a story as satisfying and comforting as a family Sunday dinner."
~*Caridad Pineiro*
NY Times & USA Today best-selling author

"I loved how Ms. Quinn wove intelligent humor and family issues into a heartwarming romance that is by every definition sweet and tender."
~*Jennifer Shirk, author*

Moonlight and Violet

The Perennials, Book Two

by

M. Kate Quinn

Moonlight and Violet: The Perennials, Book Two

COPYRIGHT 2011 by M. Kate Quinn

Cover Art by *Kim Mendoza*

The Wild Rose Press
PO Box 708
Adams Basin, NY 14410-0708
Visit us at www.thewildrosepress.com

Publishing History
First *Last Rose of Summer* Edition, 2011
Print ISBN 1-60154-890-7

Published in the United States of America

Dedication

To Margaret,
my authority on life, in and out of the kitchen.
And, to Bethy, my Dragon Slayer.

Chapter One

The moment she stepped foot into her parents' home Violet Terhune knew something was up. The aroma of her mother's signature tomato sauce wafted to her nose with the familiar scents of the family's traditional Sunday feast. Only, this was Wednesday.

"Ma?" Violet called from the entry. She tossed her purse onto the seat of the slip-covered sofa. After the stuffy train ride in from the City, she was glad for the coolness in the room. It was one of those unusually mild June days, the kind where all the windows in the house were open and the breezy air swirled through the rooms, making itself at home.

Violet looked around. She called out again. "Dad," she said, then waited. "Anybody home?"

Violet crossed the living room, the same scene it had been for more years than she could remember. Her father's tan brushed corduroy recliner sat empty in front of the white-washed brick fireplace. Her mother's canvas bag of crochet yarns was plopped beside the leather hassock.

Through the arched doorway into the dining room she saw the table was covered with a starchy Battenberg cloth. It was set with her grandmother's silver-rimmed china and the intricately-etched crystal wine goblets usually saved for holidays. This was absolutely no ordinary Wednesday.

Violet thought about the way her mother had sounded when she called two days ago to invite her over for dinner tonight. There had been a hint of urgency in her tone. At the time Violet had chalked that up to her mother's typical zeal for food preparation. It could have been that pork chops were on sale at the Shop Rite and her mother thrilled at the thought of serving them as their entrée.

Violet felt a familiar stab pinch at her insides. She never understood the penchant for cooking. If the trait was hereditary it had missed her by a mile. In spite of her mother's attempts to ignite a culinary spark in her eldest daughter, Violet did not burn with the desire to chop and slice and dice her way through gastronomic bliss. Penny, her baby sister, however got the cooking gene and a slew of their mother's other domestic traits. She even knew how to make a pretty impressive version of that aromatic sauce that wooed now from Ma's kitchen, the heart of Josephine Terhune's existence.

Dad's favorite music, one of those Irish tenor's woeful ballads, crooned out from inside the kitchen.

Violet made her way through the dining room and pushed open the swinging door revealing a familiar scene. Late-day sunshine filtered in through the gingham-curtained window above the double sink. The Formica countertops brimmed with stainless utensils, glass bowls, and a variety of jars to rival an apothecary. A heap of bright green basil sat on the thick wooden chopping board ready for its fate.

Her mother stood at the stove, a white enamel relic from God-knew-when, yet it gleamed like new. She stirred her masterpiece with a dexterous turn of her wooden spoon. Garlic and oil, onions and oregano, tomatoes and cheeses now bubbled over a low flame, and Violet, salivating over the intoxicating smells, was still in awe of the fact that each ingredient had surely been added without measurement. A pinch of salt, a palm-full of grated imported Romano, a drizzle of red wine. The woman never consulted a cookbook.

"You have to *feel* the food," Josephine always said. "You have to know *in here*,"—she'd add with a point to her temple and then finish the lesson with a hand to her heart and say—"But you have to know *in here*, too."

Now, Josephine turned to the doorway and pointed a finger at her eldest child. "Violet, for God's sake... You scared me half to death."

It was clear to Violet that the little spitfire of a woman was anything but scared, but her flair for the dramatic demanded the phrase. She wore a bright smile. Her face was still absent of wrinkles, even though she was pushing toward the ranks of septuagenarian. *It was all the olive oil,* is what Josephine always said. *No Oil of Olay for her. No siree.*

Josephine made a face when the tenor, Violet now recognized as Michael Daly, hit a high note in his melodic reverie of the Shannon River. Violet felt her mouth twitch with an impending grin. Her Italian mother had never learned to appreciate her Irish husband's taste in music.

"Charlie," she said to her husband. He sat at the kitchen table with his jigsaw puzzle splayed out in front of him. "Turn down that music. I can't hear myself think. Look, Miss New York has arrived."

That was Violet—*Miss New York.* Only, she was not a title holder of any pageant. And, the name was said with the same acridity as if her name was Benedict Arnold. Violet worked in the city as a feature writer for a small women's magazine, *Today's Hearth.* The fact that she now lived and worked in New York made Violet, in Josephine's eyes, a defecting chickadee from mama's New Jersey nest.

Charlie reached over to his CD player and turned the knob. A grin broke out over his affable face. He blew Violet a kiss then pushed his wire-rimmed glasses back up to the bridge of his nose.

"Hey, Dad."

"There's my girl." It made Violet's heart swell. Here she was forty-four years old and her Dad was still calling her *his girl*. In spite of his love for his wife's domestic excellence, Violet knew her father also appreciated that the only thing his eldest child would ever do with a cook book was diagram its sentences.

"What's going on around here, Daddy-o?"

Charlie nodded toward Josephine. "Ask the boss."

Violet crossed the room and stood beside her mother's small frame. "Okay, Ma," she said, thinking that either her mother was shrinking or she was growing taller. She didn't know which would be worse. "So, spill it."

"What do you mean?" Josephine asked with staged surprise. "Who says something's got to be going on?"

"Oh, come on, Ma," Violet said with a little chuckle, playing along with her mother's theatrics. She peered into the sauce pot and picked up the nearby wooden spoon that now sat in the ceramic chicken-shaped spoon rest. Violet sunk the spoon into the ruby mixture and stirred around like she was at the beach and the spoon was her metal detector. She lifted a find to the surface of the sauce.

"Ah, ha," she said.

"Ah, ha, what?" her mother asked.

"Sausage *and* meatballs."

"So?"

"So, it's Wednesday. And, you don't make a meal like this on Wednesday, and you don't set the dining room table, and you don't call me and give me a special invitation to come here for dinner, in the middle of the week."

"Can't a mother make a nice dinner for her

family?" Josephine asked, still with that odd grin on her face.

Violet closed an eye and twisted her mouth to one side. "I smell something cooking, and it's not just your sauce."

Charlie looked up from his puzzle and gave his daughter a wink. "You can't fool this one. She's too smart for you, Josie. She's on to you."

"Okay if she's so smart, when is she going to learn how to cook?" Josephine turned to Violet, her knuckles pressed to her hips. "When are you going to make *my* sauce? You're not getting any younger you know, Miss Big City."

Violet rolled her eyes and looked to her father for help. Charlie had turned in his spindle-backed honey-pine chair and faced the two women. He sat, smiling, expectant, like a child waiting for his favorite TV show to begin. The man had enjoyed the sparring between the two over the years too much to intervene. Violet knew she was on her own.

"Ma, why would I want to copy your sauce when I can come here and enjoy the real McCoy?"

Josephine smiled. Violet was hopeful that the compliment would end the discussion.

"You going to explain that to a potential husband?" Josephine asked. Her chin lifted and her shoulders raised high. She reminded Violet of a mad hen with puffed up feathers. This conversation was not over. Violet sighed.

"Come on. Don't start. It's been a long day."

"Ah, that city's taking the life out of you. You can't marry New York City. You can't make a family with New York City. When are you going to come back home and settle down?

"The Georgios down around the corner are selling their house. They just put all new windows in and added on a new deck. You could make a nice life there, Violet. You could get married and have a

5

family. It's not too late."

"Ma..."

"It's not! You see them in Hollywood? They're all having babies when they're in their forties. It's the modern thing to do. Nobody has babies early, like when I had you."

"I'm happy in the City. It suits me."

"Yeah? Good. I hope you and the City live happily ever after," Josephine said. She snatched the wooden spoon from its resting place and resumed stirring the sauce, this time with added gusto. "I'm not going to be around forever, you know. What are you going to do for meatballs and sauce after I'm gone? You going to buy Ragu?"

"You're not going anywhere for a long time. And when that day comes, in a billion years, I'll have Penny make sauce for me." Violet knew fully that she was playing right into her mother's hand.

"Huh! Thank God I have one daughter with some common sense."

The doorbell rang as if on cue. Violet heard her sister's familiar high-pitched chirp, a thirty-seven-year-old baby bird swooping back to the nest.

"We're here," Penny called out in sing-song. "Where is everybody?"

Penny appeared at the doorway to the kitchen, holding a foil-wrapped dish, undoubtedly some fabulous confection made with her pretty little hands. Beside her was the man of her dreams, Benjamin Layne. He held a large bouquet of spring flowers wrapped in clear cellophane in one hand and a bottle of champagne in his other. He grinned at Josephine with his winning, *I'm-a-dentist* smile.

He was not just the man of Penny's dreams, but it was apparent to Violet that this was the man of Josephine's dreams, too. Whenever Ben was around Josephine gushed with a school-girl's giddiness. Violet watched now as her mother flapped her arms around as though she was trying to take flight.

"Here *they* are," Josephine said as if she had just found her lost earrings. "Here they are."

Penny and Ben rushed at the wiry little woman and the three of them embraced like a team huddle.

Charlie got up from the kitchen table and gave Violet a look. He shook his head, his eyes alight with amusement. Violet went to him and gave her Dad a hug.

Violet and her father were the same five-feet-eight height, and they stood now, eye-to-eye. She gave him a long look. She also had his deep-sapphire-blue eyes. It had been his idea to name her Violet, a badge for having his eyes as well as his dark Irish looks. "What's this all about?" Violet whispered to him.

"Well, now that these two kids are here, maybe we'll all find out," Josephine said in response to Violet's question. The woman still had the hearing of a bloodhound.

"It's time for a toast!" Ben said, wielding the bottle of champagne with the triumph of Prince Charming's sword.

"Well then, let's go into the dining room," Charlie said. He pushed open the swinging door.

Josephine led the parade. Her husband was still at the kitchen doorway when Josephine called to him, like a doctor demanding a scalpel, "Charlie, bring the antipasto!"

****

It was a rock the size of a wisdom tooth. At least, Violet thought, this dentist probably had to extract a slew of them to afford such a ring. It was dazzling. As was the happy couple. Penny and Ben would soon become man and wife. They were already dentist and hygienist. Partners in livelihood would now become partners in life. It was sweet enough to give Violet a cavity.

Mr. & Mrs. Benjamin Layne. Violet closed her eyes and let the thought sit in her head. Her baby sister would forever be known as Penny Layne, the title of a Beatles hit. A title of another hit from the Fab Four popped into her head—*"Help!"*

"To Ben and Penny," Charlie said, raising a champagne flute that typically only saw the light of day at Christmas and Thanksgiving. "Congratulations!"

Everyone raised their glasses. As they took their polite little sip of the bubbly liquid, Ben made one more announcement. "Now for the *big surprise*," he said with his shockingly-white smile.

Penny looked to her man, her big brown eyes filled with anticipation. She turned to her mother and clapped her hands in rapid succession.

"Oh!" Josephine said. "Did you hear that? There's a big surprise."

Violet took a large sip of her champagne. She figured she might need it. *Maybe Ben has finally gotten Penny that pony she's been yapping about since she was eight.*

"Well, everyone," Ben said. With the dramatic pause of a game show host and the matching grin, he continued, "We've already made plans for our wedding."

Penny beamed her electric smile, nearly outshining the crystal chandelier that hung over their heads. Violet wondered if the happy couple had monogrammed whitening trays.

She reached over to the antipasto platter and stole a fat black olive. Josephine, with her brown spotlight hawk eyes saw Violet's hand and reached to swat it. Luckily, she was too far away. Violet popped the olive into her mouth with an exaggerated turn of her wrist and savored the salty morsel.

"The wedding is going to be in August. August 14th," Ben began. He reached over to give Penny's hand a gentle kiss. Penny tittered in a tone so high she might have been a helium balloon with a leak in it.

"And..." Ben continued, "We've booked The Pines in Vermont. We've made arrangements for all of us and our guests to stay for an entire week of wedding festivities."

Violet felt a stab in her chest so fierce, so real that it could have been the blade of her mother's best carving knife slicing her insides in two. Her mind buzzed with denial. *The Pines?* She swore all those years ago that nothing, absolutely *nothing* on earth, would ever get her to return there. *This can't be happening!*

She took a long sip of her water feeling as if she was drowning in it. It was as though she were moving and seeing things in slow motion. Violet forced herself to snap out of it. She physically shook her head and sat up straight in her chair. She needed to have a clear mind so she could finagle a way out of being any part of this.

Josephine pressed a hand to her ample bosom, and closed-eyed, softly called to Mary, the Madonna. It was nothing new. She usually spoke to the mother of God on special occasions like births, deaths, and such.

"Well, well..." Charlie said, running his hand over his still-thick head of hair. Violet noticed that it was now more gray than black and wondered when the ratio had changed. She touched her own hair, still jet like Charlie's had been. She inwardly acknowledged there was an occasional coarse gray, poking through here and there, ready for plucking.

"It's been a long time since we've been to The Pines. This will be fun. Good idea, kids."

"It was Ben's idea," Penny said, dripping with pride. "Can you believe this guy?"

"My sister is going to have a fit when she hears

this," Josephine said. "When her daughter got married they had a reception at the American Legion. Wait until she hears this one. Madonna."

Josephine enjoyed a healthy competition with her only sibling, Marguerite, even now that they each flirted with seventy. Violet couldn't help but smirk. Poor Marguerite would get an earful later. At least her aunt could hold over Josephine's head that Violet was still unmarried—a spinster by anyone's standards. And Violet was sure, Marguerite would remind Josephine of that when she was going on and on about the news of Penny's nuptials.

"Let's see," Charlie mused. "We haven't been to The Pines in how many years? Penny you were going into gymnastic competitions and we stopped going. What year was that?"

"Oh, who can remember?" Josephine said. "I'm going to put on the water for the ravioli. Everybody, come on, have some of the antipasto. Take some bread."

Violet remembered what year it had been, in spite of all the time it had taken to wrench the memory from her consciousness.

The last time they vacationed in Vermont at The Pines it was August, nearly twenty-five years ago. It was the year that Logan Monroe broke her heart into a million irrevocable pieces with the news that a local girl was pregnant with his child, and he had decided to marry her.

Just like that.

Nine summers of tender, young love. Nine winters of desperate letters and phone calls. Cherished visits to each others' homes, eventual college dates, ski vacations, promises for their future, love professed for eternity—all of it, halted in an instant.

It had taken much longer than an instant to get over the shock. Violet finally found a way to bury that whole chapter of her life like the rotten corpse that it was.

And, come hell or high water, she was not going back there to exhume it.

Chapter Two

"Benjamin and I had this long discussion about our childhoods," Penny said. She stabbed a meatball with her fork and passed the platter to Ben, the charming culprit of this bright idea. "I told him all about The Pines and what wonderful memories we have from all those summers. And that's when he came up with this incredible plan."

The meat platter made its way to Violet and she willed her hand to stop shaking so she wouldn't wind up with meatballs in her lap. Penny knew the summers at The Pines had ended dreadfully for Violet, and if she'd thought beyond her own gaga world she'd remember that.

"Oh, how we loved those summers in Vermont," Josephine said dreamily. She closed her eyes and smiled at whatever memory of perky little Penny probably came into her curly gray head.

"This is a dream come true," Penny gushed.

"No, Darling," Ben said, touching Penny's head of cinnamon curls. "*You* are the dream come true."

There was a collective "Ah," around the table. Violet's "Ah," however, sounded more like a reaction to a splinter. She washed it down with a sip of red wine.

"I dug out the old photo albums of our vacations," Penny said, reaching over to grasp Ben's hand. "Remember when I moved into my townhouse I took that box from the attic? It was so much fun going through all the pictures."

"I remember you were pretty handy with that camera of yours," Charlie said. "You were quite the little photographer."

Penny did her little chirp. "Remember my Swinger?" she asked. She then began to hum the old-time jingle that went with the popular camera. "It was my favorite birthday present."

"Ah, the Polaroid Swinger. I had one, too," Ben chimed in. "What were the words? Something about it being more than a camera, that it was almost alive. Right?"

"Yes!" Penny squealed. "Oh, Ben, we have so much in common!"

Everyone at the table laughed. And why not? It was a special Wednesday with a special event on the Terhune family's horizon. Violet's face felt frozen, as if the fake smile she had plastered on it would never go away. The more she anticipated the upcoming affair, the more her face felt like it would crack and fall to the floor in shards.

Ben whispered something to his bride-to-be and Penny nodded, her red curls bobbing like springs. He handed her a wrapped package that was about the size of a book.

Perhaps it holds a pair of gloves or maybe a couple pairs of panties, Violet thought. She felt a glimmer of delight tickle her insides. *Now that would be something. What would Mama say to the prized groom-to-be if he presented darling little Penny with token panties for an engagement gift right in front of her family? Maybe she'll throw the loaf of garlic bread at him and demand that the wedding be called off. Could happen.*

"Everyone," Penny said in a tone that spoke of a call to order. When the chatter around the table quieted, Penny smiled in Violet's direction, her dark brown eyes all a-glisten.

"I have something for you, Violet. But first, I would like to officially ask you to be my maid of honor."

Josephine applauded again. Then she made a kind of whooping sound. For a second Violet thought the woman might have swallowed an olive pit.

"Well..." Violet said, clearing her throat. She looked at the box extended toward her from across the table. She was convinced that her idea about panties had to be wrong. Obviously, unmentionables were not an appropriate token gift for a would-be maid of honor. And, neither were gloves unless the wedding was going to be a cotillion. But, who knew what other bright ideas this dazzle-mouthed duo might have concocted. Violet stretched her arm across the table and grasped the package.

"Open it, open it!" Penny trilled.

It was heavy. Violet started to wish the package actually did contain something ridiculously lacy that would catch her contours and chafe her raw. Because, so far, everything else about this was rubbing her the wrong way. The hairs at the back of her neck did their telltale prickle like the fret of a laundry tag. That was never a good sign.

She peeled off the wrapper gingerly, in long slow tears, watching diligently as each pull of the paper unmasked what she held. Her heart stopped in her chest when she recognized the red leather cover. *Where has this been? When did it re-surface?* Her girlhood diary now sat unabashedly in her grasp, the chronicle of all her so-called wonderful summers at The Pines.

It had been a Christmas present from her beloved grandmother. A thought zoomed through Violet's head about the irony of such a gift. The book, meant to record memories had been given to her by a woman who eventually fell victim to Alzheimer's, the disease that wipes memory clean. Violet traced the stitching, touched the brass lock and then the little nub of a button beside it. It was locked. As it should be.

14

"The lock's stuck," Penny said. "God only knows where the key went. But, I'm sure you can jimmy it with a bobby pin or something."

"Where did you find this?" Violet asked, not letting her eyes leave the book in her hand. Her voice sounded hollow to her own ears, haunted by the ghost at her fingertips.

"In the box that was in the attic. It was with all my pictures."

Violet looked up and scanned everyone's faces. She read their expressions to see if they had picked up any clue to the fact that she was feeling rather ill. She felt as if Ma's meatballs had turned to lead in her belly.

She would have been better off if this *had* been a box of panties, and she'd been asked to don them right there and then. Four pairs of expectant eyes waited for Violet's reaction. She needed to dig deep to pull off a believable version of what they wanted to hear.

Her eyelids fluttered closed and she breathed in the succulent aroma that normally belonged to a Terhune Sunday. The truth sat in her head like a tumor. There was no way out of this blessed event and all that went with it. Like a cluster of basil with its tender leaves on the chopping block, Violet needed to accept her inevitable fate.

"Thank you, Penny. I had forgotten all about this thing." Violet turned the diary over in her hand, making her wrist relaxed, loose. She kept her voice steady. "A nice memory to hold onto. Thanks."

"You're welcome," Penny said. She looked over to Ben and gave his hand a squeeze.

"And, yes. Of course I would love to be your maid of honor." She had succeeded in pulling a cheery tone out of thin air.

The merriment resumed as if someone had pushed an "on" button. The room was again filled with the energy of good news. All the while the diary sat in Violet's lap. Waiting.

"Violet?" Benjamin asked, as he sipped his cappuccino during dessert. As she suspected, that foil-wrapped plate Penny had carried into the house contained a fabulous dish—marble cheesecake she undoubtedly had prepared in her spare time between x-raying the jaws of Benjamin's patients. "You think you'll have any trouble getting an entire week off for the wedding?"

Violet thought of her job at the magazine. She felt her mouth pull sideways, her classic reaction to the mere mention of *Today's Hearth*. Things were precarious these days. Violet's boss, the head of the feature department, was all gloom and doom. Ted Solomon blamed the internet for the slower sales quotas.

He was a sixty-year-old snail that refused to embrace progress. He still dictated memos to his secretary rather than key them into his laptop. He was a throwback to the old days at the magazine and Violet knew that included a work ethic that did not call for a whole week off to go to a wedding.

Somehow she would find the way to work it out. She knew a wall when she was backed up against it. And there was no wall more rock solid than the united force of her family.

"Oh, I'm sure it will be fine," Violet said. She wondered if she sounded convincing.

"You think that Mr. Salami of yours will let you go?" Josephine asked. She started to clear the table of dessert dishes.

"It's Solomon, Ma."

"Josie, be nice," Charlie said, though his eyes beamed with amusement. After all these years the man still got a charge out of his feisty wife.

Josephine shrugged. "I just think that man could be nicer to Violet. He's always giving her grief.

How many times does he send her messages on that blueberry of hers?"

"Blackberry, Ma."

"Oh, who cares what kind of fruit he talks on," Josephine said. "Why doesn't he just call you on the phone? Wouldn't that be easier?"

"Please," Violet said as she stood to give her mother a hand with the dishes. "I just got him to communicate on his Blackberry. It was like pulling teeth."

Violet looked over to Benjamin who was in the middle of kissing the top of Penny's newly-diamonded hand. "No offense there, Ben," she said.

Ben lifted his head from his kissing pose. "No offense taken, Violet. I enjoy any reference to being a dentist. I love what I do."

Now there was a concept, Violet thought. *Loving what you do.* She had always wanted to write, to make a difference with her words. She had big ideas of what she was going to do after she graduated college. When she got the job at the magazine she thought she was on her way.

Instead she had spent the last decade writing nonsensical articles about how to make a pinecone wreath for the holidays and how to set your table for High Tea. These concepts may have been valid to some women—women like her mother Josephine and her little red-headed clone—but to Violet it was drivel. Yet, that drivel paid her enough to have a nice apartment in the City. It was the one place that Violet knew might someday give her an opportunity to really write something with some substance, some purpose.

She carried a stack of dessert plates into the kitchen and placed them beside the sink. Picking up a dish towel, she stood at the ready as her mother carefully dipped each dish into the water.

"No dishwasher for this china," Josephine said,

as she did every time the set came out of the breakfront. "It would chew them up for sure."

Violet placed each plate onto the kitchen table after she dried them. Josephine, whose arms were immersed in sudsy water nearly up to her elbows, turned to her daughter. By the cock of her head Violet knew she meant business. "So, you want to tell me about the diary?"

Violet stopped drying the dish she held, and stared at her mother. Did a mother's radar ever diminish? Violet knew better than to feign ignorance.

"It's my diary from when I was a kid. You know me, Ma, I've been putting pen to paper since I was born."

"What was with the face?"

"What face?"

"When you saw it you had a face like you just stuck your hands into a dead chicken."

Violet tossed the towel onto the counter. Her mother would gnaw on this until she was satisfied with her answer. She wasn't about to tell her mother the truth.

How freeing it would be to just yell it out and declare that she hated the whole idea of going up to Vermont to revisit the past. And that she couldn't wait to throw that blasted diary into the nearest dumpster. Violet bit her lip. She wasn't sure just how much playacting she could muster in one night.

"It's silliness, that's all," Violet said with a shrug and a re-plastered smile. "The ramblings of a kid. But I know Penny meant well by wrapping it up like a present and all."

"What's in there? Stuff about that Logan boy?"

'That Logan boy' is now forty-six years old. And yes, Violet thought, *the diary was loaded with Logan.* "Ancient history," Violet said. She gave her mother a little nod, hoping she seemed nonchalant.

18

Josephine smiled; the kind of closed-eyed lipless smile that Violet knew meant she was satisfied. Violet had played it well enough and her mother would now drop the inquisition.

"Violet, you'll probably read it and laugh," Josephine said. "You'll crack up."

"You're right, Ma." Only Violet had no intentions whatsoever of reading a single syllable of that historical tome.

****

On the ride back to the City, Violet tried to distract her thoughts from the past.

She wondered about what kind of maid of honor dress Penny would choose for her. Since they would be up at The Pines did the lovely bride and groom want a woodland theme? She tried to imagine it. *Maybe Ben will dress as a wood sprite and Penny would be a fairy of some kind—yes! A tooth fairy!*

Violet wiped the smile off her face when another image entered her mind. Logan Monroe was there in her head, blond, sun-browned, young and handsome in cut-off blue jeans and a white tee shirt. It was a vision that hadn't crept into her head in a long, long time.

She pushed the automatic window button and let in some cool evening air. Hopefully, the chilly rush would scatter any thoughts of Logan and those days back when.

The diary sat beside her on the passenger seat, looking like a long lost friend. She thought of tossing it out the window, but with her luck someone would find it, read it and post it on Facebook. She toyed with bringing it home and burning it in her fireplace, but the fireplace was gas and the logs were made out of some synthetic material that didn't actually burn.

When she pulled into her parking garage she thought to leave the diary in the car, but it was in her hand when she unlocked her apartment door.

Violet flipped on the living room lamp illuminating the tidy space in warm, yellow light. She tossed her purse and her leather tote onto the sofa and kicked off her sensible, city-walking shoes. Her feet ached as did her head.

She padded to the kitchen and snapped on the light over the small center island. How she loved this square granite-topped surface. For her it was more of a workplace than a cooking zone. She ran her hand over the cool stone slab and looked around the tiny room with its clean lines and smooth planes.

There were no utensils cluttering her space, no bottles of crushed leaves and dried whatnot littering her open shelves. This was how she liked her kitchen. The place had been hers for over a decade. *A decade!* Violet shook her head. *Where did all the time go? What do I have to show for all that time?*

She noticed the diary still in her hand. She tossed it onto the counter like a hot potato.

Violet pulled a ceramic mug from the cabinet by the sink and filled it with water, a routine she had down to a science. She stuck it in the microwave and pushed the "fast cook" button. When the bell rang she withdrew the hot mug and plunged a packet of herbal tea into the steamy liquid. Presto, she had tea. All in all, it took about a minute.

Her cook top was free and clear of any cumbersome tea kettle. The copper-bottomed pot her mother had given her for Christmas one year was still in its box, stuffed up on a shelf in the coat closet under her bucket of hats and gloves.

She tossed the soggy teabag into the trash and slid onto the wrought-iron-framed counter stool. Her eyes found the diary. It was amazing that something so old could still have such energy. It was as though the book called to her, beckoned her to hold it.

Violet touched her fingertip to it tentatively, as

though it might burn her skin. Slowly she traced the gold-embossed words emblazoned across the leather in fancy script. *My Diary.* She forced her hand away, wrapped her fingers around the handle of her mug and lifted it to her lips. But her eyes were still on the diary.

Her finger reached for it again. This time it found the little brass button, the only thing holding the contents away from Violet's eyes. She pressed it, waited then pressed it again. She tapped it rapidly, as if giving signals in Morse code. She wondered how many clicks and pauses it took to spell out *idiot.*

She took a long swig of her tea, felt the warmth of it surge through her. She hoped the tea would bathe her in logic. But the chamomile had no mercy. Violet wacked the button with the heel of her hand. Nothing. She pressed her elbow to it and held it down. When that didn't budge it, Violet stood up and slapped her now-empty mug onto the lock. A hunk of ceramic broke off and shot across the room. The lock stayed stuck.

A mad woman now, Violet yanked open the top drawer of her island. A measly selection of spoons and spatulas rattled around in the big space. She lifted an egg beater, examined it for its strength, then threw it back into the drawer.

At the very back, behind the never-used package of wine glass rings, she found what she needed. She lifted the stainless steel meat mallet into her hand and almost laughed diabolically. It had been one of the more affordable items for purchase at a co-worker's home cooking party, her attendance at such an event nothing short of preposterous. She never thought she'd find a use for the device, but now with the weight of it in her hand, Violet was sure of its purpose.

One good whack and the lock sprung open like a jack-in-the-box. But what jumped from the pages of the old book was no Jack. It was Logan Monroe.

****

August 16, 1975
Dear Diary,

I thought this was going to be the worst vacation ever. I mean all the way up here I kept thinking how everybody in the whole world gets to go someplace cool for vacation like Disneyland or Hawaii, but we have to go to the woods. The woods! And my parents were singing campfire songs in the car during the entire ride and Penny joined in because she's five and she's an idiot. I wouldn't sing.

I just kept looking out the window watching the scenery change like a fast movie thinking how I could have stayed with my best friend, Libby, for the whole two weeks. But my parents said, "No, this is family time." They don't get that when you're twelve, you don't want family time. You want your best friend.

When we finally got here, the first thing I noticed was the sign at the end of the long driveway. It's a carved hunk of wood shaped like, what else, a pine tree, and it says "Welcome To The Pines," and my first thought was, "get me out of here." But then we pulled up to the entrance of this big building that looks like somebody made it out of Lincoln Logs and the owner and his son came out to greet us. And that's when everything changed.

He's fourteen and his name is Logan. He's tan, the color of an acorn, and he has thick straight blond hair with bangs that keep falling into his eyes. He has the bluest, prettiest eyes I've ever seen. And they were looking at me! Libby is never going to believe this.

Chapter Three

Violet was groggy when she awoke the next morning. She had fallen asleep with her bedside lamp on and the diary on her chest. She flipped the book onto the floor with a swipe of her hand, tugged off the covers and pushed herself out of bed.

Hopefully a steaming hot shower would shock some sense into her. She had to get to work early. She had a mission.

Violet walked through Ted Solomon's office doorway swinging a bag of donuts. She knew the way into this man's heart, if he really did in fact possess one.

Ted was a barrel-chested, squat man with a ring of gray hair encircling his bald head like a fringe. Thankfully, he had stopped combing those long strands over the naked skin of his head in that pathetically feeble attempt to look non-bald. To Violet's—and everyone else in the Feature Department's—relief Ted Solomon had finally accepted his baldness.

It was just seven-thirty, a full half hour before the rest of the staff would arrive. Violet wanted to get the man alone so she could ask him about time off for the wedding week in August. Violet's thoughts went right to the diary. *So much for tossing the blasted book into a dumpster.*

Ted was at his computer, hunched in front of the screen.

"Good morning," Violet said.

Ted spun around in his ergonomic chair. "Hey, you're early," he said. "Did you hear me using your name in vain?"

"No, why?"

"This stupid computer just won't cooperate. I hate it. I can't open the attachments on any of my emails."

"Maybe we need to call the tech guys again," Violet offered as she pulled a wheeled task chair over to Ted's work station.

"I'd rather throw the damn thing out the window," Ted said.

Violet put the brown paper bag on the work surface in front of Ted.

"What's that?" he asked. His voice was still filled with frustration.

"Two jellies and a Boston cream."

"You trying to kill me, Terhune?" Ted asked, with one eye squinted closed. He sounded suspicious but his mouth turned up into a reluctant smile.

"You don't have to eat them all at once, Ted."

"So, what brings you to the office early, with your bag of sugar?"

"Can't a girl just be nice?"

Ted narrowed his eyes. "Oh sure. Like I said, what's up?"

Just then Ted's Blackberry sounded and he pulled the device from a leather pouch clipped at his waist. He shouted into it as though it were a walkie-talkie. Violet felt a chuckle forming in her throat. She got up from her chair and walked across the room to give her boss some privacy with his call. No easy task considering he was screaming nearly at the top of his lungs.

Violet eyed the framed black and whites that lined the long wall of Ted's office. The man was great at the helm of the magazine's feature department. But his love, Violet was sure, had to be photography. She never tired at studying the shadows in his images, the multiple shades of gray that created mood as much as it captured moments in time.

Violet continued to give an ear to Ted's yelling as her eyes feasted on a photograph of a large barren tree in winter. Ted snorted with a tone of disbelief and her nose for news came alive.

She pulled her eyes from the frames on the wall and stepped over to the drip coffee maker on the counter. She proceeded to listen to Ted's responses while she scooped grinds into the paper filter, hoping not to lose count as she paid more attention to Ted than to his special blend of dark roast. Whatever this was about, Ted sounded furious. And that made Violet nervous about having to ask for the week off in August.

When Ted hung up from the call, he tossed his Blackberry onto the counter. He ran his hand over his bald head and closed his eyes.

"Coffee's on," Violet offered.

Ted looked up at her with surprise as if he had forgotten she was in the room.

"Violet, we're in trouble." Ted's voice was low, soft even. He almost never called her by her first name. He sounded defeated, tired, and old. Violet crossed the room and sat back in the chair beside him.

"What's going on, Ted?"

"We've run out of time. Corporate's going ahead with the merge."

Violet's heart fluttered in her chest. Rumors had zoomed around the office for weeks that their parent company planned to either merge or abandon some of their magazines dependent on the circulation numbers.

She knew that *Today's Hearth* was losing its readership to other venues in spite of recent campaigns to boost sales. Many magazines were in the same boat. But, wasn't a merger better than a collapse? "And *Today's Hearth* is merging with whom?"

"*Country Charm*," Ted spat, as though he had just cursed.

Violet let out a little groan. *Country Charm Magazine* was simple and basic, and involved ladies' household advice that appealed to what Violet believed was the bygone homemaker. Women just didn't put up preserves or make quilts for wedding gifts any more. Today's woman was busy. She had a schedule a mile long, a job to do, aside from a desire for nesting. At least *Today's Hearth,* with all its annoying domestic focus, spoke to that woman.

How could the parent company possibly think merging the two magazines would be a viable solution to fledgling sales? To Violet, this was not the solution to save the outdated *Country Charm.* This was the sure way to bury it and have it drag *Today's Hearth* right along with it into the grave. "That's crazy."

"It's suicide," Ted said. He reached into the paper bag and retrieved a jelly donut.

He held it out toward Violet and she shook her head. They needed more than sugar to solve this problem.

"So, when is this going to happen?" Violet asked.

"Yesterday," Ted said, his mouth full of jelly and dough. Granules of sugar peppered his lips.

"Yesterday!" Violet said. "What do you mean, yesterday?"

"As of the close of business yesterday, phase one began for combining the two magazines to come up with something entirely new."

"What do they plan to call this new magazine? Modern Frankenstein?"

Ted laughed sardonically and shrugged a shoulder. "Guess we'll find out at the big meeting."

"What big meeting?"

"Ten o'clock, our conference room. All the head

honchos."

Violet's heart sank. The future of *Today's Hearth* would be determined by a bunch of suits that thought women only found happiness in their glue guns and tubes of glitter.

"By the way, Terhune," Ted said, lifting the donut bag. "You never told me the reason for these *heart attacks in a bag*. What'd you come here so early to say to me?"

She had resigned herself to the reality that there was no way around being part of Penny's marathon wedding hoopla. Even if it did mean coming face to face with Logan after all these years. But she also knew this was the worst possible time to petition Ted for a week off from the troubled magazine. "It can wait, Ted." She took a deep breath in spite of the fact that she felt suffocated.

****

The top brass sat around the highly glossed conference table, all of them in dark, pinstriped suits—even the women.

Stacey, their office manager, and Shari, Ted's secretary, had somehow managed to pull together a continental breakfast, a feat that impressed Violet as though she were a kid at a magic show. One minute the announcement had been made that the head honchos were coming and the next, these two office genies had produced a spread of cut-up fresh fruit, halved bagels, and a variety of muffins.

This was a skill Violet just didn't possess. If prepping for this meeting had been her job, she'd have raided the vending machines in the lunchroom and provided enough water and pretzel sticks for all. Again, she wondered how the instinct had bypassed her. Sometimes she felt like a freak of womanhood.

What she did have was words. She loved the sounds of words, their origins, their meanings, their emotion. To Violet there was the same pleasure in poetry and well-written prose that Penny or their mother found in a perfectly flakey crust.

Violet also knew how to read the faces on the well-dressed intruders to their magazine's world. She believed that this was a sham, not a meeting at all. This was not a forum to express ideas. These people were not here to bat around the strategies of what to do with the merger of two magazines. It had already been decided among them at some meeting they had held in their own conference room at corporate headquarters.

Violet sat beside Ted Solomon and waited for him to jump in and fix everything like he always did. But, the suits wouldn't let him. "Why don't you just can *Country Charm?*" Ted asked finally. "I mean, come on, people. Look at the numbers. They're a sinking ship. We're holding our own here. Besides, we've got some ideas on boosting—"

"But, Ted..." Emil Harrison, the company's big cheese, sitting at the head of the table interrupted. And this cheese smelled, as did his tone. He sounded like a parent tired of listening to his whiney kid.

Violet didn't like it. She felt the hair on the back of her neck scratch at her skin. Her jaw tightened. Ted's head feature writer jumping up and yelling like a banshee would not help preserve his credibility. But, she wanted to.

Maybe *she* could complain about the opinionated curmudgeon at her side, but it was not okay for this Emil Harrison to cut him off like an unwanted appendage.

"What, Emil?" Ted said through clenched teeth. "'But what?"

"But, Robert here has big plans for the two publications. Plans that could turn this around for both magazines. You want to be a team player, don't you Ted?"

Violet followed Ted's gaze to the man directly

opposite him. Robert Matthews, a tall, young snake in Brooks Brother's wool. He held the same top spot at *Country Charm* that Ted did at *Today's Hearth*.

His smarmy smile deserved a reaction. Violet eyed the platter of muffins at the center of the table and fought the urge to flip one of the gold foiled squares of butter right at his kisser. She folded her hands in her lap instead.

"Ted," Matthews said, as though his mouth were full of sweet, rich butter, "This merger will prove to be the best for everyone. You'll see."

"It's progress," Harrison added. All the suits nodded like a convention of bobble heads.

It was all over by noon. The big wigs exited in pairs, like pallbearers minus the casket. There had indeed been a death. That was for sure.

Violet sat alone at the conference table. She fingered the paper doily that lined the tin tray. The only thing left was half of a bran muffin and a multi-grain bagel. She snickered. She guessed with all that bull the brass had slung at them, nobody in the room needed any extra fiber today.

Stacey and Shari were back, ready to remove the remnants of the so-called meeting. Stacey, with Windex in hand, squeezed the trigger and squirted a fine mist onto the table. She leaned over and swept a fistful of paper towels across the dewy expanse.

"So?" she asked. "Violet, what's the scoop?"

"I have to talk to Ted," Violet said, looking around, only noticing now that he had closed his door.

"Yes, go see what Ted thinks about all this," Shari said. "Find out if we'll all still have jobs."

That was the million dollar question, and it didn't take a ton of math ability to figure that two staffs merged into one magazine meant too many employees, plain and simple. Violet thought about what had just occurred—people's livelihoods being decided over a friendly tray of baked goods. Where anyone stood in the land of pink slips was something Violet didn't know. But, she was going to find out.

She gave a quick rap of her knuckles on Ted's door and then went in. He stood at the window, his back to her, shoulders slumped, hands jammed into his pants pockets.

"Ted..." She walked toward him cautiously, as though trying not to wake him. But she knew Ted was not asleep. He was wide awake, fully cognizant of what had just happened.

"It's over, Terhune. For me, anyway,"

He didn't move his head, kept staring out at the buildings along the crowded cityscape. Violet looked out through the glass. She eyed the windows dotting the faces of the brick and plaster buildings. She wondered if anyone in them was gazing out, too. Was anyone else searching for answers, the kind that Ted Solomon already knew were not there?

"It's not over yet, Ted," Violet said, with half conviction. They both knew that although management hadn't so much as said that *Country Charm's* Feature Editor, Robert Matthews, would be named the head of the new magazine. It was inevitable. Ted was over sixty years old. Robert was in his thirties, and his nose was as brown as dirt. There might not be any answers out that window, but Violet and Ted both knew the writing was on the wall.

"Hey," Violet said. "I'm in the same boat." It was true. Violet, as Senior Feature Writer, would have to compete to keep her position.

Country Charm's head writer was someone Violet had never met, but apparently, this Melanie Rosen was a powerful force for her magazine. Violet had heard in the meeting that Melanie was a wonder child, fresh out of college, with credentials coming out the old wazu. Apparently she lived in an A-frame in the woods smack dab in the middle of real live country charm.

Violet was sure the girl chopped her own wood and made gourmet meals out of stuff she found in the forest. She had no idea how she was supposed to win out on such a rivalry, especially if the new magazine were to lean more toward the old-fashioned views of *Country Charm*.

One thing Violet knew, however. She would not be able to stand writing anything even more inane than she was already asked to produce. It was bad enough that she had to tap into her flair for fiction when describing the ideal dinner party, when her real dinners were often a tableau of white boxes from the take-out Chinese place. She simply could not write about the wondrous things in the country. She would rather face unemployment.

The Pines came to mind. In August she would get one heck of a dose of the country, laced with a dollop of Ben and Penny's sappy charm. Her head started to spin.

She closed her eyes against the view out the window, the thoughts of the merger, and especially against the idea of spending a week in the woods. In a matter of hours country living had somehow become the focal point of her entire existence. And, there was nothing the least bit charming about it.

All she wanted to do was go home and sit in a darkened room.

Yet, there would be no respite awaiting her in that Pottery Barn-accented haven.

Not anymore.

When she returned there an irresistible red leather book with its lock smashed open by her own hand would beckon her.

Again her resolve would crumble like the dry, fragile cornflower pressed between its pages.

****

August 17, 1976
Dear Diary,

Today Logan took me through walking trails. I watch his eyes when he talks. They shine like the sun lives in them.

We picked flowers for his mother's dining table vases, putting them in a bucket of water he carried to keep them fresh. He showed me his favorite place— the hunter's cabin near the edge of the lake. It has this open slat up along the top of the wall that looks out over the water for hunters to poke their guns out so that when they see a duck they can aim for it. I hate hunting and I'm glad that Logan's parents don't allow it at The Pines. I guess the people that used to own the property built it.

We stood together at the opening and looked out over the shiny water. Then Logan plucked a flower out from the bucket and handed it to me, a purplish blue cornflower that he said looks nice with my eyes.

I'm pressing it right here on this page so I can remember this day forever. Today is the day Logan picked me a cornflower and then held my hand on the walk back to the lodge. Palm pressed to palm, fingers laced, we walked like that until the trees parted at the end of the path.

Chapter Four

The only thing that remained the same was that the honchos had decided to keep *Today's Hearth* as the name of the newly formed magazine. Everything else was a train wreck. They closed *Country Charm's* offices, leasing out the space they had occupied with as quick and callous a move as a bulldozer's scoop at a cemetery.

Violet was saddened by the number of staff members that lost their jobs. There were a string of luncheons planned to provide chances for the ones saved from the ax to bid fond farewells to those who had been severed from their livelihoods.

Ted, thankfully, was safe. But, not in his former capacity, now being called the "Feature Consultant." Robert Matthews, as predicted, was the new head of the department. To give the insult an added jab, Ted would have to relinquish his office to make way for Mr. Apple Polisher.

While Ted wasn't out the door, Violet wished her future at the magazine was as clear cut.

Matthews called her into what had in no time become his office. She entered the room marveling at his books already lining the shelves and pictures of his family looking out from pewter frames. There was no apparent sign of Ted anywhere. It was like a heartless tornado had whipped in and had its way.

Melanie Rosen sat in one of the guest chairs. She was all of twenty-five or -six, athletically lean, very natural looking. She wore little or no makeup and donned a crisp man-cut shirt tucked into razor sharp creased chinos.

Violet looked down at her own standard lightweight business suit, purchased from the sale rack at Lord and Taylor, and suddenly felt like a throwback to Mary Tyler Moore in her television sitcom.

"Melanie, this is Violet. Violet, meet Melanie."

The two women shook hands. Violet noticed the girl wore no rings on her long well-manicured fingers. Her handshake was firm, her palm cool. She had the distinct look of intelligence in her dark eyes. *Maybe,* Violet thought, *just maybe this Melanie and I can become allies, comrades to band together and take the new hybrid publication to great heights. We're united by the fact that we're women. We might even knock Robert Matthews onto his pinstriped ass.* Violet smiled at her, ready to begin.

"I've heard a lot of good things about you, Melanie."

"Thank you."

Violet waited for a returned compliment, a verbal confirmation that they would become a Batman and Robin of sorts that would take on the whole new regime. She waited some more. But the reciprocal olive branch never came from Melanie's lips, slapping Violet's daydream right out of her head.

Robert cut into the silence with a swift slice of reality. "Ladies, here's the deal," he said. He tapped his shiny monogrammed pen against its onyx stand. "The new *Today's Hearth* has its debut in October. I want each of you to come up with a brilliant idea to launch the new format. The key is *earthy and wholesome*, with a yuppie spin. I want something that's going to make every young urban professional want to make room in her closet for a good pair of Franco Sarto boots to sit alongside her Kate Spade flats. You get what I'm saying?"

Melanie crossed her leg, pinching two fingers

along the sharp crease of her pant, and then folded her hands in her lap. Now she found her voice—her tone cool and clear like a mountain stream. "And, what then, Rob? Winner takes all?"

Violet started to feel like a contestant on a game show. *Whoever produces the better feature gets a contract to stay on board? Maybe they'll throw in a washer/dryer combo. Is this what my future will be reduced to? Wonder if I'll get the option to phone a friend?*

Robert let out a low chuckle, then shook his head at Violet's smug-faced competitor. "Melanie, you always cut right to the chase."

"Yes, and you always go for the drama."

Violet thought, *these two youngsters just need a sandbox. It's quite obvious that this is how they play together. And I'm outside the box, without a shovel.*

"There's room for both of you on the new staff, but there's just one top spot. Whichever one of you earns it gets it. Simple."

Violet nibbled on her gelled fingertip, feeling the cushiony fake coating on top of her nail. She knew one thing; she was too old to play in this sandbox. But, she needed her job and she was glad that it sounded like the magazine would be more cosmopolitan than *Little House on the Prairie*. That gave her an advantage. She would come up with just what Mr. Robert Matthews wanted. She would think of something.

"Rob, don't forget. I'm flying to California the end of August," Melanie said.

"I remember. Reunion or something, right?"

"College roommate getting married," Melanie corrected, her mouth turning into a sly grin. "But, I already have an idea for an article."

"Really?" Rob prodded, glancing over at Violet. She felt her jaw ache from chomping down on her teeth. Not only was Melanie going away in August too, but she already had a plan.

"Want to give us a hint?"

"I'll give you two words." Melanie said, her voice coated in honey.

"We're listening," Rob said. Violet smiled as if she was also eager for Melanie's stupid two words. *Maybe they will be, "I quit."*

"Wine country."

Robert leaned his upper body forward, planting his hands on the surface of what just yesterday had been Ted Solomon's desk. Then he pulled his eyes over to Violet, his look filled with the electric charge of challenge. If he wanted fear from Violet, he wouldn't get it. She nodded a quick jerk of her head.

"I like it," Robert said. "Just make sure you get your piece to me before Labor Day." Then he turned to Violet. "You have any problems with a Labor Day deadline?"

"I..." Violet hesitated, letting her eyes scan the room as she collected her thoughts. Her gaze fell onto a couple of file boxes on the floor. Picture frames jutted from them at haphazard angles. Ted's photo gallery had been packaged, ready to go. She shifted in her chair and began again. "I will be away the middle week of August."

"Will you?" Robert asked, with a tone that sent a distinct message to Violet's ears. A message that asked if she was sure she wanted to take a detour when the race had just begun.

"My sister is getting married and, uh, I'll be at a lodge in Vermont for the week."

"A lodge in Vermont? Well, lucky you, Violet. What better place to come up with a piece for a magazine that seeks to appeal to the woodsman in all of us DINK's. Looks like you've been handed a stroke of luck."

She imagined herself at The Pines, amidst all the wedding hoopla, trying to come up with an angle geared toward the young married urban professionals with double incomes and no kids—the demographic that formed Robert's acronym.

As a bonus, she would have to conjure that gem of an idea in the proximity of Logan Monroe and, undoubtedly, his wife and child—or possibly children. Maybe a dozen little Logans would be running all over the place.

After all these years just seeing Logan would be an acute reminder that there was another time in her life when she had lost the game. Yes, she had lost then, but she would not lose now.

"My thoughts exactly," Violet said, with enough conviction that she almost believed herself.

Chapter Five

Violet kept the news about her job situation from her family. This was Penny's time to shine and she didn't want to be the one to dampen the plans for all the festivities. Nor give their mother another reason to cluck her tongue at Violet's state of affairs.

So on Saturday, when it was dress shopping time, Violet glided into Debonair Bridals wearing a well-plastered smile.

Violet had trudged down Park Place, glancing appreciatively at the little square park in the heart of her hometown, Morristown. She circumvented a lineup at the hotdog vendor, waited at a crosswalk crowded with ready shoppers, then moved to the other side of the street.

Penny and their mother were already in the boutique, perusing the sample rack, when she stepped inside. The saleslady—a small framed, middle-aged blonde with a tape measure dangling around her neck like a string of pearls—turned to her.

"Well, well, this must be our matron of honor." She pushed rhinestone-trimmed glasses up on her over-powdered nose.

"Maid," Josephine corrected, with a tone as sour as a pickle and a look that matched.

"Oh, I'm sorry," the saleslady said. "I just assumed…"

She didn't finish the sentence, and she didn't have to. Violet was used to it. Most people in suburbia just figured she was either married or divorced. She didn't get that so much when she was in the City—another reason she liked living there. There were all types in New York. Everyone was busy dealing with their own lives. Everything was fast, too fast to delve into anyone's set of circumstances. That's the way Violet liked it.

Penny had a plum-colored dress draped over her arm like a wrap.

"What's that?" Violet asked, segueing from the topic of her spinsterhood.

Penny lifted the dress high allowing it to cascade to the floor. It was a flowing chiffon formal that reminded Violet of what Lily Munster's getup would look like if she had spent the day rolling around in a wine barrel.

"Don't you love this?" Penny cooed as she gave the fabric a little swish.

Violet's eyes darted to the saleslady, hoping for a possible ally, but saw she appeared just as enthralled. Knowing Josephine would be completely on board with the bride's opinion, Violet did not count on her mother to shoot down the choice.

The saleslady took the hanger from Penny's grasp and held the garment up against Violet's body. She tucked the bodice at Violet's waist to simulate how it would look when it was actually on her body. Violet's mouth felt as if it was full of cotton, preventing her from commenting. All she could do was stand there like a dumb plum.

"Look at the way this complements your skin tone," the proprietor gushed. "Oh, and with your black hair, it's breathtaking."

It was *breathtaking* all right. Violet's mind buzzed. This wasn't a dress for a grown woman. This was a prom dress for a wino.

"Violet," Josephine said in that tone that resembled a scold. "Speak up. What do you think? The lady doesn't have all day."

"Oh, take your time. And, please call me

39

Monique."

"Thank you, Monique," Josephine said. Her voice was coated with the honey she saved for complete strangers. Then she turned back to Violet. "Well?"

"Penny, is this really what you had in mind?"

"You don't like it," Penny pouted. Violet knew the business of that protruded lower lip. That lip had worked wonders for the girl as far back as Violet could remember. She needed a strategy or else she'd find herself looking like a walking grape of wrath.

"I think it's nice, but it's a bit of an overstatement."

No one spoke, but it appeared that they might be listening. This gave Violet hope that they entertained her line of malarkey. Her lungs released pent up air and she continued. *Heck, I'm on a roll.*

"I mean," Violet said, taking the dress and folding it over her arm. "The focus is on you, baby sister. Not me. I think this would be ideal for some swanky event... But I don't know. I'm just not sure it would fit up at The Pines."

All eyes knew to turn to Josephine. Violet was impressed at Monique's speedy observance that she was the one to convince. It was apparent that Josephine was the authority of all things big and small. And this ditty was definitely something big. This was a Barney costume, for heaven's sake.

"The last thing we want is to take away from the charm of The Pines. Don't you agree, Ma?"

Josephine sniffed in a breath of air then looked over to Monique. "She has a point."

"Well, how about we look for something a bit less showy?" Penny asked, taking their mother's lead.

Violet felt her muscles relax. Relief and satisfaction washed over her. She didn't win often, so when she did it sure was sweet.

"I agree," Monique added, taking the dress back to the sample rack.

"Violet's from New York City. She knows these things," Josephine said, for Monique's sake. Once in a blue moon she could find a reason to think Violet's move to the City had something positive in it. To Violet's surprise this was such a time.

Meanwhile, Penny's lower lip had protruded further. Now her head was bent down toward the floor. Violet sighed and went to her.

"I think we should concentrate on your gown first and then we can find something for me that will complement yours."

Penny brightened at the refocus. Monique took the cue and ran with it. In a flash the three Terhune women were ushered back to a large, lushly carpeted dressing room with mirrored octagonal walls. Josephine and Violet sat in little slipper chairs while Monique brought out a variety of bridal gowns and helped Penny into them one-by-agonizing-one.

By three o'clock they had a winner that even Violet had to admit was perfect. The lacy bodice accentuated Penny's small frame, her curves, and narrow waist—a body completely different from Violet's long, straight lines.

She watched Penny pirouette on the velvet stand in the center of the room. The wedding portrait that adorned her parents' bedroom wall popped into Violet's head. A replica of the bride their mother had been, Penny would step into a duplicate role of wifedom and find it as comfortable as the right pearl-studded white satin heels she'd chosen for her size five-and-a-half feet.

Violet never pictured herself as a bride or a wife, not anymore anyway. There had been times—years ago—after everything about Logan had been tucked safely into a closed corner of her brain, when she had dated more regularly.

She had even toyed with moving in with one boyfriend a couple of times. But now—aside from the occasional dinner with Martin Knowles, when he was in town—she shied away from any active pursuit of love and its trappings.

She had thrown herself whole-hog into her work. The merger of her magazine with the dreadfully wholesome *Country Charm* was like having to face a balance sheet of her life, where there were too many debits and not enough credits.

Penny spun around on her little stand like a ballerina in a jewelry box that had been wound too tight.

"What's the matter, Violet? I thought you liked this one," Penny said.

"I do."

"Then why do you look funny?"

"I was just thinking that it's getting late, that's all."

"You going to turn into a pumpkin, Cinderella?" Josephine asked.

Violet didn't bother to correct her mother in the details of Cinderella's story. What did it matter that Cinderella didn't turn into a pumpkin at midnight? You didn't need fairy tale accuracy to know Violet's evening ahead would not include a prince's ball.

Her night would involve a bag of low-fat chips and the one thing she had mastered from her kitchen, homemade antioxidant-rich guacamole. Mashing an avocado into a slime-colored pulp with a dash of this and that was something even she was capable of.

She'd dig into a good book, something that would pull her into its world and out of this one. Yet, there was another book that waited for her at home, its call became louder with every page she read.

"No special plans, Ma, but, you know, I have to get back to the City."

"Madonna. You and that city. Your sister needs you here," Josephine turned to Monique, who stood again at the doorway to the dressing cubicle. "Let's find a dress for the maid of honor."

Since Penny's dress was cut close to her frame, a lacey sheath, the dress they chose for Violet was the same. Even Violet had to admit it didn't look so bad, and gave the illusion that she had a more girlish curve than she possessed. The color, miracle of miracles, Penny had selected was a rich, subtle midnight blue. Violet stood in front of the mirror, flanked by her sister and mother. Monique peeked in from behind.

"Perfect!" Monique said as she clutched her chest. She touched Josephine's shoulder. "That's the one. Don't you agree?"

Josephine remained silent as she surveyed her eldest daughter's image in the mirror, her eye keen. Penny and Monique waited for the word, like farmers waiting for Juan Valdez's approval on a sackful of coffee beans. Violet dreaded what would happen if her mother didn't like the dress. It would be back to the rack to fish for another one.

"Ma?" she prodded, braced for it.

"Yes." Josephine said. "Madonna, this is it."

"I think so, too," Penny chimed in, like it mattered whatsoever.

Violet let out a long sigh of relief. Their day at Debonair Bridals was finished, at long last.

"Violet…" There was such a soft, warm tone in her mother's voice as she called her name, that she felt a stab of panic.

"What's the matter? You sick or something?"

The older woman cleared her throat, straightened her stance. "That color looks nice on you. That's all."

"Thanks, Ma." Violet felt silly when a lump suddenly appeared in her throat. Even at her age a woman could be moved by a compliment from her mother—especially when they didn't come easy.

While Monique helped Violet out of the dress, Penny poked her head into the dressing cubicle.

"Oh my God, Violet, you know what I forgot to tell you?"

Violet met Penny's eyes in the mirror, "What?"

"Guess who I talked to yesterday?"

The hair on the back of Violet's neck pricked its warning. She kept her tone casual. "Who?"

"Logan Monroe." Penny's face lit with delight in delivering the juicy morsel of information.

Violet licked her lips, pausing to respond as Monique adjusted the dress back onto its cushiony satin hanger, and then exited the booth. "Did you?" Violet pushed an arm through the sleeve of her boat neck tee.

"Yes," Penny said, the word bursting from her lips like a bubble.

Violet shoved a leg into her jeans, fixed on her task.

"He asked for you." Penny was sing-songing again.

Violet fumbled with the metal snap at her waist then pulled up the zipper. She slapped her thighs for good measure. In a minute she'd be out of there.

Josephine appeared at the curtained doorway, her arm holding the fabric aside, a little gray-haired sonar, detecting a tidbit worth hearing. Violet, crouched on a little wooden stool, tugged on her white cotton socks then pushed her feet into her sneakers.

"What? No comment?" Penny coaxed.

"Um…" Violet lifted her head after she tied her laces. "That's nice."

"That's nice?" Penny asked, hands on her curvy little hips. She giggled that little-girl twitter that surfaced whenever she was up to something.

"Yes," Violet said with a polite cadence. "That was nice that he asked for me. And, how is he?"

Josephine stepped into the cubicle with her daughters, letting the curtain drop behind her, closing the three of them into the tight space. Their images met Violet's eyes in the multi-paned mirror. They were wall-to-wall Terhunes. "Ma, what are you doing? We can't all fit in here," Violet protested.

"Sure we can. So, what did this Logan say?"

Violet started to feel as if she was in a confessional. All they needed was Our Lady of the Sorrows' Father Dalton to be on the other side of that curtain. How many Hail Mary's would he assign for confessing she wanted to clap the trap of her little bride-to-be sister?

"He runs The Pines now, but we knew that," Penny said.

"During our conversation about dinner selections, he just blurted it out."

"What? What did he say?" Josephine asked.

Violet flipped the strap of her purse up over her shoulder and nudged her mother toward the curtain. But, Josephine had turned to cement.

"He said 'how is Violet doing?'" Penny said. "And I said she's doing great and that she lives in New York and works for a magazine. And he said that was good to hear."

"Okay, Ma? You got the scoop. Now can we go? I have to give Monique a deposit."

"Wait," Penny said, touching Violet's arm. "That's not all."

Violet stood still and waited. She knew there was no getting around these two little women even if she did tower over them. Penny had to have her say.

"I asked him how he was doing and he said he was doing well. And I asked him how his family was and he told me that his daughter, Jessica, just graduated college and she's helping run The Pines."

Violet hadn't known his daughter's name. She knew Jessica's mother's, though—Bonnie. Suddenly Violet remembered her last conversation with Logan and how things had ended between them.

The image of Logan's face, wrought with sadness, came into her head. His words had filtered in like smoke curling up under a closed door. Somebody named Bonnie was pregnant...it was a mistake...but there was nothing he could do...had to do the right thing.

Violet felt her chest constrict even now. The walls of the dressing cubicle pressed in on her, squeezing the air out of Violet's lungs.

"Well, that's nice. Does this place take American Express?"

"And then he told me he's a widower."

Violet met her sister's eyes. She tried to read the look on Penny's face. Was there a flash of sympathy in her dark eyes? And was the sympathy for Logan or for Violet?

"His wife died?" Josephine flashed a wide-eyed gaze at her older daughter, ready for her reaction.

Violet could feel a warm flush climb up her face. The tiny room was full of hot air. She knew if she didn't say something now they'd stay in there until she did.

"When?" Violet asked, not wanting the answer, yet holding her breath until it came.

"In childbirth."

****

Violet drove back to the City in a numb state, making all the right turns and stopping appropriately at lights when they changed to red. She was on automatic pilot.

She did not will her mind to rehash the conversation in the dressing cubicle, but the stun of learning Logan had been a widower all these years was there in the car hovering over her.

46

At home finally, as she stepped into her own little haven, she felt herself emerge from the fog and was surprised at her feeling of anger. She felt mad, but for the life of her she couldn't understand why. Why should she react at all, really? What happened to Logan had nothing whatsoever to do with her.

She went into the kitchen, suddenly ravenous, craving carbs. She pulled a loaf of multi-grain out from the fridge and untwisted the tie. Instead of unwinding the little wire she made it even more secure. She had to twist in the opposite direction to get to the bread, firing her frustration.

Violet was acting frenzied but her self-awareness didn't quell the feeling. She yanked out a slice of bread and took a bite. Pulling the peanut butter off the shelf, she sunk a butter knife into its thickness. She slathered a layer onto the bread then licked the knife clean.

Two bites in, it came to her. The realization of her own self-directed anger stuck in her brain exactly like the glob of Skippy plastered to the roof of her mouth.

Reacting to news of Logan betrayed the woman she was now. Logan did not belong in her thoughts. Images of him should not be popping into her head. And, she had no business allowing memories from the pages of that ridiculous old diary to conjure feelings that were long dead.

Violet went to the drawer where she had stashed the book and flipped it open enjoying the sharp sound of the binding's crack. Damn it, she would read the entries, all of them. She'd devour every word, swallow them, digest the memories. And then they'd be gone. Her effort would be the cure to these adolescent, bothersome emotions. This was like getting the mumps again and the medicine, although bitter, would render her immune at last.

****

August 16, 1977
Dear Diary,

I'm almost ashamed to say that this is the happiest day of my life, but since I'm just telling you I'll admit it. It is 100% the happiest day of my life!

You know how sometimes a good thing comes from a bad thing? Well, that's what happened today. Today we heard on the news that Elvis Presley died. Elvis dead! I still can't believe it.

I couldn't wait to talk with Logan. So I went to find my mother to tell her I was going for a walk and found her standing at the dresser in their bedroom, dabbing her eyes with a tissue, crying.

"Ma?"

She turned around so quickly she almost lost her balance and had to hold onto the furniture to brace herself.

"Madonna! Violet, really," she said. She held her hand over her heart like she was doing the Pledge of Allegiance. "Don't sneak up on me like that."

"Are you crying?"

"No."

"It looks like you are."

The rims of her eyes were red and her cheeks were wet. She dragged the wad of tissues over her face. "I don't know what's come over me," she said into her tissue. "I'm just so upset about poor Elvis. He was so young. What a shame."

She seemed relieved when I asked if I could go for a walk. To tell you the truth, I was relieved, too. Penny was taking a nap, so I was glad I didn't get stuck bringing her along.

I ran down the path to the cabin. The whole time all I could think of was how my mother looked. I mean, my mother's always the one that we all lean on. It's like she's the boss and we all know it, even Daddy. So, it's freaky, I guess, to see her looking all sad and little in her red-checked pedal-pushers.

48

Logan was fishing. The blue-and-white plastic bobber floated on the surface of the water. I walked up to him cautiously, not wanting to scare away any fish that might be coming to take his bait.

"Hi," I whispered, breathless from the run and from just being near him.

"Hey, Violet."

And, I don't even know why, but I burst out crying. Just like that. I started bawling. Logan dropped his fishing pole and the end of it slipped into the lake with a plop.

"Violet, what's the matter?"

"Elvis died."

It sounded lame and ridiculous. It was like I was this big Elvis fan or something, and I'm not. I mean, I'm sad that he died and everything, but I could not figure out why I started crying so hard. But, all I could see in my mind was my mother standing alone in her bedroom crying into her Kleenex. My father sometimes calls her "The Little General." But, not in a mean way. Whenever he says it you can tell he's proud of her being so feisty.

But, today there she was. The Little General was a pile of tears because Elvis Presley died too young. She looked like a tiny little lady and nothing like a general in any way.

I held my hands over my eyes while I cried like a big fool. And, then Logan put his hands over mine and peeled my fingers away from my face. He leaned down and kissed me. At first it was a gentle, soft little kiss, a brush of his lips against mine. He hesitated for a second and then his arms were around me and my arms were around him.

When we pulled apart we were both breathing hard like we had run a far distance.

Chapter Six

On Monday morning, Violet's heart tugged when she saw that Ted was settling in at the cubicle right next to hers. The man had had his own office, a room with a window and a comfort station, and now his space was an eight-foot fabric-walled square. She put her things down on her desk and stood at his make-shift doorway.

"You have to admit it's cozy," she said.

Ted swung around in his chair and gave Violet a lopsided grin. "Okay, Pollyanna. Whatever you say."

Ted's files lined a milk crate. His coffee mug, desk calendar, an elephant-shaped brass clock were all bunched into a corner on the laminate countertop. His framed photos, still in the cardboard box she had seen in Matthew's *new* office, sat at Ted's feet. This boxy space looked more like a storage shed than an office.

"You need a hand?" Violet asked. "I could, you know, help you nest."

"Ah, leave it," Ted said.

Violet went over to the photographs and pulled one from the box. It was a black-and-white photo of a duck on a pond. The duck's white feathers were distinct, eye-riveting in contrast to the muted grays of the water and the grasses around the pond. The bird was a beacon in a cloudy world.

"You should hang these, Ted. The walls in here should support them."

Robert Matthews, in his million-buck-looking charcoal gray pinstriped suit, sauntered up and stopped beside the cubicle. At his side stood Melanie

Rosen, a vision in crisp linen trousers and a white sleeveless sweater. Violet wondered if the girl had knitted the damned thing herself on her coffee break. She'd probably sheared the sheep first this past weekend.

"Good morning, Violet," Robert said.

"Hi, Robert." She then turned to Melanie. "Good morning."

Melanie nodded, a smile so disingenuous Violet thought for sure it would pop off her face and fall to the floor like a faulty Mrs. Potato Head.

"Violet," Robert said. "Melanie and I were just talking."

Violet did not like the way the two shiny new staff members virtually ignored Ted. Apparently, their mothers didn't spend too much time on manners, let alone tact. Her mouth twitched with a desire to tell them they should be ashamed of themselves. But she knew any mention of their slight would only offend Ted further.

Robert continued. "By next Monday's staff meeting I'd like a breakdown on your idea for the October spread. Nothing formal. Melanie's already briefed me on hers, and I'm delighted with her angle."

Melanie beamed up at Robert. Violet felt her stomach churn. The half a bagel with light cream cheese she had for breakfast knotted inside her belly, tossing around like a rock in a tumbler.

"Oh, I've been working on my idea as well," Violet said. She could see Ted looking up at her from his chair. He had that glint in his eye that told he knew that she was bullshitting. Violet couldn't con a con artist, and Ted was the best of them. She hoped Robert was not on to her bluff.

"Wonderful!" Robert said. "It's a pleasure to work with such competent people. Melanie, tell Violet what you've been working on."

"Well," Melanie said, her chin high, her eyes glancing up sideways to Robert's face.

Violet mused, *If the girl had a tail she'd be wagging it. Maybe she's part poodle, one of those hybrid designer dogs, a Mela-poo.* She forced her mind to stop for fear she might reach over and scratch Melanie behind an ear.

"I've decided to incorporate the spa experience into Napa getaways."

"Nice," Violet said with as little enthusiasm as she could without seeming rude. After all, her mother had rammed manners and tact down her daughters' throats since they were born.

"Oh, and that's not the best part," Robert said. He turned to his eager pet. "Tell her."

"I've been working on the spin of frugality—because of the economy and the flavor of the magazine. The piece is going to be sort of a do-it-yourself. Bring your own scented oils, candles, and bath salts to create the atmosphere of a spa without the extravagance. I'm working with reps in the beauty industry to come up with some packages they can offer to our readers."

Violet swallowed hard. Even she had to admit that the idea was a good one. It was exactly what Robert Matthews wanted, and everyone present knew it.

"That sounds interesting," Violet said. She looked at Ted who nodded in dull agreement. His eyes told her he was more interested in how *she* was going to get out of her self-painted corner.

"So, what's your idea, Violet?" Robert asked.

Violet bit her lip and glanced over at Ted. He remained silent with his eyes fixed on her. She looked down at the frame in her hand, focusing onto the image of the duck on the pond, gliding along in his merry way, peaceful, happy, with nobody around to divert his path.

"Birding," Violet said.

"Birding?" Melanie's tone was laced with enough disbelief to cause Robert to cock his head to the side as though he couldn't possibly have heard right.

"Yes," Violet said with more conviction. "Birding. It's quite an up-and-coming pastime. It's always been a favorite among the elite, but now people of all walks of life are becoming interested in the idea of studying birds and their habitats. It's involving yourself with nature, yet has the feel of sophistication."

Violet's eyes met Ted's and transmitted a look that questioned if her line of crap sounded at all valid. His twinkling eyes declared she had told a good one. Satisfied that Ted approved of her baloney, she waited for Robert's reaction.

"I love it!" he said. He turned to Melanie, her mouth now pinched into a little bow. "You two are brilliant. This is going to be one interesting competition."

Violet felt the weight of the frame in her hands. She had conjured that concept out of a hat. Now she actually had to pull a rabbit—no a bird—out of that same imaginary chapeau.

When Robert and Melanie walked away, Violet plopped onto a double-stacked set of copier paper boxes that stored Ted's belongings. Ted's face was bright with amusement.

"Well, well," he said, leaning back in his chair. "Now wasn't that just, shall we say, *ducky*?"

"Ted, what am I going to do?"

"You're going to write a fantastic piece on birding." He could not suppress a laugh that escaped from his mouth like a belch.

Violet shot him the evil eye. "I don't know where to begin with this."

"Get on the internet and find out everything you can about birding and put your spin on it. Nobody can spin like you, baby."

She shook her head. Ted deserved more respect than he was getting, especially from those newbies. This displaced man who had been her boss, her advocate, her coach for all these years gave her heart a good pang. Violet reached over and gave his chair a shove. The squat little man turned around in one full revolution before she put her hand on the arm of the chair to halt it.

"Looks like you can spin pretty good, too," she said.

"Tell you what. Go do your research and we'll do drinks after work. You can fill my head up with everything you know about birding,"

"A couple of bird brains—that's us," Violet said as she set off to begin her task.

****

Back in her own cubicle Violet Googled "birding in Vermont." She was going to have to find a way to incorporate this angle with her week at The Pines.

She learned that there were several resources for birding enthusiasts in and around the area of Bennington as well as other towns near the lodge. Her idea needed to be fleshed out by the following Monday. She spent the morning reading website after website, making notes, printing information.

By lunchtime her neck hurt and her stomach grumbled. She got up from her chair and peeked over into Ted's cubicle. His computer screen was black and the lights along the underside of his cabinets were off. She hadn't even noticed that he left. She saw the post-it note on his screen. "*Flew the coop*—See you at Durkin's at 5:00."

Violet went back to her desk and unwrapped the other half of her bagel from breakfast. She munched and turned back to her screen although she had had it up to her eyeballs on Vermont's birds. Instead of looking at pictures of the Hermit Thrush or the Red-

Throated Loon she keyed something new into the search box. She typed in "The Pines" and waited while the little hour glass pulsed on the screen.

The lodge had no website. It showed up on Violet's screen as an address with a little map and an arrow pointing to the location. But, no site. She wondered why a vacation spot wouldn't take advantage of the internet's ability to attract people to its doors. After all, wasn't that the point of operating a lodge? People? How better to have vacationers learn about your establishment?

Next she Googled "Logan Monroe." Nothing. There were a ton of Monroes listed, several of them in Vermont, but none of them were Logan.

She typed in "Bonnie Monroe" to see if her obituary would pop up. It did not. Weren't deaths a matter of record? Didn't it have to be listed somewhere? Maybe Bonnie never took Logan's name, Violet thought. Maybe she kept her maiden name, but what was it? Violet wracked her brain. Had she ever heard Bonnie's last name mentioned back then? She could not remember.

She Googled Logan's daughter and finally got something. Jessica Monroe had been listed in an article in a Bennington newspaper back in 2006. It said that she was one of a half dozen students from Southern Vermont College working on an environmental cleanup project at a small park in a town called Drury.

There was a photo of the students but it was too small and blurry for Violet to really see what the girl looked like. From what she could tell Jessica was blonde like her father. Violet squinted. So, this was Logan's daughter. She was taller than the two other girls in her group. She appeared slim, with narrow shoulders. Violet felt a stab when the thought occurred to her that Jessica's build was similar to her own. It made her wonder if Bonnie had been built like her, too.

Violet wadded up the waxed paper wrapper from her bagel and tossed it like a ball into the trash. She sipped the last of her vitamin water.

She shook her head. What was she doing? Researching these people was a waste of time. They meant nothing to Violet. What did it matter if Jessica Monroe was tall or short or blonde or brunette? What did it matter to her if Logan was missing the boat on advertising his lodge?

Violet rubbed her temples. Apparently, she wasn't immune enough yet to this damned man. Her head had started to throb. Violet knew that the day would soon come that she would see for herself if Jessica looked like her father—and, worse, she would see Logan.

Chapter Seven

The bar at Durkin's was crowded and nearly every brown leather-upholstered stool was occupied. Violet scanned the room in search of Ted. It was half-past five and she knew the man would probably be on his second Guinness by then.

She walked around clusters of people, all suited professionals. The din of their happy chatter a tribute to the fact that it was indeed Happy Hour. And then she spotted him. Ted sat at the corner of the bar with his briefcase beside him on the next stool.

"Hey, Ted," she said as she walked over. "This seat for me?"

"Well, I don't know," he said. His smooth tone confirmed that the half-empty beer in front of him assuredly was his second.

She knew the man was kidding but she played along with the best-sounding indignation she could muster. "What do you mean you don't know?" Violet asked. She removed Ted's briefcase and took a seat.

"That's prime real estate you're sitting on. I could make some dough subletting that seat."

"Too late. It's mine now."

Ted snickered. "So, what else is new? Story of my life."

The bartender made his way over to the two of them. "Hi, Violet," the big ruddy-faced Irishman said to her. He tossed a compressed paper coaster on the bar with a Frisbee-like jerk of his hand. "What are you having today?"

"It's a martini day, Kevin," she said.

"Serious stuff," he said. His mouth curved up into a wide grin. "One of *those* days, huh, Violet?"

"It was one of those days all right," Ted chimed in. "You can say it was 'for the birds.' " Ted laughed at his own reference and brought the glass up to his lips.

Violet narrowed her eyes at him then looked over to Kevin. "Yes," she said. "Today *was* 'for the birds.' So, in honor of the occasion make that Grey Goose you put in my martini."

"You got it," Kevin said.

"Oh, and he's paying." She pointed a finger at Ted.

"Shit," Ted downed the rest of his beer. "Kevin, you might as well get me another one. I got a feeling I'm in for it."

When Kevin brought their drinks over, Violet ordered a corned beef sandwich for the two of them to share. She knew drinking on an empty stomach was a bad idea and this was more than likely Ted's third beer.

"So, Ted, you have to help me." She was serious now. "I need to have my spiel ready for Monday."

"You mean you have to get your ducks in order?" Ted laughed again.

"Please stop making bird references. You're not helping."

"Okay." Ted turned his stool toward her. "Let's talk about this."

"Thank you."

"Okay, so what did you learn about birding?" he asked.

"Well, a lot really. Enough to make *my* head spin. There's plenty of opportunity for me to sell the idea to Robert. I mean, it's got all the stuff he's looking for. Outdoorsy and sophisticated, but not too over-the-top."

"You need to add one more thing in your spiel."

"Okay, what?"

"Moolah."

"Moolah? What do you mean?"

"Magazines are in business to make money. They make their money when they present things to the consumer that they simply *have to have*. So, if you do your job in convincing the world that they're nobody unless they go birding, then the magazine gets advertisers to pay big bucks for all the bells and whistles that go along with it."

"Yeah." Violet liked the thought so much she put down her half of the sandwich and gave her hands a little clap. "I'll get some names of manufacturers of equipment and clothing and accessories and stuff."

"Binoculars," Ted said, "Boots, hats, jackets, books on birds. You can have a field day. And, of course, the most important is cameras. A good birder needs a good camera."

"Speaking of cameras," Violet said. "Have I ever mentioned that you are a pretty damn good photographer?"

Ted smiled with his lips closed. His mouth was full of corned beef on rye.

"You love it don't you, Ted?"

Ted swallowed and washed it down with a sip of his beer. Violet could tell he was pacing himself. The sip was a tiny one.

He didn't confirm that he loved photography, but his eyes did. "I always wanted to enter the world of publishing with camera in hand. Go figure."

Violet thought of the photo of the duck that prompted her birding idea. The image of all Ted's frames in that carton popped into her head.

"Come with me to Vermont," she said. "Be my photographer."

Ted was mid-sip when Violet's words met his ears. He almost dribbled the beer down the front of himself. "Okay now I know you're cuckoo."

Hunkering down on her seat, she leaned closer to him. "Ted, I need you. Your pictures will help me win this ridiculous contest. Together we'll blow Little Miss Melanie Nature Nerd out of the water."

Ted cocked his head to the side and pulled the corners of his mouth down in a contemplative curve. "Vermont, huh?"

Violet slapped his shoulder and gave a little laugh. "I knew you'd do it," she said.

Just then Kevin approached them and took away the large oval dish that now had just a sprig of parsley and a strip of crust left in it.

"Anything else, folks?" Kevin asked.

"Yeah," Ted said as he dug for his wallet. "Don't let me have three beers any more if I'm with *this one*. She takes advantage of my good nature."

The three of them laughed at one of the most preposterous statements the man had ever made.

****

Violet drove Ted home because, in her estimation, he seemed a little too jolly to be left to his own devices. "What are you, my mother, now?" he asked, although he willingly slid into the passenger side of Violet's Saab.

While Violet made her way through the streets to Ted's part of town, they drove in silence. Cars darted in and out like bees in a hive. Horns wailed in what seemed like a conversation among a gaggle of angry geese. She took a deep breath. Now *she* was making bird puns. She gripped the wheel more firmly. She had to stop that stuff. She needed to be serious about this venture. This bird article was going to decide her fate.

Then her mind flipped over to the other topic that would not go away. Violet shook her head. Talk about cuckoo. She hadn't seen him since she was twenty. That was a long time ago—a lifetime ago.

She pulled up in front of Ted's building. Luckily

there was a fire hydrant and she pulled into the "no parking" space.

"Home sweet home," Ted said, putting his hand on the door handle. "I'll see you in the morning, Terhune."

"Ted, thanks for agreeing to help me. I really appreciate it."

Ted's mouth twisted sideways and he gave her a long, serious look. "Can I tell you something? Remember that time when your friend, what was her name, Lizzie..."

"Libby," Violet corrected. A jab speared her gut.

"Yeah, Libby," Ted continued. "Remember when she died?"

Violet nodded. She hadn't thought about that in a long time, although she had thought of Libby often. It was funny that whenever Libby came to mind she was young and lively like she had been as a girl. She was strong and fit. Her auburn hair was rich and full on her head like a crown. Violet seldom thought of Libby when she had the yellow hue from the chemo on her tissue-paper skin, or when her head was covered in that too-perfect page-boy wig. Violet had mentally found a way to put that piece of history behind a locked door. But sometimes, like now, that door popped open.

"What are you getting at, Ted?"

"You had this sad look in your eyes for a long time." Ted shook his head. "A really long time. It was like something inside you was missing. Something you couldn't get back."

Tears stung her eyes. *Yes,* Violet thought. *Some things you just can't get back.*

"I didn't want to make you cry, Terhune. I'm sorry."

"What made you bring that up?"

"Well, lately you've got that look again."

"I do?"

Ted nodded. "You look like somebody's gone again. Somebody important."

A tear dribbled down her check. She swatted it. Her mumps theory might be backfiring. Instead of becoming exempt from the past, she was showing signs of a relapse, like her fever had spiked again. *Ah, Libby*, Violet's mind called. *I need you here again to keep me sane.*

When Libby died not only had Violet lost the companionship of the best friend anyone could hope for, she also lost the one person who knew it all, and had been her strongest supporter.

Violet looked over to Ted through the blur of her tears. His image was skewed, distorted to a wavy ghost-looking figure. Although Violet knew that she would always talk to Libby in her mind, a sudden impulse told her it was time to stop talking to ghosts and let someone else be her friend.

Ted took his hand from the passenger door's handle. He settled into his seat, facing Violet. "Tell me about it, Terhune. Come on. I'm listening."

She wiped the wetness from her eyes. Ted's image was clear to her again. His eyes held hers. "I got all the time you need, kid."

Violet shifted the car into park, took her foot off the brake and let her back relax against the leather seat. "My sister found my old diary, and I've been reading it."

"And?"

"And it's all about this guy who, uh, who meant a lot to me."

"What happened to him?"

"He married someone else."

"Oh."

"It was a long time ago, Ted, and I haven't thought of him in years, but now with this diary..."

"Why are you reading it if it's making you upset?"

"I have to."

"Why?"

"You know how when you get a childhood disease, you know, like the mumps…"

"Okay."

"You're looking at me like I'm nuts. Listen to my theory. It makes sense."

"This should be good."

"Once you get the mumps, your body builds up its own antidote and you're cured from ever getting it again. I'm reading the diary so I can binge and purge. Be over it once and for all."

"Why bother now? What's so important about binging and purging stuff about this guy after all this time?"

"Because he owns the lodge where we're headed in August."

"Shit."

"Exactly."

"Okay, so spill it. Let me be the penicillin in this cockamamie plan of yours. Tell me what's in this diary."

****

August 25, 1978
Dear Diary,

Tonight Logan and I sneaked out of our rooms after our families were asleep. Logan told me about the Mute Swans that sometimes show up on the lake and that he wanted me to see them. Apparently there's a lot of hoopla going on about the swans because they are taking over the local waterways. It's like they're getting out of hand and nobody knows what to do about it.

We darted down the path to the cabin like thieves afraid someone might spot the beam of our lantern. Peering out the opening in the wall we looked across the inky surface of the lake. It was still, but in the silence we could hear the sounds of movement.

There was something going on under that slick wet surface. There was life under its dark, glistening blanket. Trees bowed over the lake like they were saying their prayers. Were they praying for the swans to show, just like we were?

Then they came into view, gliding along in silent majesty. Logan reached over and touched his pinky to mine. We turned and looked at each other knowing we should not speak for fear the swans would scurry away.

When the swans had gone, Logan took out his penknife and handed me the lantern to hold. I watched as he worked the blade on the project he had begun days ago. The cool night had chilled my skin, but it was Logan's task that gave me goose bumps.

"Hold it still, Violet," Logan whispered. His face looked so serious. "I'm almost done."

I placed my other hand at the base of the lantern to keep it steady while Logan worked the point of the blade into the plank on the wall, chipping splinters of oak onto the floor of the shed.

I watched his hand reworking the first letter, the "I." Then he moved to the space beside it and cut deeper into the heart shape already begun in the wood. He defined it with the tip of the knife, blew into the heart and crumbs of wood sprinkled from the cutout. He placed his index finger into where he cut and swept the space of any lingering debris.

Then Logan made a new cut, a long slice downward then another cut upward. He dug the tip of the knife into the large "V." Then he cut the "T" working the knife like an expert. My heart swelled at the sight of my initials there in the wood right next to the heart. The message was permanent, indelible, forever. Logan loves me.

Chapter Eight

By the time Violet was sitting in her pajamas, curled up on the sofa with a mug of tea, she was wondering how one little martini could have made her spill her guts to Ted Solomon. She closed her eyes. She was tired.

She picked up the remote and pressed the "on" button and the television came to life. She flipped through some channels until she got to the evening news. She had missed the important stuff at the top of the hour and now they were onto the fluff. She sighed out loud and put her mug down onto its coaster on the coffee table.

The story was about a dog that found its way home after running away nearly two years earlier. The owner, being interviewed by the reporter, gushed happily into the bulbous microphone poked at her mouth. When they panned back to the newsroom the two anchors at the desk bantered about the amazing pooch. Violet hit another button and changed the channel.

She had had enough of fluff pieces for one day. She would work hard on that birding story because so much depended on it, but she still felt that hollowness inside her. She didn't know what her writing passion was, but she knew what it wasn't. It wasn't the desire to get people with some extra cash to spend it on a high-end pair of binoculars.

She thought of Libby. Now would be a good time to be able to pick up the phone and wallow just enough for Libby to tell her to snap out of it. Libby had been great at that.

Violet, in spite of her unwillingness, felt her thoughts drift to the days when her friend was nearing the end. Libby had only been thirty-seven, newly married, and in her prime. Violet shook her head, disbelief slapping her as the image became clear. How much easier it was to envision Libby as she was before the diagnosis. The sick Libby was painful to remember.

It had been seven years now. She thought of their last moments. Libby's last words to Violet were about love. "You need to promise me that you'll find happiness," Libby had said from the hospital bed set up in the den off her kitchen.

She couldn't climb the steps to the bedrooms any more. Libby's husband, Danny, had discreetly left the room to give the two friends a moment alone. He and Violet knew there were not many moments left and Danny, with his haggard appearance and sad eyes, was willing to let Violet have her share.

"Don't you worry about me, Libby," Violet said, her smile feeling awkward on her face.

"Well, I do. You need me to keep you out of your own way." Libby gave her friend a sappy smile. Violet's heart ached.

"Hush," Violet said and reached over to wipe Libby's perspired brow. "You want a sip of water?"

"No, I want to say this...and I want you to listen." Violet heard the resolve in her friend's weary voice.

"Okay, I'm listening."

"You need to let somebody in. I've been a crutch to you."

Violet opened her mouth to protest, but Libby held up a slack hand. Violet closed her mouth and let Libby continue. "We've been there for each other since we were little kids. Ever since that one girl in kindergarten lied to the teacher and said I wet my pants when I had fallen in a puddle on the playground. You stood up to her. Remember?"

"Donna Burkhardt," Violet said. "She's a biker chick these days."

"Well, that just figures."

Violet noticed Libby's eyes fighting to stay open.

"Lib, you want to take a nap?"

"Not until I get this out."

"Okay."

"So, it's me and you, Violet. It's always been me and you. And, now it won't be."

Violet felt her breath lock in her chest. The truth in Libby's words was too hard to process but there was no sense in denying the fact anymore. She stayed quiet.

"You need someone."

"I have lots of people, Libby. Honestly. Don't worry."

"You have lots of family and lots of work friends, but you need somebody in here." Libby reached to point her index finger to the center of Violet's chest. Her skeletal arm was lost in the fabric of the pink brushed-cotton pajamas she wore. Violet's eyes filled with tears and she put her hand over Libby's, curled her fingers around it, and cradled Libby's hand in her own.

"Here is where you live," Violet said to her friend, giving the bony hand a gentle squeeze. "In here."

Libby smiled. "I know and I'll always be there. But I can share your heart. Remember all the time I shared it with Logan?"

"Yes," Violet said in a barely audible whisper.

"Make room in your heart again, Violet."

"I will, Libby."

And then Libby closed her eyes and slept.

Violet looked up at the clock on the wall as she brought herself back to the present. She really needed to turn in for the night although she knew sleep would not come to her anytime soon.

Her head was a scrambled mess now. She had the report she needed to work on for Monday, to present her ideas to Robert Matthews. And she had to hope and pray that when she got to Vermont she would be able to deal with the one man she had let reside in her heart—right beside her Libby—all those years ago.

Violet clicked off the television and doused the lights. She padded off to bed with the thought that she needed to take a trip to the cemetery to talk with Libby. She could tell her how now Ted Solomon knew why it was going to be tough revisiting The Pines. She would go to the cemetery on Sunday on the way to Penny's future in-laws' house for dinner.

Violet rolled her eyes as she turned on the bathroom light and set out to perform her evening routine of brushing, exfoliating and moisturizing, a series of tasks that seemed to get longer in duration and more involved every year. Violet looked in the mirror in the stark bright light. "It's a bitch to get old," she said out loud.

****

"So, can you believe it, Lib? I'm heading back to Vermont." She actually laughed when she said the words out loud. It felt good to talk to her friend.

Violet had brought a bouquet of summer flowers to Libby. There was another gently wrapped cluster of blooms in her car awaiting Penny's soon-to-be-mother-in-law. Dinner was at two o'clock and Violet had plenty of time to get to their house in Chatham.

"Lib, I know you're laughing up there in heaven," Violet said. "The kid's getting married to Mr. Wonderful and doing it at The Pines. Doesn't it just figure?" She shook her head then touched two fingertips to the top of the granite headstone. "Be with me, Libby. I can't do this alone."

A small brown bird, wings spread wide and free,

glided in the air overhead. It circled the rows of headstones as though looking for just the right one on which to perch. And, then it darted upward and disappeared in the branches of a sturdy elm. Violet felt a surge in her chest. She turned to leave, satisfied that her plea had been delivered on tender wings.

She drove through the pretty, well-maintained neighborhoods and found her destination.

Mrs. Layne, a stately woman with ash blonde hair cut into a smart bob, came to the door. She gushed at the bouquet when Violet handed it to her, her mouth a broad grin that exposed yet another set of startlingly white Layne porcelain.

"Oh, how lovely. Thank you, Violet."

"You're welcome, Mrs. Layne. How nice of you to have all of us."

"Please call me Deborah. Everyone's in the living room."

The house was a study in wallpaper. Every room's walls were either striped, floral, or pin-dotted. Violet had the thought that a hangover would be doubly bad in such a house. The living room was done in coordinating patterns of raspberry.

Violet's family sat shoulder-to-shoulder in a line on the satin-striped sofa. Benjamin, at Penny's side, had an arm slung across the back of the seat. Josephine flashed that look that had always come into her brown eyes whenever they either had company or they themselves were the company. The look said to *behave*. Violet breathed out. She was in her forties and her mother was still willing her to toe the mark with a simple glance.

It was true that the Laynes were a clan to impress. Violet got that much from her mother's stern look. There may have been a time years ago when she would have thought it amusing to embarrass Penny, to bring out a picture of her from when she went through her "chubby stage" back in elementary school perhaps. But, hell, Violet knew there was no joke good enough to compare with Penny and Ben's bright idea to drag the whole group to The Pines.

She crossed the room and shook Benjamin's father's hand. He was an older version of his son with the same brilliant smile. He, too, was a dentist and his wife ran his office for him. Violet wondered if all the oral brightness in the house saved on their light bill. Although the question would be a delicious one, she knew better than to ask.

Ben's father, Roland, as he asked to be called, introduced Violet to the other guests in the room. Roland's brother and his wife, George and Shirley, sat in wing chairs near the fireplace. They were one of those couples that wind up looking like brother and sister. With them was their middle-aged *single* chiropractor son named Franklin.

The second they were introduced, with that emphasis on 'single,' she knew why her mother had flashed her that look. This was a set-up. Violet could just feel it. Against her better judgment she pulled her eyes over to meet her mother's. The woman grinned like a jack-o-lantern. This was trouble. Big trouble.

Franklin shook her hand with a nice, firm handshake. But the rest of him looked weak and needy. Violet could not pull her eyes away from his large ruby red lips, the kind of clownish mouth that looked like the waxed lips you bought at the candy store for Halloween.

She saw him look to his mother after he said hello to her. Shirley even nodded at him with what seemed like a gesture of encouragement similar to a parent convincing a reluctant kindergartener to board the bus on the first day of school. Violet forced herself to keep a smile on her face.

When they all entered the dining room Violet saw that there were place cards set before each plate. Her eyes scanned them and to no surprise she was seated beside Franklin. His mother sat on the other side of him. She watched in disbelief as the woman reached for a folded napkin and placed it on her grown son's lap. Violet's eyes strayed to the doorway into the kitchen. She wondered if this dental haven had a back door.

"So, Violet," Franklin drawled. "It's no surprise where you got your name."

Josephine's rosy mouth, colored with her favorite Revlon shade, still held its insufferable curve. A heated blush crawled up Violet's face.

"Your eyes really are violet blue," he said.

She could have been mistaken but Violet thought she saw his mother pat Franklin's leg under the table. *Oh brother,* she thought, *what next? A biscuit?*

The conversation during dinner centered on the upcoming wedding and all the fanfare that would be going along with it. They discussed floral arrangements, musicians, and menu items for the reception as well as the wedding breakfast and the rehearsal dinner.

The mention of Logan Monroe rolled off Penny's tongue as though it were any inconsequential name. With each reference Violet felt as if she was being poked at by a cattle prod.

All the while Violet felt Franklin's eyes on her. Whenever she allowed herself to glance his way, she was appalled at the sight of his oversized rubbery lips twitching at her.

Coffee and petit fours were served out on the screened-in veranda. As Violet stepped into the room she felt a pinch on her arm like an insect bite. Unfortunately, it was no wasp. It was Josephine. "Be nice to that boy, Violet. He's a catch," her mother whispered.

"Ma, stop."

"He's a chiropractor. That's almost a doctor! And he has his own house right here in Chatham. Just down the block."

Violet wanted to say that *of course the man lives on mommy's street. Apron strings only stretch so far.* Instead she took a seat at the table, as far away from Franklin as possible. She accepted a tray of desserts from her father, seated next to her.

Shirley and Josephine sat together, heads close, mouths moving quickly. Violet turned to her father who happily bit into a little square confection with pale green icing. She whispered into his ear. "Dad, do something with her, please."

His mouth full of cake, Charlie Terhune flashed his deep blue eyes with the life-long million dollar question—"Are you kidding me?"

"Please, Dad. This is embarrassing." And then it got worse.

"Violet," Deborah said in a tone as sweet as the fondant frosting on her little cakes. "Franklin was telling us earlier how much he's looking forward to the wedding."

"Great," Violet said.

"He's the Best Man, you know," his mother added.

"Uh, no. I didn't know. That's, uh, nice."

"He's looking forward to seeing a bit of the scenery up there. Aren't you Franklin?"

Coffee dribbled over Franklin's ample lips and sped down his chin. He quickly placed the cup back in its saucer with a racket, then pulled his napkin from his lap and pressed it to his face.

"Yes. Yes I am."

"Terrific," Violet said, the word sounding exactly to her like fingernails raking a blackboard.

"You could probably give him a tour, Violet. You

know, show him around," Josephine added with a nod of her little curly head.

"Well, sure, if there's time." Violet said. "I mean we'll all be so busy with the wedding and all." She turned to Penny for help, which she already knew was ludicrous, but she was desperate. "*This* maid of honor takes her job seriously."

"Nonsense," Josephine said. "You'll have plenty of time. It'll be nice for both of you. You know, since you'll both be there without a partner, and everything."

Before she could think Violet blurted out a response. "But, I do have a date."

Josephine looked startled, and Violet couldn't blame her. She was pretty startled herself.

"You do? Since when?"

"Since, um, the other day."

"So who is this date?"

"Ted."

"The Salami?" Josephine spat the word as if someone had served a plate of Hormel Genoa when she had been expecting filet mignon.

Around the pretty cross-stitched clothed table, all eyes were on her. Violet gave a little laugh. "My mom teases me about my friend, Ted Solomon. She calls him Salami, but it's all in good fun."

The eyes around the room darted like a frenzied family of flies looking for a way out. And, that's just how Violet felt. She needed an escape hatch.

"Violet, that's so nice that Ted's joining you," Penny suddenly piped in. "I know how much you admire him." Penny then turned to the others around the table. "Ted is Violet's boss at the magazine. He's a brilliant man. He's probably the main reason *Today's Hearth* is as successful as it is."

Violet fixed her eyes on her little sister and gave her a silent, heartfelt, "Thank you." However, she could not keep the shock from her gaze either. The kid had saved her ass. Not only was that rare, it was almost unheard of.

Violet excused herself and found the powder room. Naturally, its walls were covered in a papered pattern of hydrangea blooms. She closed the door and dug her cell phone from her purse.

As she listened to Ted's phone ringing she studied the tiny little white tiles on the floor. They looked like clean bright teeth.

She shook her head. She was stranded in the land of oral hygiene.

"Hello?"

"Ted, it's me, Violet," she whispered into the phone. She turned on the faucet to drown her voice.

"Why are you whispering? You in church or something?"

"I'm at the in-law dinner."

"Yeah, so?"

"Well, remember how you agreed to come with me to the wedding?"

"You mean do I remember how you took advantage of a poor defenseless man who happened to be enjoying a few beers? Then...yes."

"Ted, I'm serious. I know you're coming to be my photographer, but you also have to be my date."

"Why Terhune. This is so sudden," Ted said.

Violet could almost see the sinister grin on the man's face.

"They're trying to fix me up with the groom's cousin."

"So that's what this is all about," Ted said, letting out a string of chuckles.

"His name is Franklin."

"They actually call the guy Franklin?"

"Yes."

"And he's Benjamin's cousin? As in Benjamin Franklin?"

"Oh my God."

"Think he wants to show you his lightning rod?" And then Ted laughed so hard at his own joke that he started coughing.

"Ted, if I didn't need you, I'd kill you."

Chapter Nine

Violet came prepared for Monday's meeting. Although Melanie Rosen arrived with a full-fledged PowerPoint presentation outlining the anticipated consumer satisfaction and frugality of self-appointed spa getaways, Violet's less technology-oriented spiel on her idea was well-received. Thanks to her dry run with Ted, Violet played up the opportunity for advertisers to jump on her birding bandwagon. The only glitch was when she announced that Ted Solomon was going to accompany her on the trip as her photographer.

"Ted's not a photographer," Melanie said through a sideways smirk. "You're bringing him to mentor you through this project."

Melanie turned to Robert Matthews who sat at the head of the long mahogany conference table with a laptop open in front of him. "Rob, is this acceptable?"

"Why wouldn't it be?" Rob asked.

"You're the one that made this a challenge between the two of us, so if you make it a game, Rob, you need to define the rules. Can one of us bring a mentor along for the ride and still have this be a fair playing field?"

Violet looked to Rob. His face was not easy to read. Violet knew that he had a connection to Melanie that gave her an advantage of her own. Rob carefully ran his pinky-ringed hand over his perfectly coiffed head.

"Melanie, as far as I'm concerned, however you two produce what this magazine needs to elevate its readership is fine with me. For all I care, you can go hire Martha Stewart to ghost for you. Hey, ingenuity always wins, Melanie. You know that."

Violet let the air that had been lodged in her lungs release in a slow steady leak so that neither of the dynamic duo would detect that she had been scared for a minute. She could not go up to Vermont without Ted. Not only was the man going to help her with the magic of his camera, he was going to keep her from having a mental breakdown with all that awaited her at The Pines.

****

Violet's frou-frou maid of honor dress hung from the hook in the back seat of her Saab, covered by a thick white vinyl garment bag. When she turned corners the bag swayed like a ghost with a swishing sound reminding her of its presence. As if she needed to be reminded.

She drove up the New York State Thruway. Images flipped in her mind like a slide projector clicking its way through a wheel of photographs from a family vacation. With each picture she gripped her steering wheel tighter.

She searched radio channels for a song she could sing. She ran through lists of toiletries in her head to make sure she had brought everything she needed. Anything to distract herself from what she knew was swiftly approaching—Exit 23.

Violet saw the sign and turned in the direction of Troy/Bennington. In spite of the churning that tied her insides into a knot, she traveled along the lush green landscape, marveling at the scenery around her.

She turned onto Colchester Road. Taking it to the end, she saw that there was a new sign at the entrance. It was wooden, like the one that Violet remembered from her childhood. But, this one was fancier with engraved gold lettering that announced boldly that she had arrived at The Pines.

The drive into the complex was no longer a rutty dirt road. Now, Violet travelled along a paved private roadway. Attractive wrought iron lanterns lined the way, like soldiers at attention. She scanned the parking lot for familiar cars feeling the need to be in the midst of company. There was security in numbers, especially when you went back in time.

Benjamin's shiny black sedan was there, easily recognizable with its vanity plate that boasted his initials as well as the letters of his credentials. Violet's father's Jeep was there, as well. Knowing her family was there should have helped, but it didn't. She still felt like a marching band was parading through her gut.

Violet pulled her car up to the entrance of the lodge, put her car in park, and just sat there. Everything looked new. And why wouldn't it? It had been a lifetime ago when she had last visited. The weathered siding had been replaced with beautiful honey-colored logs that looked clean and bright.

There was a grand-looking bank of windows along the front that gave Violet a good view of the lobby. That, too, was totally transformed. She saw stuffed sofas and chairs covered in rich green fabric, and plenty of wooden tables with textured ceramic ginger jar lamps sitting neatly with their pleated shades. The large stone fireplace still adorned the far wall.

The front desk was larger and statelier. There were two females behind the glossy wooden counter, each wearing hunter green golf shirts.

Violet stepped out of her car and stretched, stalling the inevitable. She shut her door as quietly as she could. She could not help but remember every single time she had arrived at this destination. Each time the sound of her father's car door had brought Logan to greet them.

She braced herself as she went around to the trunk and popped it with a touch to her remote. By the time she pulled out her laptop and briefcase she started to wonder when it would happen. The anticipation was killing her. She turned toward the doorway to the lodge and waited. Still no Logan.

Okay, she thought. She'd take this little gift of time. It would be soon enough that she would have to see him. She went into the lobby and looked around. It was a beautifully appointed space with a nice mix of hominess and sophistication. *Who did this*? she wondered. This was a far cry from the rustic cabin-like retreat of yesteryear.

Violet approached the registration desk and the two young females overseeing it. Violet gave each girl a glance and knew without a doubt that the one nearest her was Logan's daughter. She had his eyes. They were the blue of a spring sky, clear, startling, riveting. She was tall and slender with a mane of wheat-colored hair pulled back into a ponytail. The name embroidered on her shirt confirmed it. *Jessica.*

"Welcome to The Pines," Jessica said with an easy, genuine smile.

"Thank you." Violet distracted herself by digging into her purse for her reservation information.

"You're part of the Terhune/Layne wedding?"

"Yes."

"Name?"

"Violet Terhune." She waited for Jessica to look up from her computer screen and show recognition. *Surely she had heard her name before. Had Logan not mentioned to his daughter that this wedding included a major blast from his past?*

Nothing. Jessica continued to tap keys on her keyboard. The girl had that same little wrinkle in her brow that Violet remembered would appear on Logan's forehead when he was concentrating on something.

When Jessica looked up her eyes were still friendly and welcoming, but absent of any bells going off at the mention of the name Violet Terhune. "All of our rooms are smoke-free," she said.

"That's not a problem," Violet replied.

Jessica handed Violet her room key folded into a little card. "Your room is a honey," she said. Leaning closer, she gave Violet a cute little smirk. "It's my favorite. Better than the bridal suite, even."

"Really?" Violet brightened. "How so?"

"You have a view of the lake, beyond the woods. We have a lovely lake here."

Violet felt her heart stutter. "Yes," Violet said softly. "I know."

Recognition flashed into Jessica's gaze, "That's right. Your whole family used to come here every summer. I keep forgetting."

"Yes, it was a long time ago, and things sure have changed around here," Violet said. "But I was pretty sure the lake hadn't been moved."

"Oh, you just wait," Jessica said. "You won't believe how different the place is."

Violet walked across the lobby to climb the large staircase, its patterned burgundy and green carpet a stunning contrast against the fine wood of the banister. She found her room at the end of the hallway and was equally impressed when she opened the door.

Her room had a fireplace and was done in jewel tones of blue and gold. The bed was a four-poster of antique mahogany. A large chest of drawers against the wall was accented by an elaborately etched mirror.

Violet put her purse and laptop onto a small table and went right for the French doors on the far wall. She turned the latch, pushed the door, and stepped out onto a small balcony. She didn't remember any rooms having balconies. They must have been another of the add-ons.

Out across the balustrade Violet saw the sunlight-glistened lake beyond the trees. The woodland was even greener and denser than she remembered, thick with trees of all varieties. But the pines towered higher than all the rest.

A lone bird flew above the treetops, its wings spread wide against the cloudless sky. Violet remembered her supplementary mission. She needed to produce a story on birding retreats inspiring enough for her readership to scramble for their binoculars and more importantly, their wallets.

She was sure The Pines could benefit from her piece. The way the place had transformed into a retreat for sophisticates was just the backdrop Mr. Robert Matthews was looking for. This was going to be a piece of cake—albeit a five-tiered white-frosted cake, decorated with roses, and topped with a little plastic bride and groom.

A tall male figure emerged from the woods. He wore a baseball cap on his down-turned head. She saw that it was not Logan when the man lifted his head. Her heart relaxed from its quickened state. She stood at the railing, hand on her chest, wondering how long it would be before Logan did arrive in her line of vision.

When the bellman knocked at her door she jumped. She knew she needed to get a grip. After proffering the appropriate tip and thanking him for delivering her belongings, she said to herself, *For crying out loud, you've got a whole week to get through. You can't freak now.*

She studied the itinerary that Penny had forwarded to her email. This evening at eight there was a welcome reception for all the wedding family and guests. The printout indicated it was being held in the Garden Grove.

That was also new. There hadn't been any

Garden Grove all those years ago, the same way there hadn't been any balconies, fancy lobby. Or bellmen to deliver your luggage. She shook her head. Life was change, that was for sure, and change definitely had found its way here.

After organizing her belongings, checking her email, and reviewing the notes for her magazine piece, Violet realized she was avoiding leaving her room.

Her stomach growled its call for food. She looked at her watch. It was nearly four in the afternoon and she hadn't eaten a thing since breakfast. She wished she had thought to bring a box of granola bars with her. Now she had no choice but to go seek some sustenance. She decided to call the bride.

"Violet!" She closed her eyes as she sat on the bed's lush coverlet. Penny sounded so happy Violet thought the girl might spontaneously combust.

"Have you eaten anything?" Violet asked.

"Are you kidding? Mom's here. Of course we ate."

Violet chuckled. Josephine never went anywhere without a stash of food. The woman was a walking automat.

"I'm starving. What do you have?"

"Come on over to our room. The bridal suite is at the far end of the north wing. Can you believe the way they changed this place? It's like a country manor."

"I know," Violet said. "Things are definitely different."

"Well, hurry. Daddy's just about to open a bottle of wine."

****

The bridal suite was lovely and spacious, but Violet concurred with what Jessica had told her. The room overlooking the lake was better. This suite, however, had its advantages. There was a mini-kitchen and a bar on one side, and a sizeable sitting area with a sofa and easy chairs. Again, Violet marveled at the decorator's taste. The suite was a sumptuous blend of creams in varying fabrics, accented by taupe taffeta pillows, and vanilla-scented candles in cut glass holders scattered throughout.

Charlie Terhune stood at the bar wrestling with a corkscrew and a bottle of chardonnay.

"Hey, Daddy-o," Violet said. "Need some help there?"

"Nah," Charlie said through clenched lips. "I got it." The cork popped from the mouth of the bottle and Charlie proceeded to pour splashes of the golden liquid into wine glasses. At the other end of the bar, Josephine stood in her peach-colored French terry pant-set working on a slab of Münster. She sliced through the cheese with a paring knife and arranged the paprika-edged squares onto an ironstone dish.

"Charlie," Josephine said. "What did you do with the crackers?"

"I didn't touch them, Lamb Chop," Charlie said, lifting his dark blue eyes to meet Violet's. They shared a little smile.

"Well they're not in the bag," Josephine said. "And, I know I put them in there."

"What bag, Ma?" Violet stepped closer to where her mother was working.

Josephine pointed the paring knife toward a cluster of shopping bags on the floor. "In one of them."

"Let me look," Violet began to rifle through the bags. There was tea—both regular and decaffeinated—a box of artificial sweetener, potato chips, and a bottle of ginger ale.

"No crackers, Ma."

"I know I brought them. Why else would I bring cheese?"

"Maybe you put them in the cabinet," Violet moved now to stand beside her mother, dwarfing her. She sensed Josephine's heightened emotion—panic almost—and it confused her. *After all,* Violet reasoned, *it's just crackers.* Violet opened the cabinet above Josephine's head. She went from door to door in the little kitchen, but found no crackers.

"What are we supposed to do with all this cheese and no crackers?" Josephine asked. She waved the paring knife in the air like a conductor who was angry at his orchestra.

"Eat it." Violet grabbed a slice from the plate. "I'm famished."

"Cheese is good to absorb the wine," Charlie said as he handed Violet a goblet. They clinked their glasses together creating a nice tingling sound.

"To the bride and groom," Charlie said. He looked over to Penny who was making notes on her own copy of the week's itinerary.

"Don't eat too much, you two," Penny said. "There's a reception tonight, don't forget. Ben's parents just arrived. His aunt and uncle are here already."

Josephine's attention turned from the missing crackers. "How about Franklin?"

Violet cringed.

"I'm not sure, but I'm going to guess if his parents are here, that he is, too."

"That's a given," Charlie said with a laugh.

"Charlie," Josephine scolded. "Don't do that. Franklin's a great catch for somebody. Any girl—who wants to have a nice life and doesn't want to live like a gypsy in a dirty, crowded city, and be all alone all the time—would be lucky to meet a nice doctor like him."

"He's not a medical doctor," Charlie said.

"He's almost a doctor, okay? Almost."

Violet had walked over to the refrigerator to see

if there was anything else to eat besides the Münster. When she opened the door she saw that there was a bag of seedless red grapes and, lo and behold, a box of Triscuits sat on the shelf right beside them.

"Hey, Ma," Violet said retrieving the box and waving it toward her mother. "You keeping these things on ice for a reason?"

Josephine's mouth dropped open. She darted a look to her husband who remained motionless across the room. She turned to meet Violet's amused gaze. She even clucked her tongue at the precious bride-to-be when she let out her routine high-pitched chirp.

"Who put those in there?" Josephine asked.

"I'm going to guess it was you." Violet said.

"Okay Miss Wisenheimer, okay," Josephine said. "Maybe I'm just flustered about all the wedding plans. Pour me some of that wine so I can calm my nerves."

Violet turned to her father to share their usual conspiratorial look of amusement and was surprised to see that his eyes were filled with concern. Violet took a big sip of her wine. Maybe it would calm her nerves, too.

"Does everyone have a copy of the little map they give you at the front desk?" Penny asked. "So much has changed around here I want to make sure everyone knows where they're going."

"Don't worry your pretty little head, Penny from Heaven," Charlie said to his youngest daughter. "Here have some wine."

"The Garden Grove is out that way," Penny said, ignoring her father's offer and pointing out a dormer window.

Violet looked at the window and knew instinctively where her sister was pointing. That was the direction of the hunter's cabin. It was there that Violet had spent her most memorable moments during her visits to The Pines. There she had laughed until she cried, cried until she was spent, loved for the first time, and then felt her own heart shatter into a million bits.

It was the setting for all that and more. And thanks to her sister's discovery in the attic, it was chronicled in a diary that Violet could not help but continue to read.

****

August 18, 1979
Dear Diary,

I knew immediately that there was something wrong with Logan. He seemed weird since we arrived and when I met him in the cabin tonight the look in his eyes confirmed it.

I sat down on one of the old sofa cushions Logan swiped from a renovation project his parents had done. He sat down on the hard wood floor, his back up against the wall. His arms were folded over his knees, hands clasped. And, he just stared straight ahead with his pretty blue eyes full of clouds.

"Okay," I said. My chest was tight like I was wearing a harness. "What is it?"

He blinked the clouds away and really looked at me.

"I don't know where to begin," he said and reached up and gave his thick hair a quick shove from his forehead.

"Just say it, Logan."

"I took Caroline to my prom."

"I know that, Logan. You told me, remember? I wanted to come, really I did, but I had finals and our school's spring musical was that weekend and I was in the chorus. So, I know you took someone else. It's okay."

"Well, I, uh, I'm sort of seeing her."

The words hit me like a ball of ice in my face. I could actually feel the stinging on my skin. All I could think was that Logan was in love with someone else.

We just stared at each other for what felt like a long time. I could almost hear both of our hearts thumping like natives beating out drum messages from one village to another. Only, I didn't want this message.

"What are you telling me?" I finally managed to ask.

Logan shrugged. "I don't know," he said and made a sound that could have been a little laugh, but he was not laughing at all.

I waited. I just sat there and waited for him to be ready to tell me. That's how it is with Logan. He thinks long and hard before he will speak his thoughts. It's like he has a judge and jury in his head and he waits until all the facts are presented before he makes his closing remarks. So, I waited because I knew eventually he would tell me. He always does.

"It's just that she's here, Violet. You know?" Logan said several minutes later. I could tell by the warmth in his voice that he had wrestled everything he was thinking and that he had a good grip on it now. "I mean, last night we went to the drive-in. We went to see Life of Brian. You know, the new Monty Python movie."

"How was it?" I asked, sounding wounded but I didn't care because I felt wounded and he should know that.

"It was hysterical if you like Monty Python. I happen to love Monty Python. She..." He stopped then, cleared his throat like he could dislodge the word "she" from his sentence and swallow it, make it go away. But then he continued. "Caroline didn't care for it."

"Logan," I said and scrunched myself closer to him. "Listen, I see people in New Jersey. We've had this conversation. I mean, we're kids, we have to go

out and stuff."

"I know," he said.

"So, what are you telling me now, Logan?"

"She really likes me, and she doesn't know about you. And I feel like I'm, I don't know, lying to her or something."

"Well, we wouldn't want Caroline to be upset would we?" I spat, then pushed myself up from the cushion on the floor. I bolted out the door.

I ran and ran all the way back to my room here and I cried silently so Penny wouldn't hear me, which is not easy to do when you want to wail.

Then I heard the noise outside the window right above my head. I sat up, dried my eyes with the heels of my hands and peeked out the heavy plaid curtain. I saw his lantern and the glow it cast illuminated his arm and his upper body. I could see his face in the shadows. He was staring up at me.

I didn't even put my shoes on. I slipped out the door and padded down the stairs to where Logan stood in the grassy courtyard. In a moment I stood in front of him, panting, my chest heaving under my baggy tee shirt.

"I love you, Violet," he said, his voice sounding choked, painful. "Only you."

I didn't speak a word, didn't breathe a syllable, didn't move a muscle. I stood there and let tears of relief spill from my eyes. This is what is forever etched on the wall of the hunter's cabin. And Logan did not forget.

Chapter Ten

Violet took her wine glass with her as she crossed the room and looked out the window. She flipped the latch of the plantation shutters and gave them a gentle swing open. She let her eyes go to the place in the scenery where she knew she would be able to spy the little wooden building. She thought that the many years' growth of the trees would probably camouflage the structure, but she would be able to see at least a piece of it.

She sucked in her breath causing her family to dart to the window. Her parents and sister peered around her as she stood motionless. It was gone. The small wooden shack had apparently been replaced by the new Garden Grove, the same dining location that awaited them for the evening's dinner. Why it bothered her so much not only confused, but annoyed her. She felt the inner sting of self betrayal. *Who cares*, she tried to muster. *Who cares?*

"Oh, look! That must be the Garden Grove, where we're having dinner tonight." Penny shrieked, misconstruing Violet's reaction as one of appreciation. Penny gave Violet's shoulder a little squeeze. "It's lovely, isn't it?"

"Let me see," Josephine said, getting up on her tiptoes. "Give a girl some room."

Violet stepped aside to allow her diminutive mother to see. Josephine called out parts of the scene like a tour guide to Charlie who was too far from the window to see for himself.

"Daddy, it's got lanterns all along the walkway. Tonight it's going to be amazing," Penny gushed.

"Charlie, there's grapevines. What do you call those canopy things?"

"I don't know. Awning, maybe?"

"No no. It's something else. It's a fancy word." Josephine turned around and looked to Violet. She was so wrapped up in the thrill of the setting outside the window of the bridal suite that she failed to notice her eldest daughter had turned to stone. "Violet," she said. "You play with words all day, what do you call that roof thing with the vines on it?"

Violet turned her head as though she were submerged in mud, the goo of her own unwanted reaction slowing her response.

"Violet, what's the matter with you?" Josephine said.

The words snapped Violet back to life, lifting her from the depths of her thoughts. "Nothing, Ma," Violet said with conviction she didn't feel. "I was just racking my brain for the word you're looking for. It's *pergola*. They call that a pergola."

"That's it!" Josephine said, the smile returning to her face. She pointed her finger up in the air as though she had pulled the word from out of her own thoughts. "Pergola!"

"This evening's going to be magic," Penny said. She checked her watch. "Oh, my. It'll be time before you know it."

Violet downed the rest of her chardonnay.

****

As predicted, the lighted walkway was breathtaking. Violet approached the Garden Grove knowing she was the last of her family to arrive.

All the time she had been showering and getting dressed she had tried to come up with a good enough reason to ditch this party. She wanted no part of any of it. She didn't want to dine in the open air restaurant.

Her low black sandals clicked loudly as she walked along the flagstone floor covering the place where the hunter's cabin had stood for so many years. It felt disrespectful, like walking over graves in a cemetery.

Add to that the fact that invariably she would have to run into Logan. She may have been able to avoid him so far, but it was only a matter of time when she would have to come face-to-face with the man. She wished that Ted Solomon was here already. If nothing else the man could divert her attention from all the memories that hung over her head like the grape vines on that Josephine-approved pergola.

At the end of the lighted path she saw Franklin at the bar getting two glasses of wine. Violet smirked. It had to be that one of those beverages was for his mommy. That was the other reason she could use Ted right now, to help her dodge Dr. Franklin Layne.

The happy betrothed couple stood at the buffet table, heads together, white dishes in their hands, making buffet choices in tandem. Violet let her eyes scan the restaurant. She hated to admit it really was outstanding.

On the periphery stood a man with closed eyes and a look of sheer rapture on his face as he sliced his bow over the strings of his violin. Violet watched the people around her as if watching a movie on a screen. Everyone was engaged in conversation, greeting each other with joyous sounds that floated on the air along with the gentle notes from the musician's strings.

Violet found herself in the center of it all, yet totally apart from it. The ripe-tomato-colored lightweight fabric of her A-line dress, coupled with her naked arms chilled her in the evening air. She wished she had thought to bring along a sweater.

Lanterns overhead drenched her in their yellow glow.

As she looked in the direction of her destination—the bar—she saw him, and stopped dead. Tall, broad-shouldered, and wearing a dark suit, Logan stood erect next to the bar. His eyes were fixed on her. His still-blond hair fell forward over his brow just as it had when he was a boy. He reached up and gave his hair that familiar push up over his crown, as though perfecting his view of her.

Violet held her small evening bag in front of her gripped tightly in both hands like a brick or a shield of iron. Try as she might air would not pull into her lungs even as her chest heaved. The violin's notes cried to her, encircling her as if the strings from the instrument had magically soared across the room and snared her, making her unable to run from the scene.

But the violin did not bind Logan. Rather, it seemed that each note that met her ears served as a vehicle for him to glide toward her on the legato. The satin bag in her hands may as well have been a dishrag wrung of its saturation.

With all the guests contributing to the palpable movement of energy, the two now stood together in the center of the floor. The lantern directly above their heads spotlighted them in a single circle of light.

Then it was as if everyone and everything around them disappeared. Time hid in the shadows beyond the golden glow that encircled them. It was just Logan and Violet standing in the hue; their feet planted on elegantly positioned tiles.

"Violet." His voice was deeper, richer, the sound of a man.

The sound of her name coming from his lips worked as a release to the tightness that held her immobile. She felt her hands loosen on the poor misshapen purse she held. Her lungs yielded to the welcoming air that filled them.

Violet studied his eyes; saw their familiar blue brightness, their thick dark lashes accenting them like a fringe. She smiled, unable to help herself. After all, this was Logan—her Logan. All the time that had elapsed meant nothing at this moment.

Logan's mouth turned up into a grin exposing that one dimple that always stayed hidden in his cheek until it felt like revealing itself. Violet's heart, remembering how to react to its presence, quickened. "Good to see you, Logan," she said, extending her hand.

Logan clasped his fingers around her hand, and their palms touched with familiar warmth. "You haven't changed," he said.

Violet gave a little laugh and let her hand fall away from his. She reached up and tucked a stray lock of hair behind her ear. "This lamplight is playing tricks on your eyes."

"It's funny you should say that," Logan said. "When I saw you standing here, for a minute I thought I was seeing things. I mean, I knew you were coming, but seeing you here sort of stunned me, as if you were a mirage and any second you might disappear."

A constriction squeezed inside her, an imaginary caterpillar had woven its silken threads around her heart. She was not a mirage, nor was he. But, disappear? Yes, by week's end they would disappear from each other's lives yet again. Something in that realization clicked in her head making her stiffen in her total response to him.

This was nothing more than a revisit to a time that no longer existed. This was not reality. This was not truth. So, in that respect Logan was right— this was a mirage.

"I wanted to talk to you about something," Violet

said. Her voice had lost its balmy resonance. Now she sounded like herself—a grown woman with a job that needed saving, and a mission to work that pursuit into this week-long wedding-fest.

"Sure," Logan said with his dimple winking at her like a beacon guiding her through a fog. "Let's get you a drink."

He pressed his hand at the small of her back, applying just enough pressure to make Violet aware of his touch, as they made their way over to the bar. Logan greeted the bartender who called him, "Boss."

"What would you like?" Logan asked, his hand still at her back. She could feel the definition of his fingers through the thin fabric of her dress.

She thought a double shot of tequila was probably in order, but she remembered the one time she'd indulged in a silly dare during a long ago Happy Hour at Durkins. Her head had nearly spun from her neck. Violet knew that would not do now. The last thing she needed, with this big tall blond at her side, was to lose her head. "Red wine," Violet said.

"Cabernet okay?"

She nodded, thinking that Logan's taste in libations had elevated since the days when they shared a six-pack of Bud in the hunter's cabin. But, she reminded herself, that was then and this is now.

When the bartender produced two goblets of the burgundy-colored wine, Logan finally let his fingers fall away from her back. Violet felt her breath suck in. Although she wanted to think her reaction was relief, she knew it was something more like yearning. She dismissed the thought with a clink of her glass against Logan's. "To Penny and Benjamin and to their beautiful wedding at The Pines," she said.

"Cheers," Logan said, and they each took a sip from their glasses.

"The place sure has changed," Violet offered.

"How do you like it?" Logan asked. It might as well have been the dimple talking because that was all Violet could see. Her eyes were fixed on the little pucker.

"It's amazing," she said. "Really, I'm so impressed."

"Thank you," said the dimple. "Well, really you should thank my daughter. This was all her doing. She's practically running the place these days."

"I met her," Violet said. She felt a pang at the mention of his child, now a young woman herself. "Jessica. I met her when I checked in. She was at the front desk."

"Okay, who's talking about me?" a voice called from over Violet's shoulder.

Violet turned to see Logan's daughter, Jessica, wearing a black button-down vest over her starched white pleated shirt. Her wheat-colored hair was wound into a tight knot at the back of her head. Jessica's eyes were identical to Logan's; in the same way her own deep blue orbs looked back at her whenever Violet locked eyes with her own father. It was one of the special connections Violet and Charlie Terhune shared.

By the way Logan lit up when Jessica appeared, Violet could tell this was another special father/daughter team. "Hey, Jess," Logan said, offering his cheek to his daughter's quick kiss.

"You using my name in vain again?"

"Not at all. I was praising you, if you must know. Jess, this is, uh, an old friend of mine, Violet Terhune."

"Hello, Jessica. We met when I checked in."

"Yes, I remember," she said. "You're the sister of the bride."

"Yes," Violet replied. "And your Dad was definitely praising you. I commented on the lovely

95

transformation of the lodge and he gave you total credit."

Jessica smiled broadly. She had no dimple. "It's been a total labor of love," she said, raising her hand to the bun on her head. She fiddled with a bobby pin that had poked up from the smoothed strands.

"Well, it certainly shows."

"Thank you."

Violet turned her gaze to Logan who continued to beam at his daughter. "Which brings me to what I wanted to talk with you about," Violet said. She turned to Jessica. "It sounds as if I should run this by both of you."

"Shoot," Jessica said.

"I'm doing a piece for my magazine, *Today's Hearth*. It's going to be an in-depth look at the hobby of birding, and ideal places to stay that are driving distance from New York City.

"I'd like to incorporate The Pines as a spotlight to my story. My photographer will be joining me here tomorrow. For your putting up with our nosing around the place, The Pines would receive incredible exposure. The publicity could bring visitors here in droves."

Jessica opened her mouth to offer a response that Violet was sure would have been exuberant, based on the smile on her face and the shiny look of expectation in her Logan-like eyes. Violet saw those eyes cloud over, and saw the smile disappeared as she looked beyond Violet to meet her father's gaze.

Logan's mouth formed an angry frown. Violet recalled that Logan had been prone to black looks only when deeply affected by something. He had been one of those boys that saved negative reactions for things of upmost importance. The small stuff never fazed him. Something about what she just proposed had to be *big stuff* if that arc of his lips was any indication.

"Absolutely not," Logan said with a stern, authoritative snap.

"I beg your pardon?" Violet was taken aback by the sharpness in his tone.

"I'm sorry, Violet," His tone softened some, but his voice still held a firmness that spoke of finality. "I won't allow The Pines to be subjected to such a presentation."

"But, Dad..." Jessica was silenced by his penetrating stare.

"I don't understand," Violet said. "Wouldn't free publicity be a good thing?"

"Yes, it would, but..." Jessica stood with her hands at her slender hips. "But for some reason this stubborn man won't let us have any kind of national advertising, including a website."

"Logan, that's crazy. Why not?"

Logan's mouth now went from an upside down "u" to a straight pencil-thin line. If his face were an electronic heart monitor, Violet's victim of an idea would be decidedly dead.

"This discussion is over. If you'll excuse me, Violet, I have some work to do."And he was gone.

Chapter Eleven

In the wake of Logan's hasty exit Jessica excused herself. Violet did not miss the frustration in the girl's demeanor. Violet stood alone in the golden spotlight, now vacant of the momentary magic it held just minutes ago. Gone like the wine in her empty glass.

"Looks like you need another drink," she heard a voice say. It was a familiar voice with the sound that comforted as much as a blanket on a cold night.

"Hey, Dad."

"What are you drinking?"

"Red wine, uh, cabernet," she said. A picture of Logan popped into her head, the sensation of his fingers at her waist coming to her, real as real.

After they had new drinks Charlie and his eldest daughter strolled over to an empty table and had a seat. Violet let him steer her as if she was blindfolded. In a way she was, because she certainly could not see what had just happened.

"Have you eaten?" Charlie twirled his wrist making the ice cubes circle in his glass of vodka and soda on the rocks.

"Not yet."

"The food's good. Have the chicken marsala. Everyone's raving about it, even your mother."

A wry smile danced over her lips. She and her father both knew that a culinary rave from Josephine was rare praise indeed.

"How's Ma holding up tonight? She enjoying herself?"

"She's getting tired, I think. But, yes she's in her

glory. By the way, she drops that word you told her every chance she gets."

"What word?"

"Pergola," Charlie said, with a chuckle. Then he raised his voice an octave, doing his best rendition of the woman he loved. "Oh, don't you love the pergola? Pergolas are so in vogue these days. Oh, I would just love to have a pergola over my patio!"

Violet laughed. She looked around to find her mother. Josephine stood at the opposite side of the patio in a smart periwinkle linen skirt suit with a cropped jacket. Violet watched her mother gesture with her hands as she spoke animatedly to her sister, Marguerite. Marguerite was short, like Josephine, only she was larger-boned. Her blonde-dyed hair was styled like a frothy whirl of cotton candy.

"Mom seems to be enjoying Aunt Marguerite's company," Violet said.

Charlie nodded. "When those two get together it's amazing. If they were beavers they could saw through a tree in no time the way they work their jaws."

"Daddy!" Violet admonished, only she was laughing at his comment.

"Your mother's a piece of work."

"She was pretty riled up today about that box of crackers," Violet said.

Charlie's smile faded and he stared down at the drink in his hands. Then he looked back up at Violet with trouble in his midnight-colored eyes.

"What, Dad?"

"She's forgetting things." Sharpness jabbed at Violet like a blade. It was more the look in her father's eyes than the words he spoke.

"What do you mean? Like what?"

He shrugged. Violet reached over and touched his arm.

"Last week your mother forgot where she put her pocketbook. She got all flustered and went around the house like a tornado looking everywhere."

"Did she find it?"

"She had put it in the oven."

"In the oven? Seriously? I mean, was the oven on?"

"No, thank God. But the oven! It's...well, it's odd. That's all."

"You know how Mom is. She's been so consumed with the plans for this wedding. That's probably all it is."

"Maybe you're right," Charlie said, and managed a smile. "Maybe it's nothing."

Violet looked back across the room at her mother in the pretty suit. She was sure it was nothing more than the Little General running on overdrive.

****

Violet was glad when the evening ended. She walked with her parents back to their suite and could not help but keep her eyes on her mother. The woman seemed fine, tired perhaps, but they were all tired.

It had been a long evening and for Violet it had been an especially stressful one. Seeing Logan had been a mixture of emotions. On the one hand she had been thrilled to see him, talk with him, look into his eyes. But his reaction to her piece for the magazine had completely shut him down. *What businessman turns away from free publicity?*

Obviously there were things about Logan Monroe that she did not know and would never figure out. After all, her time to know him had passed.

"I saw you talking to that Logan boy," Josephine said as they made their way down the corridor to their respective rooms. Her tone was nonchalant, but Violet was not fooled.

"Yes," Violet said, hoping that's as far as the topic would go, though she knew the chance of that was nil.

"He certainly aged well," Josephine said, with a sly lilt to her tone. Her carefully selected words dangled like a morsel hooked on the end of a fishing line. The woman may be confusing her pocketbook with a pot roast, but she wasn't forgetting how to cast bait at her eldest child. "He's still quite handsome."

Violet fiddled in her evening bag in search of her room key. She knew from experience that opening her mouth to reply would render her as captive as a dead flounder. She ridiculously continued to give attention to the interior of her little purse. Ridiculous considering the pouch was the size of a beanbag and the only things in it were her cell phone and her room key. But, she kept her eyes on her task and her mouth shut.

"That is, if you like blonds," Josephine mused. "I go for the tall, dark, and handsome ones. You know, like Gregory Peck. Now, *that's* handsome."

Violet withdrew her room key and snapped her purse closed. She glanced over at her father who shook his head. The look in his eyes said exactly what Violet was thinking. *Josephine was on a roll.*

"Now, to me, I think Franklin's attractive. Don't you think so, Violet?"

Violet reached over and tucked her arm through her father's. She pulled him close, seizing a way to edge a way out of this conversation. "Not as attractive as Daddy, huh Ma? You shouldn't be shopping around when you've already got the best looking man in the whole place."

Josephine pursed her lips and waved a hand at her daughter, as clear a concession as if she were holding a little white flag.

Back in her room, shoes kicked off and her dress back on a hanger in the closet, Violet sat in a chair in her nightshirt. She looked out the French doors into the darkness of the night. Reliving her reunion of the evening, she saw Logan in her mind, his blond hair a stark contrast against the dark jacket he wore. She envisioned the way he carried himself as he strode across the flagstone floor. He had the gait of a self-assured man, a grown-up. He was no longer the jaunty athletic boy who waited for her every August of her growing-up years.

The moonlight poured down in bluish beams through the thick of trees outside her window. This was the one thing that did look familiar to Violet in this former rustic retreat in the forest.

This grand inn with its paved walkways and balconied suites was foreign, yet the view from where she sat was one that she remembered well, and it brought tears to her eyes. The light penetrating the darkness bathed every tree, every branch, the leaves, and the needles on the pines. This was the moonlight in the forest she remembered that had belonged to her. This was her gift from Logan Monroe.

****

August 16, 1980
Dear Diary,

It's funny how I knew. I just knew. On the drive up here I could feel Logan waiting for me and knew what would happen when we were together.

Tonight when we met at the cabin I saw it in his eyes. It's funny how we never discussed it beforehand. Not during our phone calls, not in our letters. Don't ask me why we both knew it would happen, but we did. Sometimes we don't even need words. We just know.

It started to rain, lightly at first, just a heavy

drizzle really. The sound of it on the wooden roof was nice. It was like that light steady tapping when a drummer uses a brush on his snare instead of sticks. Logan and I sipped beer and listened to the rhythmic tapping and we did not speak. Like I said, sometimes we don't need words.

When he leaned over and kissed me, his lips were soft and cool against mine. He tasted like beer and salt from the pretzels. I pulled away from him to look into his eyes, searched them for the reassurance I suddenly longed for. Any hesitation evaporated the second he gave me that smile and touched his fingers to my chin.

"Do you know how beautiful you are?" he whispered.

I kissed him in response. I knew how beautiful he was and how beautiful it was to love him. And as the rain continued its drumbeat on the roof above us Logan and I entangled ourselves with each other, sealed ourselves as one in the night, and irrevocably gave ourselves to each other.

A long time later, after the rain had stopped and the big round moon hung in the night sky, Logan and I made our way along the forest's path lit by the luminescence. It was a surreal exposure, the way the moonlight poured through the trees and found us with each step. We stopped, stood there on the path. Logan cupped my face into his tender hands.

"We are two trees in the forest, Violet," Logan said. "And the moonlight is the love that could not help but find us."

And now, here I am, back in my room, tucked under the blanket of my bed holding my flashlight as I write this and my heart is full and it beats by moonlight.

Chapter Twelve

Next on the list of wedding fun was the bridal shower.

Ted Solomon would arrive this evening and together he and Violet would commence work on the magazine piece. She would create a knockout story with or without Logan Monroe's help or approval. It was quite apparent from his behavior last night that it would definitely be without his assistance.

Violet gave her hair a flip with her hand, a gesture that came as close to knocking a chip from her shoulder as was possible. She had been done with worrying about Logan for a long, long time. So, if the man didn't want free publicity for his precious Pines, well that was his problem.

She had a story to write and a job title to preserve. All those years ago she had not stood in Logan's way when he decided to marry the girl that carried his child. She would not let *him* stand in her way now.

The party was for ladies only, and Violet spied the glint of gladness in her father's eyes when she arrived at their room to pick up her mother. Charlie bid them goodbye from his cushioned chair, waving a mug of coffee, a newspaper open on his lap. The two women made their way to the dining room twenty minutes early to be sure everything was in place for the midday event.

The room was set with touches of pastels, a festive look for a bridal shower. Wait staff busied themselves with place settings and poured ice water into goblets from stainless steel pitchers. Jessica was at the far end of the room. She and another young woman were carefully carrying a large sheet cake to a nearby table.

"Oh, Madonna, don't let them drop that cake," Josephine said, clutching at Violet's arm.

"Don't worry, Ma. They've got it."

"Is that taller one Logan's daughter?"

"That's Jessica, yes."

"Pretty girl."

"Yes."

"She could use a little meat on her bones. Why is everybody so skinny nowadays?"

Just then Josephine's sister, Marguerite, arrived carrying an elaborately wrapped gift box. "What a lovely gift, Aunt Marg," Violet said, taking the box from the woman's grasp.

"It's that fancy blender Penny wanted. It's too bad there's no surprise in it." Marguerite closed her eyes and shrugged a shoulder, a gesture akin to one of Josephine's moves. "Kids these days register for everything they want and you just go on the computer and click a button on what you're going to buy. One-two-three. They take all the fun out of it."

"Huh," Josephine added. "You think that's bad. That's how girls meet their husbands these days. They go on the computer and click a button for a man. You want a tall one? Click this button. You want a rich one? You click that button."

"You pulling my leg, Josie?" Marguerite asked. "You must be."

"Violet, tell your aunt. Tell her how shopping for a blender and shopping for a man are the same thing nowadays. You just go on the computer and get one.

"Maybe they even have coupons, too. They probably have some men on clearance. You know, the ones that ladies picked but brought back with their receipt because after they got him home he didn't match the furniture."

Marguerite laughed and put a spotted, well-manicured hand to her chest. Now Josephine shrugged her shoulder making the orchid corsage she wore as "Mother of the Bride" nod up and down as though it were in agreement with the protestations.

"Violet, why don't you go click yourself a husband?" Marguerite jibed.

"I might ask you the same question, Aunt Marg. You're single, too."

Josephine laughed out loud at that one. Violet knew that her mother especially enjoyed her sister receiving a good zing. Sibling rivalry never dies.

"I'm an old-fashioned girl," Marguerite said. She held her chin high with her eyes nearly closed and fluttering as if they'd captured a couple of moths. "I prefer to be courted, like in the old days. If a gentleman wants my attention, he can come calling."

Josephine gave a nudge to Marguerite's ribs with her elbow as she nodded in Violet's direction. "This one here has a man completely interested in her attention, a doctor no less, and she's acting all snooty about it."

"Ma." Violet gave a loud sigh. "I'm not being snooty about Franklin. I just think you and his mother have greater ideas about the two of us than is realistically going to happen."

Luckily for Violet other guests had begun arriving. Penny's college roommates and sorority sisters flitted into the room like a swarm of yellow jackets all a-buzz. Benjamin's mother walked in too, with his Aunt Shirley, Franklin's mom.

"I'm going to put Aunt Marguerite's present with the other gifts." Violet leaned down and spoke to her mother. "I'll meet you at the table."

"Okay, Violet." Josephine reached to touch the cluster of curly ribbon that sat atop Marguerite's elaborately wrapped package. "By the way, what's in the box?"

Violet felt her breath catch in her throat. Had her mother really just asked her that question? She looked to her aunt, who had concern creeping into her dark, nearly black eyes.

"Ma, you mean this box? It's Aunt Marguerite's present for Penny. It's the blender she wanted. Aunt Marg went on the computer to order it, remember?"

Josephine gave a laugh and touched her fingertips to her forehead. "Of course, yes, of course. I knew that."

****

Violet placed the box on the gift table and greeted ladies as they arrived. She wanted to grab the chance to speak to Jessica before Penny appeared, and the festivities began. Violet made her way over to the girl who now stood at the entrance to the room.

Jessica smiled tentatively when she caught sight of Violet approaching her. Again, Violet was startled at the way Jessica's expression was identical to Logan's.

"Hello, Violet," Jessica said. "How do you like the room?"

"It's lovely," Violet said. "I know Penny's going to be so pleased."

"Listen, I was wondering, can we meet for a drink later, maybe? I'd like to talk with you about that conversation we had with my dad last night."

It was as if the girl was reading her mind. She could tell that although Jessica had kept her mouth shut at the time, she did not agree with her father's abrupt decline of Violet's offer of publicity. Logan had said that Jessica was practically running the place nowadays. The girl probably had a better sense about what a centerfold story highlighting The Pines would do for their business.

"I'd love to," Violet said.

"Okay, let's meet in the Lounge around five. Will that work for you?"

Violet knew that Ted Solomon would be arriving around then. The timing couldn't be more perfect for her to take another stab at having The Pines cooperate in her quest.

She thought of Melanie Rosen suddenly and wondered how her project was going. Violet figured that Melanie and Jessica were about the same age. She took a deep breath and let the air release from her lungs. The world was being taken over by twenty-somethings.

Penny arrived and all the women rose from their gilt chairs and offered soft applause. Violet affixed a corsage to her sister's shoulder and gave her a kiss on the cheek. Truly, the girl looked stunning with her coppery hair cascading down her back in lush fat tendrils. Although in her mid-thirties, Penny could easily pass for a college kid.

Her pale celadon-colored shift accentuated her curvy little figure. Violet, lacking the girlish curves, could not help but compare herself to the pretty little bride-to-be.

Penny was the spitting image of Grandma Sophia, Josephine's mother. She, too, had had a mane of red hair and according to family lore she had been the envy of all in her younger days.

Another image of Grandma Sophia popped into Violet's head—one from the disturbing times during her grandmother's declining years. The formerly feisty old woman sat silently day in and day out in her upholstered recliner staring aimlessly out her living room bay window. The once-red mane was then a sparse crown of wispy strands of white cotton.

During Violet's visits, the health aid would make them all a pot of tea. Sophia would accept spoonfuls of the aromatic liquid into her mouth, most of the tea dribbling onto her terry bib. Violet would do her best to extract words of response from her grandmother, trying to spark a memory in her beloved relative.

Once in a while a glimpse of the old girl would return in the form of a smile or a nod of her shaky head. Something would indicate that Sophia had resurfaced with the brevity and splendor of a firecracker bursting in a night sky. And when it was gone, it left Violet without her grandmother, yet again. The last days of her grandmother's life had been filled with such moments, filled with a thousand goodbyes.

Violet snapped back to the present, unable to stand the images in her mind, unwilling to consider that history could possibly repeat itself in the Terhune family. It just could not happen.

She sat beside her sister at a small table during their meal of cold salmon salad and ambrosia. Before dessert, Violet spotted trouble. She spied two of Penny's college buddies—a pair of giggling young housewives; oddly each named Jennifer—approaching their table.

One of them carried a stack of papers that she delivered to the shower guests like exam forms. She had a cordless microphone in one hand and looked so eager to use it. Violet figured this had to be the one they called "Crazy Jen."

The other Jen carried two white wicker baskets, their handles looped over her arms making her look like a milk maid. One basket was filled with chocolate candy kisses she doled out in handfuls to each table of guests, a grown-up candy-bearing flower girl. The other basket, Violet saw, was filled with little white cards. A confirming thud hit her in the stomach like a punch. Dear God, Bridal Bingo.

"Crazy Jen" called the game by withdrawing a card from "Milk Maid Jen's" wicker basket. This one hadn't spoken a word yet. She merely glanced repeatedly over to Penny, each time giggling with a scrunching of her shoulders.

"Blender!" Crazy Jen called into her microphone and the room was abuzz with participation. Violet looked down at the photocopied grid that had been placed in front of her. No box marked blender.

She picked up a chocolate. Penny grabbed her arm so hard she thought it would leave a mark. "You have it?" she asked, excited by the possibility.

"Nope," Violet said, pulling the foil from the kiss and popping it into her mouth. "Just feeling like a little chocolate."

That, apparently, was enough for the non-crazy Jen to perk up.

"No eating the bingo chips! You're the maid of honor. You should know better."

Even a smooth, succulent chocolate melting on her tongue couldn't erase the sour taste in her mouth. When Bridal Bingo was finally over, Violet counted the cluster of discarded foil wrappers accumulated on the table. Six chocolate kisses sat in her belly like rocks.

The game winner, Benjamin's mother, was appropriately pleased with her prize—a cellophane wrapped over-sized mug from Starbucks filled with biscotti and a package of ground coffee. After catching a piercing side glance coming at her from Penny's dark, narrowed eyes, ridiculous though it was, Violet found herself joining the room-wide applause with a soundless clap of her hands.

Like one rotten tooth begets another, the next round of agony began. It was time to open the gifts. Penny summoned Violet to perform one of her maid of honor duties by putting her in charge of package handling. The two Jens were kept busy with scissors and a paper plate creating an absurd hat with all the package dressings.

The bride-to-be accepted each gift like a queen

on her throne receiving offerings from her loyal
subjects. She gushed appropriately to each giver.
Then Violet would whisk the package away and grab
the next. After blenders—*Bingo!*—bath towels,
sheets, pots, and pans were enthused over like gems,
the last gift remained on the floor. It was too big for
Violet to lift, so she pushed it close enough for Penny
to undress.

It was the china service Penny and Benjamin
had put on their registry—Violet's gift for the happy
couple—a white-on-white pattern of English china
called Elegant Cottage.

Violet remembered the day she had met Penny
and their mother at a small pub in Morristown. She
had been in town that day for her annual check-up.

"The china is simply beautiful," Penny had said
with a bubble of delight as they settled themselves
at a small table. "It has embossed vines all around
the edge. Mom says the best dishes to get are white
ones because you don't want a pattern to take away
from the presentation of the food you put on it.
Right, Mom?"

Penny had looked over to their mother studying
a large leather menu. Josephine's response had been
a tight little grin that acknowledged that she was
indeed the authority on dishes, and in fact,
everything good and evil in the world of kitchens.

Violet had remembered her mother's comment
about the dishes she had chosen for her apartment—
rustic ironstone of earthy browns lavishly glazed
with a frosty swirl edging. "They look like a project
from a child's art class." Violet loved her dishes and
couldn't care less about the way they did nor did not
compete with the moo shoo pork or pan pizza she
plopped onto them.

Now Violet watched as Penny gingerly lifted a
plate from the box on her lap and held it up as if it
was a trophy and she were the victor at Wimbledon.

The ladies around the room murmured in a buzz of approval. Violet glanced over to her mother who wore the same prideful little grin she had worn on the day the china selection was made.

Violet could not help but wonder what Penny loved more—those white-on-white dishes or the approval she received from having chosen them. She sighed and took a sip of her juicy mimosa. If Josephine's approval was a contest, then yes indeed, Penny deserved the trophy.

Just then a figure walked into the room. When Violet saw him a chill brushed over her like a sudden wind. Logan made his way around the perimeter of the room toward her with great purpose in his stride. Each step Logan took matched the beat of her heart like a metronome.

"How is everything, ladies?" he asked in a low voice for just Violet and Penny to hear.

"Wonderful," Penny said. "Just wonderful."

"Glad to hear it," Logan responded to Penny, although his eyes were on Violet. In them Violet could see that although the words he spoke were congenial there was something incongruous going on in his head. "Violet, may I see you for a moment?"

Violet glanced over to Penny and the little bride-to-be offered a wink. Violet turned back to Logan.

"Sure." She pushed her chair from the table and stood. Tossing the napkin onto the table, she followed him as he backtracked around the seated women.

It did not go unnoticed that Violet was exiting the room behind the lodge's owner. It especially did not go unnoticed by her mother. By Josephine's scowl of disdain, making her look like the aroma of over-cooked broccoli had just met her nostrils, Violet knew there was an interrogation in her immediate future.

Logan stopped walking when the two had

reached the anteroom just beyond the glass double doors. In a club chair sat Ted Solomon, his camera in his lap, a black nylon backpack at his feet. The look on his face was of sheer amusement. Violet knew instinctively that whatever this was about would not be the least bit funny to her.

Chapter Thirteen

"Call off your lackey."

Violet stared at Logan. His hands were on his hips, his mouth pulled into an angry line. He reached up and gave the fallen blond lock on his forehead a jab. She swallowed hard and turned to look at Ted who now raised a finger into the air. "Uh, that would be me." An ear-to-ear grin was plastered on his insufferable face as he spoke.

"Lackey?" Violet asked. Logan continued to look at her with his angry lipless mouth. Suddenly she thought he looked like a Muppet, most certainly Bert rather than Ernie. "Logan, calm down. What's the problem?"

"I thought I made myself clear," Logan said. "No pictures. No article. Leave The Pines out of your rag mag."

"Rag mag?" Violet's hands flew to her hips now, and she squared her shoulders. Maybe *she* could question the overall importance of *Today's Hearth*—especially when she had to do pieces that were, God forgive her, for the birds—but Logan Monroe did not have that right.

Logan pointed a finger at Ted. "If I see Jimmy Olsen over here snapping pictures of my lodge again, I'm going to serve him that camera of his for dinner."

"Ted, what happened?" Violet asked.

Ted shrugged and lifted his hands in a gesture of surrender. "While I was checking into my room, I inquired into your whereabouts. I was told you were here at the shower. After settling into my room, I thought I'd take a few preliminary shots of the place.

Then Hulk Hogan came at me and offered to escort me out the door."

Violet narrowed her gaze, focusing on Logan "Seriously?"

Turning her attention to her long-time boss, she said, "Ted, we have to talk...later."

Refocusing on Logan, she continued, "First of all, this is Ted Solomon, an executive consultant for *Today's Hearth* magazine. He's doing me an extreme favor by being here to work with me on my assignment. It's absurd that you would insult this man and call him 'my lackey,' of all things, when you don't even know him."

"Well, I..."

"No!" Violet pointed a finger at him with the distinct aim of a marksman. "You listen to me, Mr. Monroe. I am not through. Ted and I have not had the chance to discuss your stipulations about The Pines not being a part of my story. As you know, he just arrived. So, calm down and give me a chance to let him know that for some cockamamie reason you don't want your precious lodge to be exposed to the world.

"And P.S., I think you're nuts."

Logan's eyes smoldered with annoyance. She watched his chest heave under his light blue golf shirt. His tongue grazed a quick swipe to his lips that had now found their way back onto his face. She ignored the way they glistened, even parted with pink appeal.

Ted started to chuckle and both Logan and Violet turned their heads in the direction of the chortling sound. "Guess she told you, huh, buddy? What's the name again? Hogan or Logan?"

Violet closed her eyes. She loved the man like a brother—an older, sometimes idiotic brother—but Ted was going to get his ass kicked if she didn't get him out of Logan's sight.

"Ted," she said and pointed toward the doorway to the dining room. "We're having cake and coffee. Come with me."

"I like cake." Ted pushed himself up from the chair. He bent to retrieve his backpack and slung it over one shoulder. "What flavor?"

"Carrot."

He made a face. "For crissakes. Can you please tell me who the hell thought it was a good idea to put vegetables in a cake? Carrots belong around a rump roast."

Violet reached out and grabbed Ted's elbow. She turned to Logan. "If you'll excuse us," she said.

"Keep the cap on that thing," Logan said, motioning toward the Nikon that hung from Ted's neck on a thick woven strap.

"What's *with* you?" Ted asked. His tone was angry and his eyes were bright with challenge. "Have you seen how many people are walking around here with cameras? Why pick on me?"

"Our guests are snapping memories for their photo albums, not working for the media."

"Enough, Logan," Violet said. She and Ted walked away from him. "We get it."

As she turned away, Violet saw that Jessica stood at the other end of the hallway. Based on the incredulous look on her face she had to have heard the entire exchange. Violet hoped that the girl had *way more* sense than her father.

Inside the dining room guests were enjoying their dessert. Wait staff poured coffee from their carafes. Violet guided Ted toward her table. Penny had vacated her seat and was going from table to table thanking everyone for their gifts. Violet nudged Ted to a chair and sat beside him.

"Don't ask me why, but the guy says The Pines is off limits."

"So I noticed," Ted said. He looked down at the

piece of cake on the dessert plate in front of him. He picked up the fork. "Is this one mine?"

"I thought you didn't like carrot cake," Violet said.

"I didn't say I didn't like it. I just don't understand it, that's all." Ted dipped the tines of his fork into the richly iced cake and guided it to his mouth, savoring the morsel. He smacked his lips. "But it is pretty hard to resist."

Violet took a bite of her own slice of cake, trying to enjoy the richness of flavor and the thick creaminess of the cream cheese frosting. The bitter taste of Logan's words soured the experience.

"By the way, I'm sorry you had to deal with that," Violet said.

Ted shrugged as he continued to eat his cake.

"I can't explain what's happened to the man," Violet continued, remembering that she had spilled her guts about Logan to Ted the night she drove him home from Durkins. Now, she felt ridiculous that her apparently exaggerated memories had led her to the disclosure. "He's unreasonable and pompous. I guess I was just a kid when I found the guy appealing, but frankly, I don't know what I ever saw. The thought of being with a man like Logan Monroe has become now makes no sense to me."

"Kind of like me with carrot cake," Ted said, and flashed her a grin.

Violet twisted her mouth sideways, looking at Ted with her fork held in midair.

"And, if you notice my plate—" Ted said with his insufferably sly tone, "—the idea of carrots in my cake may have seemed repulsive, but once I took a taste I couldn't stop myself."

Violet put her fork down and pushed away the plate of unfinished dessert. She had had enough.

"Oh, come on, Terhune," Ted said with a laugh. "Lighten up. Just admit you're still hot for the guy."

"Ted, I swear to God, I might have to shove that camera down your throat, and save Logan the trouble."

"I was there. There's an energy between you two that you don't know what to do with. So you both take it out on your poor, innocent lackey. Now is that nice?"

Jessica walked into the room. Violet stood from her seat and turned to walk away, throwing her napkin right at Ted's face. A laugh popped up from his throat.

"Is that his kid?" Ted asked.

"Yes,"

"She looks just like him. Is she an ass, too?"

"No, as a matter of fact, she's not."

"Well, there's good news. Can I finish your cake?"

Violet looked over at Ted and saw that he hadn't bothered to wait for her answer before jabbing his fork into the half-eaten wedge. He could have her cake *and* his ridiculous comparison of it to Logan. There was no truth in the idea that there might be something redeemable about this new, grown-up version of Logan Monroe. The only thing he had in common with carrot cake was that he, too, was nutty. Looking at Ted as he indulged in her leftovers, Violet decided there was a lot of that going around.

"Violet." Jessica touched her long slender fingers to Violet's arm. "Are we still on for a drink at five?"

"Sure," Violet said. "But if you plan on discussing my magazine article, trust me, your father has made his point loud and clear."

"I'm so sorry for the way he talked to your photographer. I don't know what's gotten into him. He's usually not so...you know, so—"

Violet put her hand atop Jessica's where it rested on her arm. She gave her hand a little squeeze. "Jessica, you don't need to apologize for your father. He's responsible for his own behavior." Violet felt a churn of anger spiraling in her gut. *This poor kid has to deal with that jackass on a regular basis.*

"I'd still like us to discuss your story. I'm going to try to convince Dad to allow the publicity. It's a great opportunity."

Violet could see the hope in the girl's blue eyes. They gleamed with a vitality that Violet remembered seeing in Logan's eyes when he was young. *What happened to him? What took that glow from his eyes? What had doused him like a lid to a flame?*

"Please meet with me and help me game-plan on how to convince my father to let The Pines be featured in your magazine. Please."

"Sure, Ted and I will meet you at the bar," Violet said. Although she had no hope that whatever they strategized would change Logan's pigheaded mind, she could not disappoint this pretty young girl. After all, Violet could never resist those eyes.

Chapter Fourteen

After the shower had ended, and the guests had said their goodbyes, Violet walked with her mother, Aunt Marguerite and Penny down the corridor toward the lobby. They passed the entrance to the lounge and Violet was reminded that within the hour she would meet there with Jessica.

Ted had taken a few moments to talk with the Terhune women. To Violet's surprise he had been especially polite to Aunt Marguerite as she asked questions about his camera and his photography skills. She sensed a cheeriness in her aunt since her conversation with Ted. When he bid them good day Violet heard her aunt ask Ted if he was planning to dine with the family later that night.

"Absolutely," Ted responded, giving Violet a wicked grin. "Man does not live by carrot cake alone."

Violet clucked her tongue, even now as she walked beside her mother and navigated the staircase to their rooms, *Ted and his stupid carrot cake analogies.*

Back at Josephine and Charlie's suite, the girls occupied the seating by the windows and filled Charlie in on the doings at the shower.

"Oh, Charlie, everyone has been so generous to our birthday girl."

"Birthday girl?" Charlie asked, looking not at Josephine but at Violet. Concern pinched inside her chest, a pinprick of worry.

"Ma," Violet said, "It was Penny's shower, remember?"

"Of course, why what did I say? Did I say birthday?" Josephine said, putting a hand to her chest. "Madonna, I meant shower. I know it's not Penny's birthday."

Josephine turned to her husband and gave him a reassuring smile. "Charlie, she and Benjamin are such a lucky couple. Everyone is so generous."

And the moment passed, just like that. Whatever fog had passed through Josephine's head had visited there briefly. Her next comment proved it.

"Ah, I'm so glad I don't have to worry about her."

Her last statement screamed with the implication that although she did not have to worry about *her Penny*, she still needed to concern herself with her eldest daughter, *the old maid*. Violet felt like the cheese that stood alone on Old MacDonald's farm.

"Violet and that Logan boy are arguing," Josephine said to her husband. She plopped into a cushioned wicker chair.

"Ma, don't tell fibs," Violet said as though she were the parent and the little gray-haired lady were her incorrigible child.

Violet looked to Penny for moral support, but her sister had already left the conversation behind and started writing in her paisley fabric-covered journal. The image made Violet recall the diary that haunted her with its glimpses of her past, of her soul, of her heart. She shook the thought from her mind.

"I may be old but I still have pretty good instincts." Josephine pointed to her temple. "And I know what I saw. I saw you and that boy staring at each other like you were each about to bop the other."

"We couldn't hear what you were saying to him, but it did look like you were mad," Aunt Marguerite said.

Violet shot her a look that asked, *Whose side are you on anyway?*

Aunt Marguerite mouthed an, "I'm sorry."

As Violet would have bet, Aunt Marguerite's comment had been gasoline to Josephine's spark. Josephine sat up straighter in her chair.

"Charlie, you should have seen Violet's face. If she could have given him a good wallop, she would have."

"Well, what did he do, for crying out loud?" Charlie asked.

"Nothing, Dad, really," Violet said. "He's just worried that I'm going to include pictures of The Pines in my magazine article. He's gotten his panties in a bunch over it."

Charlie laughed.

"See!" Josephine said. "She's still hostile."

"For crying out loud," Violet said, "he's acting like I want to put a nude centerfold of him in an issue of *Today's Hearth*. I mean, seriously!"

"I know I'd buy it if you did," Marguerite said with a girlish giggle.

"You are no help at all, Auntie," Violet said, unable to hold back a grin. Marguerite was just too much sometimes.

"It looked to me like he was pretty upset with Mr. Solomon," Penny added. Although it had appeared that she was busily writing in her journal, apparently she had one ear on the conversation in the room. Violet shook her head. The girl was so much like their mother it was scary.

"Was he?" Marguerite perked up at the mention of Ted.

"He doesn't want any publicity and he especially doesn't seem to want Ted taking any pictures."

"What a grouch," Josephine said. "He should just get over himself."

Violet grinned. She liked it when she and her mother, on very rare occasion, agreed on something.

"Poor Ted," Marguerite added, then clamped her mouth shut like she was hoping to swallow her words. The damage was done, Josephine had heard them.

"*Poor Ted*, huh?" Josephine asked her sister. "What's that supposed to mean? Did you hear that, Violet? Your aunt's trying to *make time* with that Salami of yours."

"I'm going to go take a nap," Violet said. "I'll see you kids later. Play nice."

Charlie gave his eldest daughter an exaggerated wink. "Take me with you," Charlie begged. "Don't leave me here with them."

Violet gave her father a kiss on the cheek. "No, it's your turn to babysit. See you at dinner, Daddy-o. Seven thirty, right?" she asked.

"If I live that long."

****

Violet stepped into the rich wood-paneled enclave and tried to recall what the space had been back when The Pines was a simple rustic retreat. Now, the deep ruby-toned carpeting and groupings of taffy-colored leather arm chairs sitting around little cocktail tables were completely alien to her memories. A square, elaborately detailed bar occupied the middle of the room. Ted sat on a leather-backed stool sipping beer from a long pilsner glass.

"Looks like you could use one of these." Ted gestured with the glass and then took a long sip.

Violet slid onto the seat beside him, putting her elbows on the bar. "These wedding proceedings are going to kill me," she said.

"You can't die. You're the maid of honor. Now how would that look in all the pictures? I'm pretty sure your sister is not going for the Weekend-at-

Bernie's look."

Violet groaned and ran her hands through her hair. "Please, don't even mention taking pictures or this crazy place might call the cops on us."

"You mean *your boyfriend* might call the cops on us."

Just then a pretty young female bartender stood in front of Violet, placed a square cocktail napkin onto the bar, and asked, "What can I get you?"

"Chardonnay," Violet said, "Thank you.

When the girl turned to pour her wine, Violet rotated on her swiveling barstool. "Do not refer to that man as my 'boyfriend,' Ted. I mean it. You'll send me over the edge."

"But..."

"Just *don't*, okay? I'm serious."

"Okay, Lady Macbeth, I hear you."

Violet knew that Ted's reference to Shakespeare's character was that the Lady's famous denials were the dead giveaways to her guilt.

She did not want to discuss Logan with Ted. Nor did she want to discuss him with his own daughter whom Violet spotted walking into the room.

Thankfully, the bartender placed an icy-cold glass of chardonnay on the napkin in front of her at that moment. Violet lifted it to her lips and took a generous pull of the fragrant gold liquid. She closed her eyes and swallowed. Maybe she could make a wish and all these people would just vanish. *Everyone except the bartender. She can stay.*

"Hi, am I late? You've started without me." Jessica smiled as she sat on the stool next to Violet. She leaned in and gave Ted a little wave of her hand. "Hi, I'm Jessica."

"Hi there," Ted said. He saluted the girl with his half-drunk glass of beer. "Ted Solomon."

"No, Jessica, you're right on time," Violet said. "Ted and I just got a head-start."

"What can I get you, Jess?" the bartender asked.

"Uh, I'll just have a seltzer with lemon," she said.

The bartender quickly produced the glass of clear bubbly liquid while the three sat in silence on their stools.

Violet was not sure where to begin with trying to convince the girl to have her ogre-of-a-father give them the green light to do the magazine spread. She looked over to Ted who merely shrugged.

Violet sipped her wine, watching Jessica tear away the little paper top from her drinking straw. She could not help but look at the girl's lips, as she leaned over and wrapped them around the straw, and compare them to Logan's. The girl had more than her father's eyes. She had his same lush, attractive mouth. Only hers didn't spew idiotic accusations like his did.

Jessica sat up straight and looked over to Violet. The girl let out a long breath. "My father can be impossible," she said.

Violet heard Ted let out a chuckle, but she did not turn to look at him. There was no sense in encouraging the man's reaction.

"Jessica, look..." Violet said. "Let me tell it to you straight.

"Our magazine, *Today's Hearth*, has merged with *Country Charm*. The new head has pitted me against a young feature writer to come up with a spread for the October issue of the new magazine. Whichever one of us dazzles him gets the top spot in the department. Ridiculous? Yes. Childish? Yes. But, it's his game and I have no choice but to play if I want my job."

"No pressure, huh?" Jessica asked, her tone sympathetic.

"So, I decided to do a piece on the hobby of birding. I thought it would be ideal. You know,

Vermont during the non-ski season—a pretty, woodsy lodge where enthusiasts can go to see all kinds of bird life. It's a perfect setting—a great idea from all angles."

"I'll drink to that," Ted added. This time Violet did turn to him and gave him her best pursed-lipped look. He gave her a one-handed wave of surrender.

"Sounds like a great idea to me," Jessica said. "And, The Pines is a great location for birders. There's a chapter of the Audubon society in Rutland. And, if I'm not mistaken, there's a seasonal bird festival sponsored by the American Birding Association."

Violet could not help but feel surprised at the girl's knowledge. Had she done homework on the subject? Or was she just some wiz-kid fountain of information? Either way, Violet knew that she and Jessica were on the same page about the advantages to having The Pines be part of her magazine piece.

"It's obvious, Jessica, that you're aware of the positive aspects of my spotlighting your lodge in our October issue. I mean, the publicity would be a tremendous boon to this place."

"I agree wholeheartedly," Jessica said with a nod.

"Then, how do we do this? How do we get past your father?"

"I'll work on him," Jessica said. Her tentative tone hinted at the futility of the idea.

"There's not a lot of time," Ted added. "I mean, it's Tuesday. The wedding is Saturday. We're all out of here on Sunday after breakfast. Violet's got to have this project all sewed up by then."

Violet looked to Jessica whose pretty, ample mouth was pulled to the side in an unhappy twist.

"I have no choice, Jessica. I have to produce this story. I can do it excluding The Pines—which would be a stupid mistake on Logan's part—but if that's

126

the way he wants it, that's the way it will be. I just truly don't get his reasoning."

"It makes no sense to me either," Jessica said with a shrug. "He's always been very protective over this place. And over me, too, but that's its own story."

Violet saw the look in the girl's eyes cloud with a kind of melancholy. Jessica played with the straw in her drink, tapping the pad of her index finger on the hollow end.

"My mother died when I was born," Jessica said softly, her eyes fixed on her fingertip. "He raised me by himself after my grandparents passed away. All he's ever had is me and The Pines."

Violet felt her throat constrict. *No,* she wanted to say to this child of Logan's. *Your father had me, too...once upon a time.* Violet said nothing. *What does that matter now?*

"How do you get your traffic of customers?" Ted asked. "Is ski season that good?"

"Ski season is good," Jessica said, sounding confident again. "And we have many loyal guests that book with us annually. It's been that way forever. Violet, you know that better than anyone. Your family came back year after year after year."

"That's true," Violet said.

"I'm curious," Jessica said, "How well did you know my dad during that time? I mean, was he pigheaded back then, too?"

Violet felt the muscles tighten in her whole body. She was not about to let Logan's daughter know *just how well* she knew her father.

"I did know him, yes. That was so long ago, Jessica, that it's kind of hard to recall. He did say last night that you've been the catalyst of the renovation to this whole place. And it looks fantastic."

A prideful grin broke out over Jessica's face.

Violet was reminded again of the girl's resemblance to the man. Mentally, the two seemed to have a host of differences—logic being a major one.

"Renovations like you've done deserve to be advertised," Ted said. "More customers equal more income. It's as simple as that, kid. Tell your old man to use his head."

"I'll try. That's all I can promise," Jessica said. "But, I want you to know I agree with your idea totally. Please remember that. I'll do my best. I can be pretty relentless if the cause is important enough. And, to me, The Pines is important enough."

"That's all we can ask." Violet gave the girl a reassuring smile. "Because of the time limit I'll have to move forward with my story one way or the other. There's nothing your dad can do about our taking photos of the woodlands outside your gates, so that's what we'll focus on for now. Let us know by this time tomorrow if your dad changes his mind."

"I will. Meanwhile, keep your fingers crossed."

And the meeting was over. Violet watched Jessica stride across the lounge and disappear through the doorway. She turned to Ted who was shaking his head.

"What?" Violet asked. "Tell me, Ted. You don't think there's a chance in hell that girl's going to change Logan's mind about this, do you?"

"Nope and her daddy's not going to like her meeting with us one bit, either."

"You're probably right," Violet said.

"When she approaches him, it's only going to make him think we put pressure on his cherished little girl."

Violet stared at Ted and wondered why she hadn't thought about that before. She swallowed hard.

"And although he might want to kick my ass if he sees me with my lens pointed at anything that belongs to him, there's only one person he's going to blame for this."

Violet downed the last of her chardonnay. "Thanks for the pep talk, Ted."

Chapter Fifteen

Violet managed to convince Penny that it wouldn't detract from her maid of honor responsibilities if she skipped the organized horseback riding trek. She just couldn't face another cockamamie activity, let alone get a gander at Franklin up in a saddle.

She had also ditched the High Tea scheduled for the ladies, using the time to get some work done.

Unable to concoct a legitimate-sounding excuse, she had no choice but to go along with the golf outing. Another of their differences, Penny was an avid golfer while Violet had never held a club.

When they arrived at the Wood Hollow Country Club, Violet was not surprised to learn that she and her dear, smartly-clad golf goddess were on the same team. To make matters worse, Franklin was part of their foursome, plaid pants and all. It turned out the man had a fairly decent swing, but every time he whacked a ball he grunted like someone had punched him in his soft, doughy belly.

The facility itself was magnificent. The grass was as green as Ireland and as lush as velvet. "How much land is this do you suppose?" Violet asked, watching a bird flutter to a tree branch.

"You can bet there's at least eighty or ninety acres here," Benjamin said with authority. "Most courses up here in New England tend to be smaller due to the wetlands."

Hole-by-hole, Violet thought about what impact a golf course had on the area's wildlife. This preoccupation didn't hurt her game, because nothing could make it any worse. The only thing she seemed to be adept at was fixing her divots. The worst of it was that Franklin kept offering her his assistance, using it as a chance to tuck up behind her and place his fat fingers alongside hers on her borrowed club.

She detested whatever genius came up with eighteen holes for a round of golf. Eighteen! By the end of the day, she was exhausted and her nose was red and sore from too much sun.

She went to bed early that evening, having slipped out from dinner ahead of the so-called golf awards ceremony, especially since she was sure Penny had come up with some sort of booby prize for her ridiculously high score. Had they been bowling, she'd have been a star.

The next day, while the other guests for the Terhune/Layne wedding were most likely still in their beds sound asleep, Violet and Ted met in the lobby just before dawn. Violet carried her notebook and printouts. Ted had his camera—lens cover in place, in case they ran into the resident maniac—as well as his backpack slung over his shoulder.

"I feel like a kid sneaking out after his parents are asleep," Ted said. "All this, so we can take pictures of our fine-feathered friends."

"Let's get moving so we can be lakeside before the sun comes up," Violet headed toward the door.

The two ambled down the trail that had previously led to the hunter's cabin. It now was an elaborately laid pathway of decorative paving stones that ended at the outdoor patio restaurant covered by that *fancy pergola* that seemed to give Josephine such a thrill.

In the dim bluish light of pre-dawn the lake glistened beyond the massive pines. The air smelled clean and new. Violet's heart fluttered at the thought of being in this place that held the hauntings of her youth. With each footfall she felt the pull of the water that awaited them. When they reached the lake the sun had risen to greet them and golden rays dappled the scenery.

"This is a photographer's dream," Ted said. He placed his backpack against a sapling and lifted the cap from his lens. "Why didn't you tell me, Terhune?"

"I did tell you, Ted," Violet said absently. She was busy taking it all in. The water served as a mirror to the surrounding trees giving the lake a deep green appearance. A mallard dunked his head and splashed, enjoying his morning bath. Ted aimed his camera at the bird and clicked away.

"You'll be sure to thank my sorry ass when you're awarded the crown of the feature department, hey Terhune?"

Violet turned to him and saw that he was on one knee, unfazed by his pant leg being muddied. He spoke with his head perfectly still as he continued to take in the view through his viewfinder.

"Shhh..." Violet admonished. "Don't talk. You'll scare them."

"Where are your precious swans anyway? You sure they're still here? Maybe they moved away, bought a condo in Ft. Lauderdale or something."

Violet rifled through her paperwork. She found the information she had printed about her long-necked friends, although she knew plenty about them already. They had been *her* swans, *hers and Logan's*. Together they had discovered the elegant white birds, and together they learned whatever they could about them. She remembered the summers at precisely this same spot when they had crouched to spy on their beautiful feathered creatures. She tried to focus on the matter at hand. She tried to concentrate on her notes, jotting ideas to flesh out her article, but all she could think about was the day all those years ago when Logan had told her the legend.

****

August 29, 1980
Last Day
Dear Diary,

Logan and I have basked in the memories of our lovemaking. We've been inseparable. We talk constantly but, like a blemish you try not to notice on someone's face, we do not discuss the end of my vacation. And now here it is...today.

Today I am going to leave here like we always do each August, but this time it will be a bigger agony. How can I do this? How can I walk away from Logan now that we have shared ourselves the way we have?

Last night we walked hand-in-hand to the edge of the lake in search of the swans. We stayed out of the cabin. We haven't gone in there since that night. It's almost like the place is holy now, a place where we need to let it be. So, we walked in the darkness to the lake and sat on a blue and green plaid stadium blanket edged in long fat fringe. We looked out at the water where a white band of moonlight cut across the surface in a wedge that spread out toward us like an open embrace.

"Do you think they'll come?" I whispered.

Logan didn't answer for a long moment. I looked at his profile, bathed in the moonlight, and marveled as I always do at his sheer beauty. Finally he turned to me and gave me that reassuring smile that always quells my fear or anxiousness.

"I learned something new about the swans," he said.

"Did you?" I asked with a thrill piercing through me. "Tell me."

"There's a Gaelic legend about them," Logan said, pulling his knees up and leaning his elbows onto them. "It's about this guy named Angus and the girl that he loves named Caer."

I looked out to the lake, fixed my eyes onto the glistening surface and listened to Logan's tale.

"Caer turned into a swan at the end of the summer and then would turn back into human form the next summer. And, Angus waited for her every year."

I felt tears pinch the corners of my eyes. I knew what Angus felt like at the end of his summers. Logan and I both did.

"Finally, Angus was told that he could marry Caer if, when she was still a swan, he could pick her out from a group of one-hundred-and-fifty swans. Try to picture that one. A hundred-and-fifty swans all together on a lake."

"It would be an awesome sight," I agreed. "Did he find her?"

Logan looked at me and smiled, reached over and took my hand into his. "Yes. He found her."

In spite of the lump that grew in my throat I was able to ask, "Then what happened?"

"Then he turned into a swan too, and they flew away together."

What I wouldn't do to be like them, to swoop away with Logan, just us two forever.

Chapter Sixteen

The swans did not show up. Surprisingly it was relief that washed over Violet like a rain shower, not disappointment, nor regret. Maybe it was that she wanted to keep the mute swans part of her good and tender memories of Logan. Besides, Ted managed to record many other species of birds for her article.

She took a deep breath of the clean pine-scented air and was now anxious to take the ride out to Rutland to gather information from the Audubon Chapter there.

"Come on, Ted, I'll buy you lunch on the way," Violet said as they readied themselves to head back up the path to the lodge. "You might want to change those pants, though, unless you're going for the schoolboy-who-fell-in-the-mud look."

Ted peered down and swatted at the patches of brown on the knees of his khakis to no avail.

"Guess you're right. I'll shower off and meet you in the lobby."

"Okay, I'll meet you in a half hour," Violet said. She glanced back at the lake. "I'm going to hang here for a couple of minutes and go over my notes."

"Will do," he said, and then trudged up the pathway.

Violet sat on a large reddish-brown rock, a plateau near the water's edge. She flipped open her notebook. Alone now, she closed her eyes and relished the sounds around her. The wind rustled the leaves, squirrels scampered through beds of pine needles, birds called to each other overhead.

Comforting, all of it. The combined sounds were

a song of her youth. *If love had a sound,* Violet decided, *this would be it. This is just what love should sound like.*

"Good morning."

Startled, Violet turned toward the voice, dropping her notebook and pen onto the ground. Logan, with his hands on his denim-clad hips and his sky-blue-colored eyes squinting in the sunlight, took her breath away.

She scrambled for her supplies. "Logan." She stood with her notebook clasped in front of her chest, as though he had caught her skinny dipping, and the book was her towel.

"Violet, did I or did I not ask you to leave us out of your story?"

"Logan, look…"

"No, *you* look. I've asked you nicely to keep my family and our business out of print. It's not a tough request. I would expect you to honor it."

Anger shot through her veins so fiercely that the rush of it was loud in her ears, drowning out any other sounds around her. *Honor?* That word triggered the venom in her. Wasn't that the word he'd used all those years ago when he told her goodbye? That it was *honor* that forced his hand?

Well, honor worked two ways in her eyes and right now she felt like honoring her urge to slap him.

"We've stayed away from your lodge," she said with a clench. "Ted hasn't taken a single shot of The Pines. The only photographs he's taking are birds. You don't own every bird in the state of Vermont, do you?"

Logan raked his fingers through his thick mass of blond hair. Violet could see his jaw loosen and his stance ease. His eyes softened and she worried that she'd lose her anger. She needed it like a warrior needs his shield. But the pent-up air escaped from her lungs and her chest relaxed.

"Violet, I'm sorry," Logan said. His tone was familiar, kind. The sound of his voice bearing the resonance of the boy she knew—the boy she had loved all those years ago—made her heart stammer in her chest. *Don't*, she thought. *Don't be the old Logan. Continue to be this jackass. It will be easier to walk away from the clod you've become—a piece of cake.*

She closed her eyes. A vision of the luncheon's carrot cake and Ted's snide comparison came to mind. She swallowed hard, looking out over the surface of the lake. She wondered if she could still swim the entire width.

"I..." Violet began and tried to clear her throat of the lump that had taken residence there. "I just don't understand."

"I know," Logan said. "I know."

"And for God's sake, Logan, don't you dare lecture me about honor. You like to throw that word around when you've painted yourself in a corner. Why don't you look up its meaning? Because, clearly you can't know that honor is about honesty and fairness and integrity."

Where the words came from, Violet didn't know. If she didn't recognize her own voice she wouldn't have believed they were hers. Regret surged through her now, not relief by any means. All she wanted to do was get out of his sight once and for all. She turned to leave.

"Wait."

The two stood in silence. He had stepped closer, his face now shaded by a leafy bough. He looked at her fully. His eyes no longer squinted against the sun's glare. The urgency in them was a startling memory come to life.

"Please let me say something," he said.

Ted would be waiting for her in the lobby in less than a half hour. She should sprint up the path. But, she knew that she would wait to hear whatever Logan had to say. She nodded.

"Sit a minute." He went to the flat rock where she had been. Balancing himself on the edge, he left plenty of room for her to sit beside him.

A zombie, caught in the lure of his damned eyes, she tentatively sat beside him.

Side-by-side they looked out onto the lake. It was hard for Violet not to feel the effects of the déjà vu of the moment. *How many times have we sat right here in this spot?* she wondered.

She turned to him and surprised herself when the question left her lips. "Why did you take it down?" she asked.

The recognition in his eyes told her he knew what she meant. It was a legitimate question, but she was sorry she had asked it. She did not want him to know just how important that little wooden shack had been to her. After all, that was a million years ago.

"I didn't want to, trust me," Logan said with a half grin. "Jessica's the one that orchestrated all these changes. She's always loved the place and since she got out of college she's taken over like gangbusters."

"She's a lovely girl," Violet said, feeling the constriction in her throat. It was true. Jessica was, indeed, a lovely young woman with a good head for business on her shoulders. But, her very existence was the reason that Violet and Logan had parted on such bad terms. Memories of the way they ended tried to crash into her thoughts. She did her best to hold them at bay.

"Well, she sure likes you," Logan said. "And she certainly likes the idea of you making a spectacle of The Pines in that magazine of yours."

"Spectacle? I'm offering you a chance at free publicity. Frankly, it doesn't make sense that you wouldn't want it."

Violet looked at his profile as he eyed the lake. The crow's feet wrinkles at his eyes only served to make the man more appealing. The laugh lines etched at the side of his mouth were as attractive. He reached up, gave his hair a shove from his forehead, and turned to her.

"I'm going to trust you with something, Violet," he said.

"That's honorable" she said. She almost smiled at her own sarcasm, but sobered when she saw the sincerity in his gaze.

"It's about Bonnie," he said.

Bonnie Creswick. The girl's full name popped into Violet's head as though it were a name she heard every day. Only it had been decades since she had thought of it let alone heard Logan Monroe say it.

"I know. She died," Violet said softly. "Penny told me you said so when they first contacted you about the wedding."

Logan nodded, casting his eyes down at his feet. He lifted his head. "Actually, Bonnie did not die."

"What?"

"I've been lying to Jessica all this time. Bonnie is not dead. She just didn't want to be a mother...or a wife. After Jess was born Bonnie convinced me to sign the papers to put her up for adoption."

Violet couldn't get the thoughts straight in her mind. The idea that Bonnie was alive, and that Jessica didn't know it, zigzagged through her head—along with the thought that Logan had been carrying a lie of that magnitude for all these years.

"So, what happened?"

"I couldn't do it," Logan said. "After Bonnie split town, I went back to child services. The waiting period had not ended. I took back my baby. Thanks to my mom and dad's help, I raised Jessica as a single parent."

Sheer anguish flooded the man's eyes. Violet did all she could not to reach over and brush the fallen locks from his brow. Instinct is fueled by memory, so she was not surprised at her hand reaching over and her fingertips touching his hand where it sat on his knee. Logan's eyes met hers. He offered a joyless grin.

"If you do a spread on The Pines and highlight us—Jessica and me—there's a chance Bonnie will show up on our doorstep."

"Well, surely if she wanted to look you up after all this time it would be easy enough. I mean, she wouldn't have to see my magazine article to know where to find you, Logan."

"That's true, but..."

"And if she wanted to find her child, all she'd have to do is a little investigating to find out she's here with you."

"Trust me, Bonnie had no interest in our daughter. None. She made that point very clear. However, what she did have a big interest in was money. That was her main reason for taking off. She didn't want to be stuck in this Podunk town in a ramshackle lodge. She had bigger plans than that, and she was determined to make them happen."

Violet clasped her hands together to keep them from shaking. The news was too much, too fast. Her mind raced.

What she knew of Bonnie was what Logan had told her on their last night together. Bonnie had been the bartender at a little saloon in town. One night she bought Logan a series of shots to go with his beers and...she had taken him home to her place.

"I don't know what to say, Logan," Violet whispered.

"If Bonnie's out there, and she sees that my twenty-four-year-old daughter and I run this place,

and she sees how upscale The Pines has become...
Well, she'll see dollar signs. It would kill Jessica to
think her own mother just dumped her. I can't let
that happen."

"I see," Violet said.

"But, you're right, Violet. There's no integrity in
it, no fairness." He paused, then snickered, "No
honor."

"Don't," Violet said. "These are irrefutable
circumstances."

"I hoped if I told you everything you would
understand."

"What I don't understand is how Bonnie could
just walk away like that," Violet said.

"Like I said, she knew what she did and did not
want.

"At first she thought she was getting a one-way
ticket out of this place. You know how I always used
to talk about leaving, going to a big-city college, and
having a writing career.

"She wanted the city, but she didn't want her
baby... and she sure didn't want me. She knew that
I didn't love her."

Violet swallowed hard and forced herself to
stand up. Her shaky knees made her wobble. Just
the mere mention of the word *love* coming from
Logan's lips was more than she could take.

What was she supposed to say? What does a
grown woman say when she realizes that the man to
whom she is speaking still resides within her? Her
heart pounded in her ears. The same heart that had
been encased in steel for so long.

Libby's death bed plea filtered into her head,
"Make room in your heart again." *Well,* Violet
thought, taking in a blurry-eyed view of the lake,
someone was there all along.

"I will keep your secret, Logan," she said. "And I
promise my magazine will leave you and The Pines

alone."

"I knew I could trust you."

Then she turned and sped up the path back to the lodge—away from the lake, away from Logan—only remembering to breathe when she reached the building.

Chapter Seventeen

During the ride to Rutland, she turned the car's air conditioning on full blast. She had aimed the air vent right at her face and hoped it would blow away any reminder of her conversation with Logan.

Through her periphery she saw that Ted's eyes were on her. She tried to ignore him but it became too distracting. "Ted, for crying out loud, what?"

"What do you mean, 'what'?"

"Why are you looking at me?"

"Why are you looking at me looking at you? You're supposed to be looking at the road."

"I am looking at the road," Violet said, turning onto a tree-lined lane. "I'm trying to find a good place to drop you off."

A laugh burst from Ted's throat. She turned to him long enough for him to see her knitted brow.

"Hey, eyes forward, Terhune."

"Ted, I swear…"

"Oh, you swear what? You swear you'll dump me off in this woodsy no-man's land? I'm not worried. You need me too much."

Violet opened her mouth to speak, then clamped it shut. Ted was right. She did need him. She needed him to help keep her head straight and to stay focused on the fact that unless she produced an article that wowed the new boss, she could kiss her job goodbye.

"Can we just concentrate on birds, Ted?"

"Sure, unless you turn our brains into solid blocks of ice. You having a flash or something?"

She reached over and flipped the knob to lower

the fan's velocity.

"Happy now?"

"I did some reading up on the birds around here. Did you know that those mute swans of yours are the ones in Hans Christian Andersen's *Ugly Duckling*?"

"No, I didn't," Violet said, her tone flat. The last thing she needed was for those white, long-necked reminders to glide into her head and conjure more memories. She was on memory overload today. "That's interesting. But, we don't need to worry about the swans. They've got plenty of birds up here besides them."

"They're also the ones in the ballet *Swan Lake*. Did you know that?"

"No, but I'm impressed with your research. What other birds did you find out about? Tell me more."

"No, now it's your turn to 'tell me more'."

She gave him a quick side glance and, as she suspected, he had that challenging glint in his gray eyes. In spite of herself she took the bait. "What do you want to know?"

"Your boyfriend took off like a bat out of hell down the path when he saw me coming back with my camera. I almost followed him but I figured I'd make matters worse. He hates my guts."

"A: He is not my boyfriend, and B: I'm sure he doesn't hate your guts. But, he was pretty ticked off about our taking pictures."

"So, what'd you tell him?"

"I promised him that we would leave him and his lodge out of our story. No more pictures of any part of the place, inside or out. None."

"So, no story?" Ted asked with a shake of his head. "Why are we going on this wild goose chase? Which, by the way, I am aware is another bird reference."

"We'll do the story, but we'll modify it. We can focus on birding without having his lodge as part of the lure. Our readers can get the birding bug without having to hightail it up to this particular lodge in Vermont. There are plenty of inns to choose from."

"Terhune, you could be setting yourself up for failure. You might just wind up *being* second fiddle to that Melanie Rosen. Can you handle that?"

Violet did not answer, but she felt her jaw ache from her clenching teeth. What Ted said was true. She could very well end up answering to the khaki-clad adolescent who already had Robert Matthews in her hip pocket anyway.

They arrived at the Audubon headquarters, a small square building set in the middle of a tarred parking lot. Inside, they examined and browsed the many display cases. Violet gathered as many free pamphlets as her hands could hold, while Ted busied himself looking at framed pictures on the walls.

A lone, narrow-shouldered man with a head of disorderly static-filled flyaway hair sat behind the wooden counter. "Good day, folks," he said.

God help her, Violet thought, *he sounds like a crow calling from a tree branch.* She turned to Ted to see if that thought had occurred to him and felt relief wash over her to see him still enthralled with the photography.

Violet filled the man in on her idea for the article. He seemed affable enough to want to be a part of the process, and maybe get a quote in the magazine. He perked right up when Violet told him she was with *Today's Hearth*.

"Oh, a magazine spread, huh?" asked the little man. "You just let me know if I can be of any help at all. Ask me anything. My name's Jacob Anders. Folks, call me Jake."

Violet looked over to Ted. He studied a large

blown-up photograph of the Hermit Thrush, which Violet already knew was Vermont's state bird.

"Let's focus on the thrush," she said. "You know, because it's the state bird."

"I'm a layman's ornithologist, so to speak," Jake said with distinct pride in his tone.

"Just a hobbyist, huh?" Ted commented, stepping up beside Violet at the counter.

"Don't mean I don't know pretty much everything there is to know about birds, though," he said with a cock to his head.

Ted looked to the wall behind the desk to another display of photographs. Ted pointed to a picture of a little bird that to Violet looked fairly nondescript with the exception of a dash of pale yellow feathers on its underside.

"Okay, Jake, tell us about that one," Ted challenged.

Jake turned around and looked to where Ted's finger pointed. He then faced Violet and Ted with shining eyes, as though he were a school boy with the right answer for the teacher. "Meadowlark, that's the Eastern Meadowlark. Thing about that bird is that they usually have two mates at a time."

For some reason Logan popped into Violet's head. She saw him in her mind, in the hunter's cabin, telling her about Bonnie's pregnancy. Violet shook the image from her thoughts.

"Two mates, huh?" Ted mused. "Guess the fact that he's got a yellow belly makes him kind of like a two-timing yellow-bellied sapsucker."

Violet shot him a look. Ted had no fondness for Logan, and the jab in her gut told her this was a comparison to him.

"Oh, that's an interesting comment," Jake said. "You know, most non-birders would say that yellow-bellied sapsuckers are just a made up bird to, you know, sort of define a coward. But no, they do exist.

They're woodpeckers."

Violet refrained from comment, hoping to quell Ted's jibes. She turned to a map displayed in a glass showcase. "Tell us about this, Jake."

He moved closer to the case, tapped the glass with this index finger. "This here's our Interpretive Trail. It's a great resource, very informative. I'd recommend you walk it, if you have the time. There are ten stations pinpointing everything from soil awareness, types of vegetation, and the birds that reside in our wetland."

Violet looked to Ted who shrugged in response. "I say let's do it," she said.

Together, she and Ted maneuvered through the maze of information stations, stopping to read the postings at each site Violet collected pamphlets offered at each stop. By the time they had looped around to the office her head was spinning with information and the heel of her left foot burned from the chafe of her sneaker. She checked her watch and saw that it was near two in the afternoon. Time was escaping them and she knew that they had to be back to The Pines in time to get ready for the rehearsal dinner that evening.

"Jake, we're running out of time, I'm afraid," Violet said. "Anything in these pamphlets I'm holding that will tell me about birding equipment?"

She fanned the pamphlets like a deck of cards. Jake perused them over the lenses of his wire-rimmed glasses.

"This one here," Jake said pointing to a tri-folded paper with the picture of a man holding binoculars on its cover. "This'll tell you all about binoculars. You want to be a birder, you got to have good binoculars."

Violet placed her handful of pamphlets onto the counter and concentrated on the one Jake recommended. She unfolded it. Just by her quick scan she could tell it was loaded with information. She refolded the paper and scooped up the rest of them.

"Oh, and that pamphlet there with the green cover, that'll tell you about birds and the environment. There's a lot in there about the importance of conservation, preservation of..."

"The article won't be so much about those things, although I know they're important. I'll be playing up the appeal birding could conjure up for some New Yorker-types looking for a getaway from their concrete world."

"Oh, I see," Jake said. "Capitalists with something to do outdoors besides walking a golf course. I get it."

"Jake, you've been a great help, thank you," she said. He took his job quite seriously. That was obvious.

"Anytime. Come on back again. And, I'll be looking for the article when it comes out in your magazine."

"Hey, how about we take a picture of Jake here in case we want to use it for the piece?" Ted asked.

"Good idea," Violet said. She saw Jake stand straighter and reach up in an attempt to tame his wild hair. "Jake, you game?"

"Sure."

Ted slung his backpack onto the counter and tugged at the zipper. He withdrew his camera case, then froze, eyes on the vinyl pouch in his hands. He swore under his breath.

"Ted, what's wrong?"

"Shit," he spat, turning the open case over in his hand.

Violet sucked in air and clutched a hand to her chest as Ted uttered what she already knew. "My camera's gone."

****

They combed the inside of the car, looked under the seats, in the crevice between them. Violet popped open the trunk although she and Ted both knew the effort was futile. Ted's camera was not in the trunk, nor in her car. Each of them had a thought of where it could be. Violet couldn't let the words form on her lips. But Ted could. "This has your yellow-bellied woodpecker's name written all over it."

She didn't comment. *I can't believe it. After I promised him that I'd leave him and The Pines out of the article, would he take matters into his own hands? That would be underhanded and sneaky. Not like Logan at all. But, then again, I have no idea who he is now or what he's capable of.*

"Let's not jump to any conclusions, Ted. Maybe you left it in your room when you went back to change your pants."

"Uh, no," Ted said. "I didn't even bring it into my room. I left the whole backpack at the front desk with the girl there."

"Jessica?"

"No, another one. It doesn't take Colombo to figure this out, Terhune. He came storming back to the lodge, found my backpack and helped himself to my camera."

"When we get back we'll go straight to the desk and ask the girl what she knows."

"Yeah, like she'll rat out her own boss, the guy that signs her paycheck. Keep dreaming."

"Let's get out of here, Ted," Violet said, sliding into the driver's seat. "We haven't eaten. After we grab a bite we can think more clearly before we head back."

The last thing she wanted to do was storm back and make a spectacle during her sister's wedding week—unless, of course, she really wanted to be excommunicated from the Terhune clan. Besides, it was quite possible that there was a good explanation for what had happened to Ted's camera. Maybe it had nothing to do with Logan at all. No sense jumping to conclusions without the facts.

"That guy's got my camera and no BLT in my belly is going to convince me otherwise. I could skip lunch. My camera's the only thing I can think about."

"Well, I need something, Ted. My head's splitting open. I have to eat."

"You're stalling."

"I'm not stalling. I'm hungry."

"Yeah, okay."

They stopped off at a little roadside diner. Ted stomped his way to the door, hands jammed into his pants pocket. Violet brought all the pamphlets in with her, hoping she could divert Ted's focus from his camera by rifling through the information.

They ordered tuna sandwiches and glasses of iced tea. When the waitress placed the dishes in front of them, Violet immediately offered Ted her pickle.

"No thanks," he said. "I'm sour enough."

"Ted, come on. Let's wait and see what we find out when we get back. We can't just rush into the place like storm troopers. Hell hath no fury like an Embarrassed Mama Terhune. Meanwhile, let's enjoy our lunch. Here take the pickle. You know you want it."

"A peace pickle," Ted said, taking the wet green spear from her fingers. He bit down into it, smacked his lips. "Okay, show me what you've got, Terhune."

She spread the pamphlets over the gray-flecked laminate table top and unfolded them like road maps open for navigating a route.

"This is a ton of information," Violet said, finishing up her sandwich and sipping on her glass of tea. "My head's spinning."

"So, you think you'll be able to wow Robert

Matthews without pushing a nice cushy lodge in your story?"

"I hope so," Violet said with a shrug. "I mean, all I can do is try. My hands are tied at this point, Ted. I can't put a thing about The Pines in this piece. And with the Princess Bride's itinerary, there's no time left in this week to get firsthand information from another inn. I'll just have to wing it, if you'll pardon the phrase."

"Yeah, yeah, I know. I don't know what he told you that made you back off, but I can see that you've promised Paul Bunyan."

"That's right," Violet said, ignoring the fact that he was taking a pot shot at Logan. She wasn't going to get Ted riled up again.

"And, if I know anything, Terhune, I know with you a promise is iron clad."

"I'm no girl scout, Ted, but yeah."

"Let's get out of here and go find my camera, kid."

On the ride back Violet was quiet as they travelled along the roadway. She could not get the word "promise" out of her head since Ted mentioned it. It was true. Violet knew herself to be a woman of her word. She did, indeed, make a promise to Logan that she would not put his precious lodge in her article. But, she had made more promises than that.

She promised that she would not reveal the truth about Bonnie, Jessica's mother. Violet also remembered that she had promised her dear friend, Libby, that she would open her heart again.

Right now, Violet' thoughts were the echoes of Logan's empty promises made to her long ago. Opening her heart only made those resonances rise to her senses making her more aware of their toll.

Breaking into Violet's thoughts, Ted said, "I guess the best thing you can do, kid, is be prepared. I mean, really, what's the worst that can happen?

You'd have to answer to that snot-nosed Melanie. So what? You'll still have a job."

An image came into her mind. She saw herself sitting in a small cubicle with the long, lean Melanie Rosen dictating orders to her like a pert young Cruella De Vil. Violet took a deep breath and let it out in a long, loud sigh.

Not only did she have to grapple with the fact that she spent her livelihood writing about things that she did not feel in her heart, but soon she might have to write those kinds of things at the marked insistence of an obnoxious, though ambitious, kid. *Can I do it? Can I really stand to just keep producing this fluff, whether I'm at the helm of the department or not?* The truth was, she didn't know.

"I've been thinking, Terhune,"

"Now *there's* trouble."

"No listen, I'm serious," he said. "I might have been handed a golden opportunity. You know how they say that one door closes and another opens? Well, that could be what's happened for me."

Violet looked over. His face was earnest. This was not another set-up for some sort of wisecrack or joke.

"Go on," Violet said, her eyes on the road, "I'm listening."

"I came into this crazy business with a camera in my hand and for too many years I forgot about it. I got so caught up in running the magazine that I just, you know, forgot what was important to me."

"So what does that mean?"

"It means that when we get back, once your piece is wrapped, I'm telling Matthews that I'm done being a consultant for his magazine. I'm going off on my own to take a stab at what I always wanted to do. That is, as soon as I get my camera back."

Violet felt a tear sting at the corner of her eye. They had reached the long, newly-paved entrance to

The Pines. She turned her steering wheel and accelerated cautiously down toward the main building.

****

August 18, 1981

Dear Diary,

Logan and I planned our future tonight. We snuggled under a sleeping bag. With the sounds of the night just outside the cabin walls, we made our plans.

He's a semester behind in school because of all the time he's had to put into the place since his dad's been sick. So, he'll graduate closer to when I do. And then we'll go to New York, share an apartment in the Village, and get writing jobs. We'll spend weekends exploring the city, honing our craft, learning new things, and just being together.

We are so happy.

Chapter Eighteen

Violet and Ted went straight to the front desk, behind which Jessica stood with a curious expression on her Logan-looking face.

"You two look like you've got a mission," she said.

Ted opened his mouth to speak, but Violet silenced him with a touch of her hand to his arm. She turned to Jessica and forced a smile. "Jessica, there was another girl here at the desk earlier. Is she still here?"

"Kathleen? Yes, she just stepped away for a few minutes. Can I help you with something?"

"Yeah," Ted piped in. He slung his backpack onto the counter. "I left this bag here at the desk for a little while this morning and now it seems that my Nikon D700 digital camera is missing from its case."

Alarm shone in Jessica's blue eyes. Her mouth dropped open and the tip of her pink tongue darted over her lips.

"Let me find Kathleen. I'm sure we'll get to the bottom of this."

Jessica disappeared into a doorway behind the desk. Violet turned to Ted.

"Can you calm down, please? For crying out loud you all but accused that Kathleen kid of stealing your camera."

"Well, someone did."

"Ted, let's hear her side of the story."

Jessica returned to the desk, not with Kathleen in tow, but with her father at her side. Logan's eyes, too, bore the look of concern. His mouth was pulled into that lipless line that meant the man was not happy.

"Violet," he said. "What happened?"

"Where's the girl?" Ted asked.

"She, uh, she's not here," Jessica said.

"Not here, huh? I thought you said she stepped away from the desk for a minute. Now she's not here? You giving me the runaround?"

"Nobody's giving you any runaround, Mr. Solomon," Jessica said, then turned to her father. Logan flashed Violet a questioning look, then turned to Ted.

"Why don't we start at the beginning? Explain to me what happened."

Ted reiterated his story and all the while Violet's eyes were on Logan. She read his expressions like a book whose pages she knew by heart.

His face was still a billboard of his thoughts. That was one thing that hadn't changed in all these years. Logan was angry and trying not to be. He was struggling with a waning composure.

"And," Ted said in conclusion, "replacing that camera will cost about two grand. I came to this place with it, and I'm not leaving without it. Or without full reimbursement."

Just then a frenzied young girl approached the desk. Apologies poured from her lips. This, Violet guessed, had to be Kathleen.

"Jessica texted me and told me to hurry back. Mr. Monroe, I didn't mean to be late from my break. I needed to make a deposit in my bank account before three o'clock. Jessica said it would be all right to run out for a few minutes. She said that it wasn't that busy and she'd watch the desk for me."

"Kathleen, Kathleen, simmer down," Logan said. "Take a breath, for crying out loud."

Kathleen did as she was told. With each breath

her eyes darted to the group around her.

"Okay, now," Logan continued. "Did this gentleman drop off this backpack here at the front desk this morning?"

"I told you that already," Ted said. "What do you think, I'm lying or something?"

Violet grabbed Ted's arm and gave it a tug. He clucked his tongue at her but managed to shut up. Violet knew it wouldn't be for long.

"Excuse me, no. I'm not accusing anyone of anything," Logan said. "Kathleen, do you remember that?"

"Yes," the girl said, her voice a shaky rasp.

"Okay, and then what?"

She shrugged then looked to Jessica. "Then he came back a little while later and I gave it back to him."

"That's all?" Logan asked.

"Yes, that's all I know."

"Did anyone check in around that time?"

"I already checked the register, Dad," Jessica said. "No."

"Deliveries maybe?" Logan asked. "You know, UPS, or flowers?"

Kathleen shook her head, her mouth a quivering pout.

"Thank you, Kathleen," Logan said, giving a long sigh.

"Am I in trouble?"

"No."

Logan turned to Ted. Violet's hand was still pressed to his arm.

"I'm sorry, but right now I don't have an answer for you, Mr. Solomon. I'll look into it further and get back with you."

"That's it?" Ted asked.

"It's the best I can do for now."

"Ted," Violet said. "Let's go. Come on. We'll

check back later. Thanks, Logan."

Logan nodded to Violet, his face still stern, and then he strode away. As Violet and Ted turned to leave, they could not help but hear Jessica's question.

"Kath, did anybody else come behind the desk this morning besides you? Think."

"Not that I know of," Kathleen said. "Except for your father."

"I'm telling you, Terhune," Ted spat in an angry whisper, his breath hot against her ear. "That asshole's got my camera."

****

Back in her room Violet spent some time trying to concentrate on reading through the pamphlets that she had brought back from the Audubon Society. Time escaped her as she jotted down notes. All the while thoughts forced their way into her head. *Would Logan really stoop to taking Ted's camera? If so, then I don't know this man at all. He's a complete and total stranger now.*

In the shower, reels of footage from the past ran through her mind. She saw herself as a teenager jumping into the lake with Logan at her side, the two of them making one great splash as they plunged into the water.

In reel two she was in school walking to class with Libby, each wearing their peasant blouses and bell bottoms. They carried their Tiger Beat Magazines with Donny Osmond on the cover. Then Donny's magazine morphed into her *Today's Hearth*. Its pages spread open like wings and it took flight, ripping free of her grasp.

She stepped out from the shower and toweled dry, rubbing the terry fabric hard on her wet scalp as though trying to wipe away the images in her brain.

She dressed quickly, fully aware now of the

time, adding a dab of her favorite fragrance, Red Door. Looking briefly into the full-length mirror she recognized the tiredness in her own countenance. Violet turned from the glass and dashed out the door, ready as she'd ever be for the wedding rehearsal.

A small section of The Grove was set up to look like a chapel with rows of seats on either side of a short aisle and a white lectern at the head. Empty flower urns decorated the area and Violet assumed that sprays would be delivered tomorrow along with the bridal bouquet and other wedding flowers.

Penny and Ben stood near the set-up with the minister, Ben's Uncle Lenny. Pastor Lenny, a lanky man in black slacks and a white golf shirt, had traveled up from his Episcopalian church in New Jersey to officiate as a family favor. The Layne family was delighted at his gesture. Violet knew her mother was not.

She scanned the room to locate her little Roman Catholic mother. Both her parents were seated side-by-side on two folding chairs off to the side. Josephine's nostrils flared with disapproval. Her mouth pursed as if it held a sourball. Violet approached them, forcing herself not to smirk. It would not do to fuel the woman's ire.

"Hey you two," Violet said, sitting down beside her mother.

Josephine's arms were folded over her chest like a Russian folk dancer. Violet touched her mother's arm and marveled silently at its rigidity.

"Ma, you okay?"

"Madonna!"

Violet looked to her father and he merely shrugged. She focused on her mother's face, surveying the lips that looked frozen in mid-kiss. However, Violet knew there was no smooch on this woman's mind. She patted her mother's arm and

Josephine elbowed her away.

"So, how do you like that, Violet? Your sister is an Episcopalian now. Madonna."

"Josie," Charlie warned, giving Violet an eye.

"No she's not, Ma. Penny's just being accommodating to her in-laws. The pastor is a relative."

"And, after all, everybody is God's relative," Charlie added, his voice calm and soothing, a warm bath of a tone. Charlie and Violet exchanged a look. By the way Josephine pivoted her head on her straight-as-an-arrow neck, they could tell they hadn't simmered the woman for a second. Perhaps they had even stirred her further.

"Fine then, let's all be Episcopalian. Call Father Michael at Saint Teresa's and tell him he's out of business. Nobody's Catholic anymore. You better call the Pope, too."

Violet spied Ben gesturing her way, flashing his sparkling white smile. "They're waving me over."

"Go ahead," Josephine said. "Run from your heritage."

Violet got up from her chair and scooted around to whisper in her father's ear.

"Dad, don't you and Ma go to Our Lady of Sorrows anymore?" she whispered.

"Yes we do," he said with a solemnity in his tone.

"Then who is Father Michael, and what's Saint Teresa's?"

"That's the priest and church from when your mom was a little girl."

"But..." Violet said, feeling her heart quicken.

Charlie touched Violet's hand and offered an anemic smile. "She's just confused, Violet. Go on, your sister needs you."

Violet walked over. Penny looked radiant. Violet could only imagine how beautiful she would look tomorrow in her strapless, beaded gown. Penny reached over and grabbed her big sister's hand.

"Everything okay?" Penny asked.

"Yes," Violet said with a grin plastered on her face. "Absolutely." There was no way Violet was going to let on that she was beginning to get scared about their mother. Penny didn't need to know any of this, not today anyway. Hopefully these episodes would turn out to be nothing, some sort of chemical imbalance.

They went through the motions of the ceremony, each participant reciting their piece. Franklin practiced the bible passage chosen for him to read, speaking with a flourish that seemed to whip his lips around like propellers. Worse yet, he kept his eyes on Violet while he recited. Try as she willed, she couldn't take her eyes off his oral gyrations. She hoped he was not mistaking the attention as any form of encouragement. Violet gulped when he emphasized a reference to love and winked at her.

She looked around the room for Ted. He was due to arrive any minute and she simply wanted him to show up, to be the anti-Franklin ruse she needed.

Meanwhile, the wait staff had set up a buffet of shiny stainless steel chafing dishes. Guests began parading into the room in a slow, steady stream. Finally, Violet spotted Ted, and rushed to his side. "Where have you been?"

"On the internet looking for a new camera. They're a hefty chunk of change. Hope that Troy Donahue of yours is prepared to cough it up."

"Please stop referring to Logan as anyone *of mine*," Violet warned. "And, we don't know for sure about your camera."

"See? You're defending him."

"I'm not. But I want all the facts first."

"You tell me what more you need to know. The guy warns you not to take pictures of the joint, he catches me with my camera, and presto it goes missing. You need any evidence beyond that, Terhune? Shit, you must have sucked at playing *Clue* when you were a kid."

Just then Penny approached them and crooked her arm through Violet's. "Sis, take a walk with me?"

"Look, they've opened the buffet. Go make a plate, and behave," Violet said to Ted before turning to leave.

Ted called back to her, as usual needing to get the last word. "I'm telling you, kid; it was Colonel Mustard in the conservatory with the lead pipe. Face it."

"Circumstantial," she replied without looking back at the man.

"That lead pipe has a telephoto lens and costs two grand."

"Not listening."

Penny started to giggle. She turned her head to look back in his direction. "Violet, do you two talk in code or something?"

"No," Violet said. "He's just being Ted."

"It's kind of funny. It's like sibling rivalry."

"Please tell me I'm not that insolent."

"Ah, you love him like an uncle."

"Watch what you say, Penny. Have you seen the way he and Aunt Marg flirt with each other? The way they're going the man might wind up actually *being* our uncle."

"Get out of here!"

"Watch them. It couldn't get any more obvious."

Penny turned to Violet then and gave her a gentle nudge with her shoulder. "Speaking of obvious..."

Violet met her gaze. "Don't start."

"Violet, listen. I'm not trying to be silly or funny now. I mean, have you seen the way Logan looks at you?"

"No."

"Well, I have. And, that man's still got it bad."

"Oh, please. Penny, you're so busy being in your land of love that you think you see it everywhere."

"Yeah? Well, too bad you can't check out your own face when he walks into a room."

Violet opened her mouth to speak, then closed it again. She felt it best to end the conversation. Any continued dialogue on the subject of Logan Monroe would only prolong her agony.

"Penny, not that I'm not enjoying our little stroll, but I get the feeling there's something besides this nonsense that you wanted to talk about."

Violet and Penny had walked arm-in-arm, an usual gesture. The foreign feel of Penny's arm crooked with hers reminded Violet that the two had not been close over the years, and she felt a twinge of uneasiness. Since when had Penny felt the need to cling, and to Violet no less? Her father's words came to mind. *Your sister needs you.* If their mother was really losing it, then, yes, more than ever the kid would be needing Violet. Maybe they needed each other.

Penny led them over the flagstone flooring and down the path in the direction of the dining room. Another first for them, usually Violet was in the lead.

"Let's go take a look and see what they've done so far for the reception tomorrow."

"Okay," Violet said, wondering why they were doing this. After all, hadn't Penny micro-managed each detail of this wedding, barring none, using as many software packages as Microsoft had to offer?

Inside the room it was dark and cool and the silence seemed reverent. This was the place that awaited the celebration of her sister's future, a future that promised to be whole and loving, secure, and not to mention plaque-free. Suddenly, Violet felt something new, a surge absent of envy or disdain. Perhaps it was even a kind of appreciation.

"It's a pretty room, huh, Penny?"

"Yes, it is," Violet could hear the awe in her voice. It reminded her of the days of their childhood when Penny would spy a butterfly in a field, or a bird on a windowsill, and utter a breathy sound.

Violet looked down into Penny's face, searching her eyes. In them she saw something other than happiness. Whatever it was tugged at Violet's heart. "What's going on, Penny?"

Penny started to cry. She put her hands over her face and whimpered like a little girl whose sand castle had gotten washed away by an errant wave. Violet instinctively put her arm around Penny's convulsing shoulders.

"I can't believe I'm telling you this now of all times," Penny said with her lower lip pouted out from her face. "I'm getting married tomorrow and I'm supposed to be happy and carefree...

"I know I'm blotching as we speak. If I don't stop, I'm going to look like I have the measles tomorrow."

"Penny," Violet urged. "Take a deep breath and tell me what this is all about."

"It's...it's about Mom."

"What about her?"Violet felt her insides clench.

"I think there's something wrong with her, Violet. She called me Nancy."

Nancy was their mother's little sister who had died in childhood. Nancy had been dead for over sixty years.

"At first I thought that maybe I heard wrong," Penny said. "I mean Nancy and Penny sound a little alike. But, no. She was calling me Nancy. And she wanted to take my temperature to see if my fever was still there. I mean, how crazy is that? What fever?"

"Oh, boy," Violet felt her throat closing.

Violet could feel Penny's fingers on her skin. They were icy cold. She covered the fingers with her own.

"There is something wrong..." Penny said, sniffling. "You know, and you haven't told me. I can tell you know something."

"Penny, honestly, I don't know much. All I know is that Dad told me that Ma's been kind of forgetful lately and a little mixed up. Tonight she made reference to her old priest from when she was a kid as if he was still the priest at her church."

"I think they're not telling us the whole thing. I think there's more going on," Penny said, panic rising again in her tone. "I'm afraid she's going to get like grandma did."

"Listen," Violet said. "You're getting married tomorrow to your dream man. Be happy. Let this go for now. We'll keep our eye on Ma. We won't let anything happen to her."

Penny wiped a stream of tears from her face.

"What if something does happen to her, Violet?" Penny asked. "I wouldn't know what to do. I mean, she's my rock."

"Everything will be okay, Penny."

"But, I'm not strong like you."

"Tell you what," Violet said, surprising herself as the words came to her lips. "I'll be your back-up rock. How's that?"

Penny met Violet's gaze and let a half smile form on her watery lips.

"You want to be my rock?"

"Sure, I'm a good rock."

"Yeah, but for me? I mean, don't I irritate you too much?"

"We're just, you know, different."

Penny's face brightened. Her mouth curved,

showing a straight line of Chicklet teeth. Violet felt another new sensation, like a tiny pebble had found its way into her chest and had taken residence. A seed perhaps. Yes, a seed.

****

August 29,1981
Dear Diary,

Penny came into my room when we got home tonight. I'm exhausted. We're all beat. She plopped herself onto the edge of my bed and bounced her eleven-year-old body up and down because I would not look up from the book I was reading and acknowledge her. I was not in the mood.

I had just left Logan and I miss him so much I ache. I want to quit college and just go be with him.

"I know what's wrong with you," she said finally, in her whiney little voice.

"Nothing's wrong with me."

"Oh yes there is."

"Okay, smartass, tell me. What's wrong with me?"

"You love Logan more than you love us."

I put down my book. "You don't know what you're talking about," I said.

"We're your family," Penny said, and a sob broke out from her throat making her sound like a cicada. "I'm your sister."

"I think I know that," I said.

"Well, it's bad enough that you have to go to college and only come home during Thanksgiving and Christmas and Easter. You can't go to Vermont, too. You can't go there and be with Logan forever."

"Penny, who says I would do that?"

"I just know," Penny said woefully. "I just know you would. And you would forget all about me."

Honestly, I looked at the kid like I had never seen her before. She sat there in her rolled-up denim shorts, her Strawberry Shortcake tee shirt, with her frizzy red hair. She was a freckled alien looking up at me with big brown eyes. When did I get to be so important to this creature? Wasn't I just the older sister that was always pushing her out of my bedroom? Wasn't I the worm in this apple of our mother's eye?

"Penny, do you really think I could forget all about you, like, even if I wanted to?"

She shrugged her bony little shoulders.

"Trust me, kid, we're stuck with each other no matter where I am and no matter where you are."

"You mean it?" she asked, sounding both hopeful and pathetic.

"Yes, I mean it."

Chapter Nineteen

Penny and Violet walked back to where guests gathered around the buffet. Ben greeted his bride-to-be by wrapping her into his big embrace. To anyone who didn't know that Penny had just sobbed like a terrified child afraid of the bogey man in her closet, she appeared perfectly happy and content. Only Violet knew she was scared that she might be losing her mother.

Suddenly Violet needed to be alone. She could not face another moment of making small talk with Ben's and Penny's guests. She could not stomach the leering eyes of the big-lipped Franklin. Across the floor Ted spoke to her Aunt Marguerite, his hands flailing in the air as whatever he said made her aunt laugh behind a demure hand.

It was a cool evening with stars scattered in the blackness above. A fat moon hung in the sky, the legendary man's face clear, appearing to watch her. Violet let the cool breeze wash over her; willing it to make her new, to erase her fears about her mother, her worries about her job, and her memories of Logan. *Blow it all away,* she said silently to the wind. *Make it all go away.*

At the water's edge Violet marveled at the stillness of its surface. She bent down and picked up a pebble from the ground, rolling it around in her palm, felt its coolness against her skin. She tossed it out as far as she could and watched the rings ripple out from where it had disappeared into the lake with a plop. She breathed deeply, inhaling the familiar smells of this place that held so many secrets of her youth. The scent of earth met her nose. It was rich, real.

"Done with the party?" Logan was in shadow, but Violet could see the look in his eyes. He took a step closer and her body stiffened. Suddenly she became aware of the chill in the air.

"Just taking a breather," Violet said, trying to sound casual.

He was just inches from touching her. "I was hoping to see you tonight."

She forced air into lungs, stayed silent. She let herself meet his gaze. His eyes were bright even in the darkness of the evening. Nothing, she supposed, could ever suppress their blueness.

"Your photographer find his camera?"

"Not yet."

"He thinks I swiped it," Logan said. "You both do."

Old board games aside, clues were clues. Ted was right. If anyone at the lodge had an interest in keeping that camera out of his hands, it was Logan.

It had not been Logan's style to do something underhanded. Violet knew that. But she also knew this man was different from the boy she had known. He was now a stranger. "Well, did you?"

"I knew it."

"Answer the question, Logan. Did you take Ted's camera?"

"No, and I can't believe you think I would do such a thing."

"Logan, we heard Kathleen say you were the only other person behind the desk after Ted left his backpack there. Unless your employee has sticky fingers, I can't guess what else could have happened to it."

"Neither can I. Honestly, I am positive Kathleen had nothing to do with it. She's a good kid. She didn't take the camera."

"Well, somebody did. After Ted picked the backpack up at the desk he came right out and put it into my car."

"I can tell you that Kathleen is innocent, and so am I."

His eyes shone in the moonlight. In them Violet could see the old Logan she used to know. He was there, in this moment. This middle-aged man before her was no stranger at all. This was the noble, kind Logan she had known. Whoever took Ted's camera remained a mystery. But, one thing Violet was now sure of was that it had not been Logan.

"Violet," he said softly, "I wanted you to know that I've thought over a few things since we talked," He shoved his hands into the pockets of his trousers and lifted his shoulders, then let them fall. "I told Jessica about her mother."

"What?" Violet put her hand over her own heart as though protecting it from any further damage.

"I told her."

"You did? Why? How, uh, how is she? I mean, how did she take it?"

Violet was surprised at how she had come to like the girl in such a short time. She didn't want to imagine her being hurt by this news.

"When the camera went missing she pointed a finger at me, too. She said that I had been acting weird about you and your photographer nosing around the lodge. She didn't understand my reluctance.

"Who could blame her, really? I mean she loves this place. The Pines' success is attributable to her diligence and love for it. And I got to thinking about what you and I said about honor and...well, I told her the truth."

"How is she?"

"She's mad as hell at me. She accused me of taking away her rights to the truth. My only defense was that I thought I was protecting her."

"What did you tell her about her mother?"

"Well, I didn't want to give her the cold hard fact that Bonnie just didn't want her. I just couldn't say those words. I was as diplomatic about it as I could be for Jessica's sake, certainly not for Bonnie's.

"I told Jess that her mother was very young when she was born and that she couldn't cope with the idea of motherhood or marriage and decided to go off on her own. I told her I have not heard from Bonnie in all these years, and that's one hundred percent the truth."

"Did she say anything about wanting to find Bonnie?"

"No. I think she's still processing all this. But, you know what she did say?" Logan gave a little laugh, clearly not finding anything funny about Jessica's words. "She feels like she's lived a fake life."

Violet felt as though there was a fist inside her chest squeezing her heart. Instinctively she reached out and touched her fingertips to Logan's cool forearm. He looked deeply into Violet's eyes.

"That's just how I feel, too," he said. "I feel like my whole life has been a fake. I'm a phony. Besides Jessica, nothing in my life is what I wanted it to be. I didn't want to run this place forever. Sure, I helped out my dad when he got sick and then took it on when he died, but I had no intentions of making it my life."

Violet felt her own pain at Logan's statement. She, too, felt like her own life had been a sham. Hadn't she thought she would write the great American novel, or at least use her craft to enlighten somebody about something sometime?

How enlightened were her readers with what she fed them with each issue of the magazine? Does anyone really care about any of it? Or do they use the pages of her articles to wrap up their used coffee grounds?

"Logan, I think everyone has regrets. Who can look at their lives and say they did everything right?"

"I know." The left side of his mouth turned up into a half smile, revealing the dimple—a sure sign of the man's tender feelings being revealed. "Everybody has regrets."

He reached a hand to her and let his fingertips draw a feathery line down the side of her face. Violet felt an electric surge shoot through her cells like a moonbeam had entered her body. She stood immobile, her eyes on him.

"Tell me about your life, Violet," he urged softly. "Tell me about who you are now."

It was Violet's turn to emit a nervous little laugh. She always did that when she felt nervous. Either that, or run from the situation. But she did not run this time. She did take a tiny step away from Logan so that his electric fingers would disconnect from her skin.

"There's not much to say, really," Violet looked away. She took in the view of the water, the ripples of her pebble's disturbance long gone away. "I write for *Today's Hearth*, as you know. I live in the City. I have a great two-bedroom in a nice part of town, safe, nice neighbors."

"How are your parents? They seem fine physically. But your mother kind of threw me yesterday. I ran into her in the lobby and she asked me if my mother had made a blueberry pie today. She said it was Penny's birthday and she wanted it for her party."

"Did she?" Violet croaked the words like she was choking to death. "Dear God."

"What's going on with her?"

"She's been acting confused lately. It's worrying

171

all of us. When we get home we're going to make sure she sees a doctor. Poor Ma. She mixed up the celebrations."

"Is there anything I can do to help while you're here?"

Tenderness filled his eyes and her heart thudded against the iron-like shield that held it firm. It was a caged, living, breathing entity that suddenly wanted out. That scared the hell out of Violet. She swallowed hard, willing herself to get a grip. "Thank you, Logan. But, no. There's nothing you can do."

She felt the sudden urge to run from this spot that had drawn her like magic. The moonlight bathing the water with its glow had beckoned her, prodded her to remember the words Logan spoke to her as a teenager. *Don't*, she said silently. *Don't do this to yourself.*

She turned to leave. With the tiny movement of her foot, Logan's hand reached over and his fingers circled her wrist. In spite of herself she looked up into his face.

"How about *you*, Violet? Are you happy?"

It was a loaded question. Words would not come. She remained silent, unable to give a quick response in the affirmative. What was the precise truth? She wasn't unhappy, yet happiness did not define what she felt inside either. What then was she? Violet felt a tear sting the corner of her eye.

"I don't know," she shrugged. "I guess I don't think about that too often."

"Do you have anyone in your life?"

"I have friends and family...plenty of people."

"Are you still friends with Libby?" Logan asked with a full smile. Logan had always enjoyed hearing about Libby and Violet's friendship, had marveled at how tried-and-true the two comrades were. He obviously remembered the two girls had vowed to remain friends forever.

In spite of the clenched feeling in her throat she spoke. "Libby died seven years ago."

Violet read the reaction that widened his stare. She saw sorrow for Libby's loss. A rush of emotion flooded her. She did not know if it was the echoes of love in her heart for Libby, or for Logan. Most likely both...but she felt love, she knew that.

"I'm sorry to hear that."

Violet nodded, eyes to the ground.

"Violet," Logan said, "I'm just so sorry."

She lifted her head. This was more than his feelings for Libby's loss. The pain in his voice was too great, too evident. Without thinking she stepped closer to him, wanting to feel his closeness. She said the only thing that came to mind. "Me, too."

Logan pulled her into his arms, and crushed her to him. He pressed her so tightly against his chest that it felt like he wanted the two of them to become one body. She held onto him, wrapping her arms around his waist.

He smelled of the woods, the air, the water, the past, the love and tenderness of youth lost to them. Tears sprang to Violet's eyes. She squeezed her eyes shut and did her best to concentrate on the steady beating within Logan's chest. His cotton chambray shirt was comforting against her cheek as was the rhythm of his heart.

How many times in her life had she heard those beats from just this vantage point? Did his heart remember her now as it spoke into her ear pressed against his chest? Did it recognize her? For, surely, Violet knew her heart thundered for Logan...only Logan...forever Logan.

She lifted her head and Logan loosened his embrace enough for her to look up into his eyes. Tears made a glistening path of wetness down his face. She opened her mouth to speak, but there were no words. Instead she reached up and cupped her hands behind his head, burrowed her fingers into his thick hair.

Logan lowered his head and touched his lips gently, softly, tentatively against hers. Violet kissed him back, pressing hard, giving him license to deepen the kiss, to crush his mouth onto hers. She matched his ferocity. Her fingers wrapped around the strands at his nape and tugged them, pulling him closer as she kissed him harder.

Yes, her heart remembered Logan, but her body did also. His lips were soft, warm, sweet. Their kiss lit a fire that catapulted Violet to the days when they stood in this very place wrapped around each other. A familiar flame began a sultry surge through her body, travelling like molten lava over a barren dessert.

She did not care that her heart and her body did not understand that it was realistically too late for the two of them, too late for Logan and Violet to be together, to have the life they dreamed of as kids. Right now, she did not care. All she cared about was his kiss, in this place, at this moment.

Their lips broke apart eventually, each of them breathing heavily. The passion they shared had stolen the very air from their lungs. With each breath that came into her, Violet felt as if she was being awakened from a dream. She slowly let her arms fall to her sides. His strong arms continued to hold her tightly. She lifted her hands to his arms and applied just enough pressure for him to know she wanted them to let go.

"Violet?" he said as he released her from his embrace. She heard the question in his tone.

"Logan," Violet sobered by the distance she had put between them. "This is crazy."

"But..."

"I can't," she said and stepped away from him.

"Really, I just can't do this. To tell you the truth, I wish I could. If I could just, um, be with you tonight and then go home in a couple of days... Well, hell, I would. But, I can't."

Violet turned and ran up the path to the Grove as fast as her little strapless sandals would take her.

In the ladies room, she splashed cold water onto her face and patted it with a coarse paper towel. She looked into the mirror above the sink. The pain that emanated from her haunted eyes filled with the blue mist of her old wound. A ruthless diary entry came to her, forcing her to remember, and she squeezed her eyes shut.

*****

August 21, 1982
Dear Diary,

I have thought seriously of taking you and throwing you away, burning you, ripping your pages out with the fury that I feel inside. But, no. What I'm going to do is write down what happened. Just in case I ever forget for even one second what Logan did to me, I can come back to this page and remember.

I immediately felt an instinctive pang inside my chest when I first laid eyes on him. Logan was sullen. I couldn't make him laugh the way I usually can. I know him so well. Or ha! I thought I did. But, I did know something was wrong. I was not prepared for the truth when he finally told me.

In short, Logan slept with a local girl by the name of Bonnie and she's pregnant with his baby. Even as I write the words I feel like I want to get sick, and my hand has tremors. Logan is going to marry Bonnie. That's what he told me. He is going to marry her!

I just stood there in the hunter's cabin staring at him in the dim light of his lantern. Suddenly, it all felt ridiculous—the dirty shack with its long slit in the wall, the Igloo cooler full of beers, the bag of chips and jar of salsa on the little resin table, the white resin chairs—it was a scene for kids, not a scene for people our age.

I'm twenty for crying out loud. Logan is twenty-two. It seems too young to be married and have a child but that's not for me to say. All I could think to do was run. I took a swift step past him and he reached out a hand and held onto my upper arm, kept me there with him.

"Please don't go, Violet," he said. I ignored his words and I ignored the pleading tone in his voice. I wrenched free, but I did not run. Not yet. Anger boiled up in my veins like I would explode.

"Do not come near me," I spat. "Do not touch me. Leave me alone. I mean it, Logan. Leave me alone."

"I can't believe this happened," he said. "I mean, I got drunk. She kept giving me shots of tequila."

"Save it, Logan," I said. I had heard his story already. Bonnie had plied him with liquor and then took him back to her place. I did not see him as a victim no matter how many times he told the tale.

"I would do anything for this not to be happening," he said.

"Well, it is!" I said.

I left then. He did not reach out to my arm again. He did not hold onto me. He let me go.

I don't know what to tell my parents. They know that Logan and I have had an ongoing relationship for the last eight years. What they do not know is that their daughter had counted on spending her life with him. I cannot tell them that I made plans and promises with Logan and that he has gone and ripped them all to shreds. They do not know that their oldest child is broken-hearted to a point where she thinks she just might die from the pain.

I have so many regrets. And, greatest of these is that my last words I will ever speak to Logan Monroe were in anger.

Chapter Twenty

The morning was brilliant, clear, and warm. A perfect gift of a day for the bride and groom. Violet did her best to let the beauty of the day fill her senses and warm her insides. She did her best to forget about Logan and the moments they shared last evening at the edge of the lake.

Every time he popped into her mind, she gave herself another task. She checked on the flower delivery, made sure her mother's corsage and her father's boutonniere were delivered to their room. She busied herself with checking on the bride and doing her bidding, good little maid of honor that she was.

"Violet, this is it!" Penny gushed as she stood in her long poufy slip and strapless bra. The girl looked like a mermaid ready for her aquatic nuptials. "Can you believe this?"

Violet smiled at her. This was her little sister, for better and for worse, till death do they part. A flash of their childhoods darted into Violet's mind. There were all the times the kid tried to read her diary, the times she picked up the extension of the phone when Violet was on the line with Libby telling secrets.

How she had resented her mother making her watch Penny when she left the house to go grocery shopping or over to Aunt Marguerite's house for a visit. She had also begrudged having to share her Barbies with Penny. Worst of all was having to pass down her pretty turquoise bike to the little urchin when their parents determined that Violet was done with it. She hadn't been so sure that she was. It all flooded her now, and then, as quickly, there flashed another series of images.

Violet remembered Penny's eighth grade dance. She was all dressed up in a fluffy pink dress. Their father thought the sweetheart neckline was too provocative for a girl of thirteen. Penny had started to cry and ran to Violet for support.

"Daddy hates my dress," she wailed from the doorway to Violet's bedroom. "He thinks I'm still a baby."

"Penny, he doesn't *hate* your dress." Violet sighed at the girl's dramatics. "It's tough for fathers to see their little girls growing up. That's all."

"He wants me to wear a sweater," Penny said, her tone still shrill. "A sweater! For one thing it's June. And for another everybody will laugh at me."

Violet had to admit that wearing a sweater over a pink dress that flared out over its starchy crinoline would be laughable. She couldn't let the kid show up at the VFW Hall dance wearing a sweater. She'd be the target of the night among all those eighth-grade weasels. Even Penny didn't deserve that.

Violet marched down the stairs of their home to the living room where their parents stood waiting. Penny tramped down behind her.

"Dad," she said. Penny stood at her side with her sweaty hand in Violet's. She had tried to pull free of it but Penny held on tight. "I checked the thermometer out the window and it's seventy-eight degrees. Penny's not going to need that sweater."

"Oh yes she does," their father said.

"Charlie, you're being an idiot," Josephine said. "All the girls will look like that; you'll see when we drive her to the VFW. They'll all be wearing dresses like Penny's."

"Dad..." Violet said soothingly, responding to his somber look.

Violet turned to give Penny another good look. She really was beautiful, a petit young version of their mother—not that Violet would admit that out loud. The dress she wore fit her perfectly, revealing the womanly curves that had miraculously shown up one day when no one was looking. Penny's expectant shiny brown eyes looked at Violet. Her mouth pouted in its pink lip-glossed shine.

"Dad," Violet said. "Look at Penny. Doesn't she look pretty?"

Charlie Terhune looked at his two girls, the one that looked like him holding onto the one that looked like his wife. He and Josephine met each other's gaze, one that Violet recognized as another of their secret communications. He smiled.

"You *are* pretty, Penny-from-heaven," Charlie said. "So grown up."

"I don't have to wear the sweater?" she asked, her face tilted coyly with her eyes on him.

"No, I suppose not."

Penny had given Violet's hand a squeeze before she'd let it go. She had clapped her hands with giddy delight.

She was making that same gesture now as she stood in her white mermaid outfit, her hair in a turbaned towel. "The hairdresser is on her way up to do our hair," she gushed. "You're first." Penny seemed to have put aside her fears about their mother for her special day.

Violet wanted to have her hair plastered up into some fancy do as much as she wanted to stick a needle in her own eye. But it was a simple enough sacrifice to make for this pretty little bride. Pride danced in Violet's heart. She closed her eyes and tried to will her very life source to knock it off, lest she find herself pony-shopping on behalf of her little sister. Could she really be playing into all this sap?

Violet swallowed hard when an ache pulsed in

her throat. The rest of Penny's eighth grade dance events hedged into her thoughts.

When the dance had ended Penny charged up the stairs of their home and tapped on Violet's door. She knew the kid would want to report to her about the night's events. So, Violet, in her faded Mets tee shirt and cotton boxers, sat atop her comforter and told Penny to come on in. Such an invitation had once been rare, but, now that Violet was in college, had been happening more often.

She stood in Violet's doorway. The French braid their mother had fashioned with Penny's thick golden-red locks was now an unraveled mess. Penny's eyes were not the bright brown orbs that Violet would have expected to see. They were filled with sadness.

Violet felt her heart lurch. She knew eighth grade dances can be heaven or they can be hell. "So, how was it?" she asked with deliberate nonchalance.

"The dance was great. Everything about it was great," Penny said, stepping into the room and closing the door behind her. Oddly, the kid didn't sound like the evening had been a great success. She sounded more like she had just gotten an inoculation at the pediatrician.

"Yeah?"

"Yes, it was perfect. Marshall Winters even asked me to dance," she said. Then her hands flew to her mouth and Penny began to wail into them.

Violet hopped off her bed and went to the sobbing puffy pink figure. "Tell me," was all she said.

When Penny pulled her hands from her face and met Violet's gaze, she appeared to be ready to confess a crime. "It's my fault," Penny had said sullenly, sniffing away the effects of her tears.

"What's your fault?"

"Logan."

The wound of Logan's impending marriage was

still too fresh for Violet to even react to the girl's words. And, they didn't make any sense whatsoever.

"Penny..." Violet began. Penny put up a hand to stop her.

"I used to wish that he would go away," Penny said.

"Every summer when you would go off with Logan and leave me at the lodge with mom and dad—or with those other stupid kids staying there— I used to wish Logan would just go away. That way you would remember that I was there and you'd spend time with me." Penny stood before her big sister, narrow shoulders hunched up, her chin tucked into herself, as though waiting to be slapped.

"Penny, what happened with Logan is not your fault."

"Yes, it is. And here I was out having the best time in the whole world and you're home by yourself because I wished Logan away."

"Penny, listen," Violet said with conviction, forcing herself to remain strong. "Logan being out of my life is not the result of your wishes."

"Well, I wish he was still your boyfriend. Then you would be happy, too."

And before she could think it through, Violet hugged the pretty little eighth grader. And she also wished that some wishes could come true.

****

The knock at the door startled Violet back to the present. The hairdresser was a short, stocky young woman wearing all black spandex. Her own hair was a wild mane the color of an eggplant's skin. Her heavily applied makeup was just short of clownish. Violet looked over to see Penny standing wide-eyed with worry.

"Hello!" the hairdresser said. Walking swiftly into the room, she hoisted her black case onto the table. With a thumb on each metal buckle, she clicked it open. Inside Violet saw various tubes and pallets of color, and brushes in all sizes.

"We're just getting our hair done, right?" Violet asked Penny.

"Well, I thought for the photos we'd have our makeup done, too."

Violet knew one thing. This chick, who looked like an Addams Family relative, wasn't getting anywhere near her face.

"My name's Bethany. Who's first?" asked the beautician. She clutched a black vinyl cape in one hand that she swished like a matador.

Penny stood like a statue in a crinoline museum.

"Hold up there, Bethany," Violet said. "Let's assess this first. We're on the conservative side and we..."

"Oh don't worry," Bethany said with another wave of the cape. "I know, I know. You see the way I look and you're afraid I'll make you up like this. Hey, to each his own, right? Fear not. I'm a genius. Trust me. You'll be conservatively gorgeous. Both of you."

Violet and Penny exchanged a look. Penny's eyes asked if they should trust this "genius," and Violet's look said they had no choice. "I'm first," Violet said. She felt like the brave big sister about to get her ears pierced to show the little sister that she wouldn't die in the process. "But, go slow and go easy. The key word here is understatement. Agreed?"

Bethany nodded and gave Violet a wink, her false eyelash coming down over her eye like an awning. Violet sat on a chair. Bethany stood behind her and fastened the vinyl cape at her neck. "You are going to be stunning. Just watch."

There was another knock at the door and Penny called out, "Who is it?"

"It's Dad."

Penny darted to the bed and pulled on her white

satin robe, cinching it at her waist. She then went to the door and opened it. Their father stood in the doorway wearing a heather gray sweat suit. The look on his unshaved face beamed with one message— something was very wrong.

"Dad," Penny said, her hand still on the door knob. "What is it?"

Violet stood up from the chair, feeling like a bat under the drape of the black vinyl. Bethany stepped aside, her comb perched in her hand like a conductor about to direct her orchestra.

"Dad," Violet said, "What's wrong?" She rushed to the door, standing beside her sister.

"Your mother's missing."

Chapter Twenty-One

Charlie Terhune was sitting in the chair that had been placed in the middle of the room for Bethany's wizardry. Bethany had retreated to another chair near the windows. She sat quietly and fiddled with the comb in her hand.

Penny paced. She circled around the small quarters as though she were about to jump out the window. Violet ran her hands through her hair hanging in straight black strands down her back, yet saved from Bethany's touch.

"Okay, Dad, tell us again," Violet said.

"When I got back from my walk your mother decided she wanted to take one of her own. She put on her jogging suit. You know, that pink-and-white one, Penny?"

Penny did not respond. She just paced.

"Okay, go on," Violet said.

"She left our room around nine. It's almost eleven and she's not back. I went out looking for her. I didn't want to worry anyone, you know, because of the wedding..."

Penny groaned and Charlie put his head in his hands.

"I should have known," he said, the sound muffled through his hands. "I should never have let her go off on her own. I was stupid."

"Daddy," Violet said, crouching down beside his chair. She touched his knee. He let his hands fall away from his face.

"I'm sorry," Charlie said. "I should have let you two know about your mother's behavior sooner. I just didn't want to alarm anyone. Or maybe I just didn't want to face it. I don't know."

"Daddy, maybe we should call the police," Violet said. Now Penny started to cry.

"Here, here, Honey," Bethany said and stepped over to Penny with a tissue from her bag of tricks. "Don't get all blotchy."

"Well, I called Logan," Charlie said. In spite of the dire situation Violet felt a jarring inside at the mere sound of his name. "And, he's got staff looking for her."

"Okay, that's good," Violet said, although she didn't think that was good enough. She felt a fear climbing up her spine like a snake, a relentless slow steady slither.

"I don't care if he's not supposed to see me yet," a teary Penny said. "I want Benjamin. Can we call Benjamin?"

"Yes, that's a good idea," Violet said. "I'll go get him."

There was another knock at the door. Violet flew to it and opened it wide. It was Jessica. Concern covered the girl's face like a mask.

"Any news?" Violet asked.

Jessica shook her head and stepped into the room. "We've got everybody out looking," she said. She turned her attention to Penny who whimpered into her tissue. "We'll find her," she said. "Don't worry. She's here somewhere."

"I'm going to get Benjamin," Violet said. "Dad, you stay here with Penny."

"I just wanted to see if you've heard from her," Jessica said. "I'm going to go back out and continue to look for her."

"I'll come with you," Violet said.

Violet and Jessica went first to Benjamin's room. He was there with his father, uncle, and cousin, Franklin. Violet saw the partially empty tray of cut bagels and halved croissants on the table as well as champagne flutes with various degrees of orange juice in them. It appeared that the men were enjoying a wedding breakfast in their room.

"Good, good morning to you!" Benjamin boomed with a toothy grin. Violet felt a tug at her heart. The last thing she wanted to do was take away that grin.

"Benjamin, I need to talk to you."

In an instant the grin was gone and worry appeared in the man's eyes. "Penny," he said with anguish. Violet felt a tenderness wash over her at this groom's first thought being of his bride.

"My mother went for a walk two hours ago and hasn't returned. We've got people out looking for her."

"What can I do?" Benjamin asked.

By this time the other men had gathered at the open doorway where Violet stood with Jessica.

"Son, what is it?" Mr. Layne asked.

"Penny's mom is missing. She left for a walk over two hours ago. Everybody's out looking for her."

"Okay, let's join them," the elder Layne said. In a moment he, his brother, and Franklin were scrambling to help in the effort.

"Don't forget your cell phones," Franklin said as he clipped his to his belt. Violet felt ashamed at herself for the thoughts she had harbored about this clan of dentists. They were so eager to jump in and help find her mother.

Benjamin went to his Penny. The others went off in search of Josephine, leaving Violet partnered with Jessica. The two walked swiftly down the carpeted corridor and took the stairs to the lobby. Jessica checked at the front desk to see if the attendants there had heard any news. They had not.

"I've already combed the insides of this place, as have several members of the staff. Do you want to go through the place again or should we go outside?"

Jessica asked.

"Both," Violet said. "We'll go down to the grove and along a couple of the paths and then, if nothing, we'll come back here and look again."

"Okay," Jessica said. "Let's do it."

The two women headed out the big main doors of the lobby. All Violet could think of was the irony of Jessica assisting in helping find her mother when the girl had just recently learned she had a mother of her own who was missing, too.

As they passed the open-air restaurant it hurt Violet's heart to see that it was ready for the ceremony. Two large, lush baskets of creamy white flowers flanked the pulpit. A white cloth runner had been placed on the stone floor between the aisles of chairs, the traditional path for the bride's entrance. One question pounded in her head. *Where are you, Mom? Where are you?*

Logan strode over to them and touched Violet's arm. Violet looked up into his concern-filled eyes. She turned her gaze to Jessica, feeling a jab at the cool detachment that clouded their blueness as she glanced briefly at her father.

"Violet, we'll find her," Logan said.

"Not by standing here we won't," Jessica said, her tone icy. Violet pretended not to notice the chill between father and daughter.

"I'm going to check down by the lake again. I've got some of my workers combing the woods."

"I think we're going to head back up to the lodge, then," Jessica said. "Violet and I will go through the place again. She could be walking around and people are just missing her by chance."

"Okay, I'll see you back there," Logan said. He turned to leave, hesitated and turned back to Violet to give her a reassuring look. Then he was gone.

Jessica and Violet trudged back in silence. Violet thought of things she might say but dismissed anything that came to mind. She was so worried about her mother and could only imagine what Jessica had been going through since Logan told her the truth about her own mother.

What this girl missed out on—Violet could not help but think—*by not having a mother.*

Violet thought of her own mom with her neatly coiffed head of gray curls and her little gold earrings shaped like rosebuds. She saw Josephine dancing around her kitchen to the music coming from the radio that still sat on the shelf above the table. Violet felt her heart ache. *This can not be happening.*

She looked over to Jessica as they walked in their steady synchronistic pace. She imagined Logan's daughter having that same thought time and time again in the last couple of days. One day Jessica had *known* she had lost her mother from infancy, and now she knew the woman was out there somewhere.

Violet looked up and around the areas surrounding the path they travelled. Her mother was out there somewhere, too.

Back at the lodge Jessica led the way. They went into the kitchen, where cooks and assistants were busily preparing the wedding feast. The stainless steel tables gleamed in the sunlight that poured in through the windows. Everyone stopped in mid-action as if they were participants in a game of freeze tag. Each and every one of those white apron-clad people had the same look of pity. In an instant, they turned away from the wide eyes of Jessica and Violet and resumed their tasks, now unfrozen.

The two women scoured the pantry, looking behind rows of shelving and inside a utility closet. They checked the ladies room in the hallway and the men's room, as well. They climbed the stairs, nearly jogging down each corridor of rooms.

They went back down in the elevator. The

silence in the little space was deafening. Finally, Violet spoke. "Jessica, do you think we should call the police now?"

"I think so."

"Me, too."

"Let's finish looking on the lower level. Then we'll go up to the lobby and call from there."

Violet nodded. She stared straight ahead at the elevators doors, waiting for them to slide open. "This is awful," she said, feeling like the words had escaped her mouth before she'd had a chance to decide if she wanted to utter them.

"I know."

The elevator doors parted and they stepped into the hallway leading to the lounge. The room was empty. Jessica looked behind the bar and in the coat closet while Violet checked the hallway that connected to the kitchen. Violet knew Jessica would not come back with Josephine in tow, and suddenly her eyes flooded with tears.

"Are you okay?" Jessica asked.

"Yes." Violet ran a finger under each eye wiping away the moisture.

"Let's check the dining room one last time." Jessica said. "Then we'll, um, go upstairs and make the call."

"Okay."

They entered the darkened dining room through the big double doors. The room's draperies had not yet been opened for the day. Despite the horror that she felt in her bones, an errant thought popped into Violet's mind. She could not believe the difference in this room from the old days. This had been the dining hall where long wooden tables had lined the room, breakfasts of scrambled eggs and toast came out of the kitchen on big aluminum trays.

This was the room where Violet and Logan had painstakingly placed two flowers each into all the little milk glass vases on the tables at dinnertime. Dinners were burgers or fried chicken and mashed potatoes with fresh lemonade, followed by desserts of Logan's mother's homemade blueberry pies.

Weddings did not happen here in those days. People dined here in shorts and summer skirts and the only music that came from the place was the sounds of the guests singing rounds of *Row, Row, Row Your Boat* with their little kids as they all sat together at a table.

Jessica snapped on the recessed overheads with a series of clicks. Each button that she pushed highlighted the room in sequential beams of light until finally the entire space was aglow with its beautiful readiness for the day's event.

The tablecloths were white linen and the napkins, folded into little peaks at each dinner plate, were gold. Yellow and white field flowers adorned the center of each table. It was a scene that could take your breath away, Violet thought, and it saddened her even more. "It's lovely," Violet breathed. She touched her hand to her heart. *Please, Mom, where are you?*

Jessica touched Violet's arm and gave her a sympathetic smile.

The room's appearance was so surprising, so totally opposite of what it used to be that Violet almost did not see her. Beyond the tables, at the piano in the back of the room sat the small figure in her a pink-and-white jogging suit.

Violet clutched Jessica's hand and blinked her eyes again and again to make sure the image did not disappear. But, it was true. Josephine sat on the little piano bench looking down at what appeared to be a haphazardly wrapped gift clutched in her hands.

"Ma!" Violet ran through the tables across the room to her mother. A sob broke from her throat and echoed in the room. "Mom!"

Josephine lifted her head and fixed her gaze onto Violet with blankness in her eyes—a frightening look that instantly etched itself into Violet's memory bank. A ghost sighting that, she was almost sure would emerge again and again. Josephine's face was wet with tears.

Violet fell to her knees and wrapped her arms around her mother. There was no time to feel the usual awkwardness in such a gesture. She breathed in her mother's scent, Este Lauder White Linen, a kind of aromatherapy to comfort Violet's nerves. Josephine felt small and frail in her arms.

"Ma, where have you been?"

Jessica came up beside Violet. The two exchanged a look of relief, shared a knowing little grin.

"Here," Josephine said.

"We looked in here a few times and she wasn't here," Jessica said. "She must have just gotten here a little while ago."

"Where were you before this?"

"I forgot my present. I had to go back up and get it." She lifted the package in her hands, a misshapen object wrapped with the comics section of the newspaper.

"What's that, Ma?"

"It's Penny's present." She sounded flustered and winded. "I've been looking everywhere for the box. I don't know what I did with it. I must have thrown it out. I don't know why I would do such a thing."

"Don't worry about that now, Ma. Let's get you back to your room so you can get ready, okay?"

Josephine looked down at her clothing and laughed. "What time's the party again?"

"The wedding's at three, so we have plenty of time."

Josephine stared blankly at Violet then looked to Jessica.

"Are you okay, Mrs. Terhune?"

Josephine looked at the young blonde woman in front of her, confusion knitting her brow. Violet squeezed her hand.

"Of course," Josephine said. "The wedding. Yes, let's go get ready."

Violet reached for the package and took it from Josephine's hands. The sharp edges pointed up over the faces of the cartoon figures of its wrapping, distorting an image of Dennis the Menace's face.

"What is this?" Violet asked.

"It's her Swinger. That's what she wanted."

Violet's heart thudded against the walls of her chest, beating with the knowledge that in her hands she held not the old-time Polaroid camera, but Ted's missing Nikon.

"Ma," Violet asked softly. "Where did you get this camera?"

"Your friend picked it up for me. You know... The Salami."

She didn't want to further confuse her mother, especially not on Penny's wedding day. There would be time later to unravel how this had happened. For now, time was running out and they needed to get ready. "Come on, let's go get you beautiful."

"Okay," Josephine said with a compliance totally foreign to the *Little General's* typical manner. She studied her mother and thought she looked more like a sparrow than a general.

"Are you tired? You want to take a nap first before we get you ready?"

"Maybe," she said. "We'll see."

"You can get your hair done last, how's that? We'll have the beautician do my hair then Penny's and then she can do you."

"Hmp," Josephine muttered, her mouth in a

little twist. "I'm not letting that creature touch my hair. I got a look at her when she got here this morning. What do I look like? A rock star?"

Violet laughed. A loud, hearty laugh—one that let all the air that had been trapped in her lungs fly out to waltz around the room that was ready for dancing.

Chapter Twenty-Two

Josephine's dress was a dusty-lavender chiffon vision that billowed from her little frame, complimenting her steely crown of curls. Violet's eyes misted over at the sight of her. This reaction to her mother was new. Notwithstanding the affection in it, the bottom line was that it was spurred by a new fear that rattled her.

"Ma," Violet said from the doorway of her parents' room. "You look wonderful."

"Hey," Josephine said with a little shrug and a turn of her head, sounding like her snappy self. "When you've got it, you've got it. What can I tell you?"

Charlie Terhune emerged from the bathroom wearing a dapper-looking black tuxedo. His hands were fighting with the satin bowtie at his neck.

"And, look at your date," Violet said to her mother. "Who *is* that handsome guy?"

Josephine looked to her husband and gave him a little smirk. "That's Gregory Peck," she said. For half a beat Violet was worried that her mother was confused again. She felt her own heartbeat stutter in her chest. But, then the older woman gave a little laugh and added, "At least to me he is."

"You two make quite the couple," Violet said. A warm surge flooded her. These were her parents. Her mother's episode of the morning was behind them, at least for now, but its effect lingered in Violet's bones.

Suddenly, both her parents looked old. She felt as though all along she had been looking at them through memory's eye and now reality's view was crystal clear. Violet went to her father and swatted his hands away from his bowtie. "Let me give you a hand," she said. Once again she gave herself a task to avoid the thoughts swirling around in her head.

"How about you let your father tie his own tie and you go get yourself ready?"

Violet was still in her sweat suit. Her makeup was done and Bethany had done with her hair just what she had promised. It was an understated sweep-up at the sides and crown, fastened with a rhinestone clip behind her head. Her hair hung long and sleek in the back.

Charlie walked over to Josephine and put an arm around his wife's shoulders. The look in his eyes made Violet's insides tumble over on themselves. Violet could always read those eyes. She saw hope in them. Hope that Josephine was going to be fine, hope that this morning's scare was not a glimpse of what lay ahead. Violet had that same hope.

"You're right. I better go get dressed," Violet said. "And check on the bride. Come on, let's all go check on Penny."

The three made their way down the corridor to the bridal suite. Penny had been calmed after seeing her mother once she had been located. Tears brimmed her eyes again at the sight of the little woman in her pretty gown. Bethany warned her again that there was just so much makeup could do to hide blotches.

Penny was ready to put on her gown. Her hair and makeup done, she looked like a little china doll with her porcelain skin smooth and pink. Her big brown eyes were highlighted delicately with just the right amount of cosmetics. Penny's red-gold locks were piled up on her head and folded into feminine rolls that sat regally across her crown. She was beautiful.

"Mom, Violet, thank God you're here," she said breathlessly.

"Thank God," Bethany agreed as she busily replaced her supplies into her case. "I don't know who I'd have to beat up if this girl started to worry her face off. She looks perfect, doesn't she?"

"Perfect," Violet agreed. "Bethany you *are* a genius."

"Like I told you," Bethany said. "And, I don't know if you've looked in a mirror, honey, but you're looking close to perfect yourself."

Violet brushed off the compliment with a wave of her hand. She *had* looked in the mirror. It was true, Bethany had done a fine job on her hair and makeup. And even *she* had to admit that she looked good—especially for a forty-four-year-old woman.

But, perfect? No. She did not feel perfect. That was for sure. That place inside her that knew there was something missing, knew that everything that should be aligned was not—and probably would never be—well, perfect. And, Bethany most assuredly did not have the answer to *that* anywhere in her bag of tricks.

"Let's get this bride ready," Violet said, and she and their mother followed Penny into her bedroom. From behind the door Violet could hear her father chatting up the hair stylist.

"So, what color exactly would you call that hair color of yours?" he asked.

"Maraschino Chocolate," Bethany said.

"Hmmmm," Charlie mused. "It's nifty."

"You hear your father out there?" Josephine asked as she stood behind Penny, fastening the fabric-covered buttons with fingers too nimble for a woman her age.

"I hear him," Penny said, standing still as her mother went from button to button up her back. "Daddy's a flirt."

"You want me to do that?" Violet asked, feeling helpless standing there watching.

"No. This is a mother's job. And I would like to enjoy it seeing as though this is probably the only chance I'll ever get to fit a daughter into a wedding gown."

Violet couldn't even bristle. She was bristled out today.

"What," Josephine said. "No response from you, Miss New York?"

"No response, Ma. It's Penny's day. Let's concentrate on that."

Josephine shrugged and let out a sigh. "Fine with me, Violet. But you know you're not doing yourself any favors by ignoring that nice Franklin. Honestly, for such a smarty-pants you can't recognize a good man when he's right in front of you."

Logan Monroe appeared in her thoughts, and memory of their embrace blanketed her like a cloak. Violet closed her eyes and willed the image of him from her mind. There was no sense in going backwards. She had a tough enough time going forward these days.

More thoughts broke into her head like an egg tapped at the side of a glass bowl. The magazine, the article, the ridiculous competition Robert Matthews made out of it all. The ideas whisked around, scrambling themselves into one big mess.

These were the issues she would tackle when this respite in the mountains was done. Home had the view from reality's vantage point. There was no sense in looking at things with memory's eyes any more.

When everyone was ready, Violet called down to the front desk to alert them that the bride would be heading to the ceremony. It was Jessica's voice that Violet recognized on the other end.

"We're all set for her," Jessica said. "Everyone's in place."

"Terrific," Violet replied. "Let's get this show on the road."

"By the way, Violet?"

"Yes?"

"I'm glad we found your mother safe and sound. You all must be so relieved."

Violet felt a thud in a chest. Yes, she was glad, grateful, for that. But, she detected a note of melancholy in the girl's tone and it saddened her.

"Thank you, Jessica, yes we are. And, thanks for all your help."

"Oh, you're more than welcome. And, uh..."

Violet waited for Jessica to continue, but there was silence on the other end of the phone. Violet sensed there was something the girl needed to say to her.

"What is it, Jessica?"

"It was nothing." And the conversation ended.

****

A lone violinist played a winsome melody as guests found their seats. Violet ushered her mother down the short aisle.

She caught Ted's eye, a playful gleam lighting his gaze. He sat beside her Aunt Marguerite, who beamed with expectation. Violet saw that Ted had his camera with him, sitting like a pet on his lap. He gave her an exaggerated wink and she smiled.

She sent the best warning look at him, hoping to remind him of the promise he made when she returned the camera to him. "Just take a few candids at the ceremony and reception, Ted, and keep your lens on the people," she had said. The man had been so elated to have his camera back safe and sound he had agreed without hesitation. He nodded at her now and tapped his camera with one fingertip. He remembered.

From the doorway Violet watched as an usher escorted her mother to the front row, Josephine stepping with regal grace along the white fabric runner. Violet felt a tap on her shoulder and looked up to see that it was Franklin, a starched penguin in his tux. His grin wiggled at her like a pair of spooning earth worms.

"You look lovely," he whispered, leaning close.

"Thank you," she replied, forcing her own mouth into a reluctant plastic grin.

Franklin extended his crooked arm toward Violet. "May I escort you?"

Violet forced her eyes not to roll around like they wanted to. But the thought screamed in her mind. *How dense is this guy?*

"Franklin, I walk in just before the bride."

He nodded and his lips made a valiant effort to close in on themselves in a gesture that indicated understanding. Violet was ashamed of herself for sounding impatient. She needed to be nicer. Maybe she could try. "But thank you anyway, Franklin."

"Sure," he said. "I look forward to seeing you later."

She could see working on the *nicer* thing was going to be a challenge as she heard herself stifling a groan. Thankfully, Franklin had already stepped away.

The music began and the procession of bridesmaids commenced. Violet watched the girl's satin-bowed backs as they stepped gingerly single-file down the runner perfectly spaced as they had practiced.

When it was time, Violet faced the aisle squarely and began her pace to the music. She took her place at the front of the room, standing right beside her mother.

She looked over to Benjamin. Even she had to admit he was one handsome-looking groom. Beside him, Franklin beamed at her, his mouth glistening, a salivating penguin eyeing his prey. She winced and quickly saw that her mother was watching.

She felt Josephine's finger through the fabric of her dress. Her mother was poking her, she knew, but she did not respond. She was no fool. So, Josephine pinched Violet on the arm.

"Ma," Violet whispered and winced at the same time.

"Oh stop, that didn't hurt."

"Yes it did."

"Well, then why didn't you look at me?"

"Because I know what you wanted."

"Yeah? Okay, what then?"

"Shhhhh. Not now."

"All I wanted to do was point out how nice..."

"Ma..."

"Can I help it if I want both my daughters to be happy?"

"I'm perfectly happy."

Josephine choked back a sound. She stopped its emergence with the wadded tissue in her hand. Anyone in the room would have thought she was overcome with emotion for the day. Violet knew different.

"Behave," Violet said.

Thankfully, the bride appeared then at the back of the rows of chairs, her arm linked through her father's. Everyone stood.

Violet saw the wide grin through the hazy blur of the tulle draping Penny's face. Her eyes were fixated on the groom. Violet glanced back toward Benjamin, his hands folded in front of him, eyes shining and filled with pride. She looked down at her mother and saw a matched look on her face. The Little General was full of pride, too. Her urge to chastise Violet for turning her back to Benjamin had magically vanished.

The minister, Uncle Lenny—the Episcopalian—had a robust voice and his elegant words commanded attention. He spoke of love and trust and honor. He bore witness to the two participants' betrothal, and guided them through their promises to each. They promised *forever*. And, then they were joined.

As the guests stood to applaud the new Mr. and Mrs. Layne, Violet felt something prick the back of her neck. For a moment she thought that it was Franklin again, poking at her. But, then as the sensation edged along her skin, she realized it was something more, something visceral. Instinctively, she turned toward the doorway.

He wore a dark suit and his thick blond hair was combed neatly over the crown of his head. Logan was so handsome that it nearly sucked the breath right from Violet's lungs. Her hands paused from clapping, held together as though frozen, making her look as though she were saying her prayers. She wanted to look away—tried to—but, her eyes would not have it. They wanted their feast. They locked onto Logan's blue-eyed stare and unabashedly stayed there. She felt a touch at her arm. It was Franklin.

"May I escort you and your mother to the dining room?" Violet snapped to attention and saw that her mother was listening.

"Oh, how nice of you, Franklin. Of course, you can escort Violet, but I see my own groom coming for me." With that, Josephine stepped gingerly from the row of chairs and met Charlie in the aisle and the two followed the bride and groom as they glided toward the doorway. The groom's parents followed, and then Franklin jutted his arm toward Violet. She had no choice but to take it.

As she and Franklin walked through the doorway her eyes betrayed her yet again as they found their ready target.

"Hello, Violet."

"Hello, Logan."

"Congratulations. It was a very nice ceremony."

"Yes, it was. Thank you."

When she and Franklin were at last beyond Logan's vision Violet felt the air release from her lungs. She hadn't been aware that it had been trapped inside her.

They entered the dining room and although it should have been no surprise to her whatsoever, Violet learned that Franklin, too, was seated at table number two. Thankfully, so was Ted Solomon, her Aunt Marguerite and her parents. Before they reached the table Franklin turned to her and leaned close as if to tell her a secret.

"That's the owner you just talked to, right?"

"Um, yes."

"What's his name again?"

"Logan Monroe."

"Right, I remember," Franklin said with a chuckle. "He must be quite the ladies' man."

Violet felt herself flush from her well-lacquered head to her French-manicured toes. She turned to Franklin and looked into his face. "Excuse me?"

Franklin chuckled again and Violet noticed that when he did so his wormy lips pursed themselves into a doughy red ball. She didn't know what nauseated her more—his looks or his words about Logan.

"I heard a couple of girls at the front desk talking about him." Franklin's hushed tone oozed with the thrill of an old lady's nugget of gossip. "Apparently, he was seen last night in a pretty heated exchange with one of the guests."

Violet stopped walking. She wanted this conversation over before they reached the table. Her heart raced.

"You mean an argument?"

"No," Franklin said, giddy with knowledge. "He was *making time* with a lady down by the lake. My guess is a guy like that does that kind of stuff all the time. You know, taking advantage of his good looks. But whoa, those two girls couldn't stop talking about it."

The image of herself and Logan in that embrace last night formed in her mind like an apparition. Yet, there was no sense trying to pretend it hadn't happen. Obviously, there was a witness. "Well, it's nobody's business, really, Franklin."

"Tell that to his daughter. She's the one who saw the two of them." Franklin touched his hand to Violet's back and gave it a gentle push in the direction of her chair. He pulled the seat out for her, keeping his hands on it. "Apparently she was hopping mad."

Violet sat in her chair with a thud.

Chapter Twenty-Three

Ted emerged through the doorway, Aunt Marguerite at his side. Violet left the table to greet him.

"Don't you look pretty," Marguerite said.

"Thanks, Aunt Marg."

"You clean up good, kid," Ted added with a nod. "I'll have to make sure I get plenty of pictures of you." He lifted his camera toward her and gave it a little wave with his wrist.

"Can I talk to you for a minute, Ted?" Violet asked.

"I'll save you a seat, Teddy Bear," Marguerite said with a bat of her eye. *Since when did Aunt Marguerite start batting those lashes of hers? And...did she just say 'Teddy Bear?'*

As Marguerite sashayed among the tables, Violet turned and gave Ted a look that asked, *What the heck was that all about?*

"What? Can I help it if I'm irresistible?"

She reached over and tapped a finger onto the camera slung around Ted's neck. "Okay, you remember the drill, right? Be careful where you point this thing."

Ted gave a little laugh. "People yes, places and things no."

"Thank you."

"So, Colonel Mustard wasn't the big blond grouch after all. I'd have bet the house."

"Guess your Clue skills aren't as sharp as they used to be, huh Ted?"

"Well, at least you can rest easy that your

knight's armor is still shiny."

Violet crooked her arm though Ted's and guided him toward their table. "Looks like my Aunt Marguerite might be sizing you up for your own suit of armor there, *Teddy Bear*."

Chatter was alive and vibrant in the dining room, particularly at Violet's table. *Darling* Franklin sat to her left. *Ugh.*

The chitchat was commandeered by Josephine, seated at Violet's right. The woman flitted from subject to subject like a bird hopping from branch to branch. No longer a frail little sparrow, Josephine was now her usual hawk.

Violet, realizing she was thinking bird-isms again, turned to Ted seated across the table beside a smitten-faced Marguerite. "Ted, I've got my story fleshed out. When can you take a look at it?"

"How's tomorrow morning after breakfast?"

"Great. I need to get it to Robert soon. Then we'll wait and see."

"Don't worry, kid. You'll blow him away."

"Thanks, Ted."

"No more shop talk," Josephine said. "Franklin, tell us about your practice. It must be so rewarding…saving people."

Violet pulled her eyes over to her father. His eyes danced. After what they had been through with Josephine earlier, who was Violet to ruin her mother's fun?

She knew this was nothing more than Josephine at center stage of an infomercial designed to sway her spinster daughter's affections toward Franklin. That kind of hard sell had not worked for Violet when Suzanne Somers gave her TV plug for that bent crowbar device that wedged between your knees to magically slim their thighs, and it wouldn't work now. Violet sipped her water and let her mother have her limelight.

"Well," Franklin said, with a shrug of one shoulder and a tuck of his head. "I wouldn't exactly say that I 'save people.' But, my work *is* very rewarding, yes."

"Oh, it must be. Wouldn't you say so, Violet?"

"Yes," she said flatly. "Rewarding."

An image of Franklin fingering a patient's spine, his mouth twisted into a big red bow, almost made her laugh out loud. She coughed behind her hand.

Pastor Lenny stood at the head of the room, near the piano that had sheltered her mother earlier in the day. The pianist, an older man with a cloud of white hair, sat silently on the bench. His eyes were on the pastor as the man tapped a butter knife against a water glass. All attention turned to Lenny.

"Let us bow our heads for a blessing," he said.

Violet looked down into her lap and folded her hands. As she laced her fingers together she noticed how cold they felt. She closed her eyes and listened as the pastor blessed the bride and groom, and the loved ones in attendance. Then he blessed the meal they were about to enjoy.

He called for Benjamin's best man to come to the front of the room to give his toast. Franklin's lips curved upward in a waxy grin. He pushed himself back in his chair and rose. Before making his way to the front of the room he turned briefly and looked at Violet.

The gesture did not go unnoticed by Josephine who responded with an elbow into Violet's rib. Violet shifted in her chair but did not acknowledge the poke. Instead she fixed her gaze forward awaiting Franklin's little speech.

Everyone lifted their champagne flutes, the bride and groom and Franklin included.

"To my cousin, Benjamin, and his beautiful bride, Penny. I knew from the moment I saw you two that you'd be together always. Remember, Ben? I came to your office for a root canal."

There was a muffled laugh that went around the room. Violet wondered where this was going. Suddenly she felt this might become interesting. *Maybe he'll go into great detail of his oral procedure, make the guests squeamish, and then I can give Ma her own jab in her rib.*

"I remember," Ben said. His head cocked to the side. Even from the distance Violet could see the crease in his brow. She looked to Penny who, too, had her regally coiffed head at a slant.

"Well, I arrived in Ben's office that day. He squeezed me into a line-up of patients a mile long. As I waited, I watched. I observed Penny and Ben interacting, watched them work side-by-side. They had this easy, warm way with each other. It was respect, affection, sincerity. They were a team of all teams."

The room sighed at Franklin's words, and at the groom leaning over and giving his bride a peck on her lips. Franklin lifted his flute higher in the air.

"To the team of all teams. We should all be so lucky."

Everyone took their sips of champagne. There were a few calls of "Cheers!" around the room. Violet took another sip of her champagne, then saw her mother's flute move into her line of vision. Josephine tapped it against Violet's glass.

"To *everyone* being so lucky," she said, with the smugness of a lottery winner.

****

Through the salad course the white-haired piano player tinkled the ivories, sending light, romantic melodies through the dining room. When he began to play *The Way You Look Tonight* Josephine put down her fork. She lifted her linen napkin from her lap and dabbed at her lips, then placed it gingerly beside her salad plate.

"Sinatra!" she said. "You can't resist Sinatra. Come on, Charlie, let's dance."

Violet hoped it would stop there but she knew that the chance was slim. When Charlie stood from his chair and took his wife's hand into his, Josephine turned to her daughter.

"We should *all* dance!" she said. She joined her husband on the small parquet dance floor in the middle of the room, joining several other couples as they swayed to the tune. Out of the corner of her eye Violet could see Franklin's hands fidget with his napkin. Then with a grand gesture he took it from his lap and tossed it onto the table with a snap.

"Good idea" he said. He rose and extended his hand to Violet. "Shall we?"

Violet looked up at him—all lips and expectation—and she knew she had no choice. So she followed him to the dance floor and let him take her into his awkward embrace. She looked over her shoulder in search of Ted with the hope that he would come to her rescue. But Ted was already on the dance floor himself, stepping with surprising adeptness with a happy Aunt Marguerite keeping his pace.

"What perfume do you wear?"

Violet snapped back to the moment. She looked up at Franklin whose eyes caressed her with such blatancy that she thought she might run from the room. But, with her luck, she'd lose one shoe in the process and this eager chiropractor would invariably show up at her door with a carriage cut from a pumpkin. She breathed out through her mouth feeling her lungs deflate.

"Red Door," she answered. Turning to the pianist, she watched his fingers move over the keys. *When would they stop? How long was this blasted song anyway?*

"Well, it's lovely," Franklin said. He leaned close

to her hair and took a deliberate whiff of her. "Mmmmm, it smells floral, wild flowers perhaps."

"Truthfully, I have no idea. I just know that I like it."

He sniffed her again. "Yes, I'm sure. Wild flowers. Violets maybe. Wild Violets."

She willed the guy at the keyboard to stop playing—to need the restroom, need a drink, or maybe even get a cramp. *Anything*, but please just end her agony.

"Are you a wild violet like your fragrance?" Franklin asked, with a wet-lipped smirk.

Violet's feet turned to cement. Her one hand dropped from his arm and her other hand loosed itself from his sweaty grip.

"I'm sorry, Franklin," she uttered. "I think I need some air."

"Let me come with you," he said.

"No," she said a bit too loudly. She cleared her throat and took better control of her tone. She knocked it down to a near whisper, "Thank you, Franklin, but no."

As she made a beeline to the doorway she heard him call after her to hurry back.

Violet pushed open the ladies restroom door and stepped into the carpeted anteroom. She still could not get over the change of the place. This was at least four times as large as the original restroom had been, and a million times more lavish.

She eyed the sleek counter with the row of oval mirrors aligned on the wall above it. Violet absently fished through the little bottles and packets in a basket filled with sample-sized products placed for the convenience of the guests.

She had a mind to tell Josephine just how her precious Franklin leered at her with his syrupy questions. She heard it in her mind again. *'Are you a wild Violet like your fragrance?'* Her stomach turned.

She'd tell Ted, but he'd never let her live it down. She wasn't that stupid. What she needed right now was—she searched through the catalogue of people in her head—Libby. She looked in the mirror. Yup, she needed Libby here with her to giggle in this lush little chamber, far from the crowd in the dining room. They would double over with laughter, holding their midsections, aching with the delicious pain of it.

In the mirror she saw sadness creep into her eyes. The deep blue orbs staring back at her with longing, regret, and—for the first time in a long time she admitted—she saw loneliness in them. Violet was lonely.

She tucked a stray hair back into the clip on her head. This was not the time for her to assess her life. This was Penny's day.

She twisted her mouth sideways when an old familiar thought popped into her head like a cherry bomb—*According to their mother, wasn't it always Penny's day?* The old resentment returned to Violet like a quick flash in a night sky. Then it was gone.

So, what, she thought. *Penny and Ma connect in ways that me and Ma don't. They're cut from the same Simplicity pattern, the kind the two of them used to thrill over on a rainy Saturday while I read my books and wrote in my journal.*

Penny had always wanted exactly what Josephine wanted for her. Violet did not. She had always bucked her mother's choices. She suspected, truthfully, that even if Franklin had been a dreamboat—rather than a clod with a life raft for a mouth—she still wouldn't want anything to do with him.

Violet decided to appreciate her sister's wedding celebration. Now, more than ever, Violet accepted the differences between her and her sister. She was grateful too, for having their mother with them safe and sound, annoying though she may be.

She stifled the thoughts of yesteryear and let them float from her like a puff of smoke. She would be glad when this week came to an end and she could be forever done with The Pines, and the ghosts it conjured.

Violet emerged from the ladies lounge feeling a need for the evening air. To let it bathe her with its cool chill—its hint that fall was on its way—would promise her that soon this summer detour from reality would be gone.

She darted like a student skipping class, past the doors to the dining room. She was not ready to rejoin the celebration just yet. Something told her that she needed a moment alone to really put this place behind her for good. She needed to say goodbye.

In the lounge, the bartender talked animatedly with a tuxedoed waitress and two male guests that Violet recognized as relatives from Benjamin's side. *More dentists, probably, or maybe another chiropractor.* They ignored her as they sipped their martinis. Violet slipped through the curtained French doors at the far end of the room. She stepped out on the balcony and welcomed the rush of cool air on her skin.

From this vantage point she could see out across the pine trees, dark pillars appearing nearly black in the shadows. Stars speckled the night sky. She studied the inky expanse, wanting suddenly to catch a glimpse of a falling star, or some sign that Libby was up there watching her.

A breeze rustled the trees, their boughs waving in reverence to the elements. It cooled her face, her neck, her arms. She closed her eyes as the light wind wafted through her hair. She felt the same ardor as her friends, the pine trees. Violet opened her eyes now. The trees, sturdy and majestic, swayed with the current, letting it travel through their needles like a caress.

"I wondered where you'd hide," a voice came out of the shadows.

Violet kept her eyes fixed on the branches of the trees moving with the wind. One tree's branch appeared to reach for the one beside it, two comrades in the night. She did not have to turn to the voice. She did not have to guess who it was. She knew— just like she knew Libby had sent him. It was Logan.

Chapter Twenty-Four

Finally, Violet turned toward him. Logan took measured steps across the cement veranda. A beam of lamplight cast a hue revealing that his hands were in the pockets of his suit pants. His tie hung loose around his neck.

"Hide?" she asked. "Why would I be hiding?"

Logan stood beside her at the railing. The evening air continued its rush, chilling her skin. Violet waited for his answer.

She tried to ignore that her heart was recognizing the man—announcing so with its rapid beats. Her foolish heart mistook them for the kids that had clung to each other in the moonlight all those years ago. That was not who they were any more. Yet her heart—her source of life—did not care about that. It knew no calendar. Time had no effect on its memory. Violet's heart knew only that *this was Logan*.

He tilted his head and let one side of his mouth turn up into a smile. His dimple appeared like a pinch in his cheek. When she saw that dimple her heart reacted to it like a bold hussy—bumping and grinding against her ribcage. She touched her hand to her chest to steady the beat, to coax the pulsing traitor to *knock it off*.

"I saw you in there," Logan said, motioning with his head toward the dining room. His hands were still jammed in his pockets. "Saw that guy putting a major move on you."

"Yeah," Violet conceded. "That was *extra charming*."

Logan shook his head and gave a little laugh. He pulled his hands out of his pockets and rested them on the railing in front of him. He rubbed his palms back and forth over the metal surface.

"You looked like you'd have done anything for a trap door to suddenly appear in that dance floor." He had that appealing tone that he used to get when they had shared a joke, or when he had been onto one of her bluffs. He could still read her.

She let a smile form on her lips. "How long will it take for you to install one? I have to go back in there."

He laughed softly. And then she did, too.

"I'm sure you can handle that Casanova."

Violet's smile faded and she remembered the conversation that she had had with Franklin when they entered the reception. "Speaking of Casanovas, I have something to tell you."

"Okay."

"Last night...uh, when we were...you know, down by the lake..." She stuttered, unable to actually say what they were doing at the water's edge. But, in her mind she saw them in their desperate embrace.

She could tell by the intensity in his eyes that an image must have come to him, too. "I remember," he said, his voice velvet to her ears.

"Someone saw us."

"So?"

"It was Jessica. And, apparently, she's upset."

Logan gave a quick rake to the shock of hair that fell forward over his brow. He jammed his hands back into his pants pockets, looking down at his feet. He then lifted his gaze to meet Violet's. "She's just angry at me in general.

"It really has nothing to do with her seeing me lakeside with my arms around a woman. Trust me, that is not the problem."

"I feel for her, Logan. She's had some startling news to grapple with these last few days. Her world's been shaken up. Maybe seeing you in an embrace in the moonlight had her thinking you were out there being a Casanova of sorts yourself. It probably made her think you're not disturbed about what has transpired between you two. You know, like you just blew it off and went on to have your jollies."

"If she were talking to me, I could explain."

Violet wondered what he would say if his daughter was on speaking terms with him. *Would he tell her it was a crazy mad moment between long-lost lovers? Would he say it was a goodbye of some kind? A closure?*

Violet did not feel closed. She felt ripped open. What had been tucked away to some far corner of her being was now present, pulsing and raw. She just knew that on the other side of this feeling would be renewed pain. Because, after all, tomorrow was the end.

She would go home to her world and enmesh herself into saving her job. She'd play by the new big shot's rules; play the game he had concocted out of vying for the coveted position.

She'd do pasta at her parent's house on Tuesday nights.

She'd go out with Ted to Durkins on Fridays, sit at the bar and share a corned beef sandwich with her former boss that had somehow turned into her buddy.

Vermont, and The Pines, and this tall handsome blond specimen standing beside her on this, her sister's wedding day, might as well be a mirage. *Because soon he will vanish.*

"I better get back in there," Violet said. She turned to look toward the French doors, then gazed back and gave him a little smile.

At least now she could go back to reality knowing that her last words to Logan Monroe were not angry ones. That had been one of her regrets from the last time they were together in their youth.

"Penny seems very happy," Logan said, ignoring her previous comment. "How do you like Benjamin?"

"He's nice. He loves her. They're perfect together."

Logan nodded. A hush fell between them, heavy and thick like fog.

This is agony. Violet needed to walk away now. But, before she could take a single step Logan reached for her and pulled her into his arms.

He said nothing. She, too, was silent and she could hear the wind through the pines. She closed her eyes and took in his woodsy scent. Violet remembered this. She would always remember this.

Logan whispered against her hair, his lips a gentle caress to the strands. Even as she heard his words she could not believe it was true.

How long had it been since she had heard anything from Keats? Not since Logan had recited them to her as a girl. *"Parting they seemed to tread upon the air, twin roses by the zephyr blown apart, only to meet again more close and share the inward fragrance of each other's heart."*

Her heart drummed in her chest, its strong beats drowning her caution. She tucked closer in his embrace, allowed the words to float through her mind and pour through her like a running stream. If she did not save herself from this mirage, she might forget her real life awaiting her return.

"I have to go, Logan." She put her hands on his upper arms, taut steel to her touch. She gave them a push but he did not release her from his hold.

"I had no idea, Violet."

"What do you mean?"

"I have spent so much time just living on

automatic pilot. You know, raising my daughter, taking care of my parents when they got sick and then passed on, running this place... It's like I just realized I've been dead—and everybody forgot to tell me."

Violet pictured herself in her two bedroom apartment after a long day at work, with her mug of tea in her hands as she watched the evening news, her stocking feet up on the ottoman. She closed her eyes again. Nobody bothered to tell her that she'd been acting kind of dead, too.

Well, except Ted. He'd been painfully honest a time or two, but she had not let his words sink in. She had managed to chalk up what Ted said as the ramblings of a man who'd had one too many drafts at Durkins.

She pulled out of Logan's arms at last and felt the chill again of the evening air.

"I never wanted this," Logan continued. He lifted his arms as though hoping to embrace the very forest around them. "I love it, but not like my parents did, not like Jessica does.

"And, now, I feel like someone has torn off my death mask.

"I remembered how much I loved to write. Remember that? Do you know I have not written one single thing in all these years? Nothing. Not a sentence."

Violet was taken back to the days when he would share his work with her. The two of them huddled in their hunter's cabin, side-by-side on a thick blanket, a lantern illuminating the words he had poured onto the page. She remembered the spiral notebooks with dog-eared covers in green, blue, black. Logan would read aloud to her. He'd held his notebook open wide, open palms beneath it as though it were an offering to her.

Violet's mind reeled as snippets of his writings

tumbled into her thoughts. Logan had written of things he knew, fishing, planting flowers in his mother's beds of topsoil. He wrote of his dreams for his future, his deepest, truest yearnings. And he wrote of Violet.

Suddenly, a phrase came forward into her mind as though Logan had penned it there—*We are two trees in the forest and the moonlight is the love that could not help but find us*. The moon had hidden behind a large cloud. Violet looked out into the dark forest. There was no moonlight to give homage to his words, but that did not mean she did not believe in their truth.

That is just what love was like. Violet remembered now, and she wished she hadn't. She wished that door had stayed closed.

"Logan, I'm glad we had this chance..." she said, although she did not know why. She wasn't glad. She was dreading having to mourn him again, and she was sure she would. It was too late now to prevent it.

Fixing on his blue eyes, gems in the lamplight, all she could think was, *Yes, in spite of myself, I am glad. Glad to be near him, glad to take in his scent and to know again what his arms feel like wrapped around my body, sensing his warmth.* "I mean...to really say goodbye. Not like before."

Logan reached up and let two fingers trail down Violet's face, lightly running the pads over her skin, drawing a line of sensation over her jaw.

She reached up and caught his wrist then took a step backward. "I really have to go. I should be in there with my family. Good night, Logan."

As she turned to leave, Logan reached out and wrapped a hand around her upper arm, halting her. She gave him a wary glance.

"Meet me."

"What?"

"Meet me later. After the reception."

"I can't," Violet said, hearing the stammer in her voice. She shook her head. "Really, no."

"Please," he begged, his word barely audible.

She did not respond but gently pulled her arm from his grasp. He let his hand fall away from her with the slowness of resignation.

Violet reached the doorway into the bar. She heard the muffled sounds of music drifting in through the closed doors of the dining room, the place where she belonged and needed to be.

She heard Logan softly call her name. She turned toward the open doorway from which she had fled.

"Violet," he said. "Midnight, by the lake."

She opened the doors to the reception. Then she listened for the click of the handle, to be sure the door was closed behind her. She hurried to her place.

The sounds of the celebration penetrated her ears. The piano's melody wafted through the air. A din of chatter sounded like the wings of a flock of startled birds that had just taken hasty flight.

Chapter Twenty-Five

Violet was in time for the entrée. The first thing she noticed was that Franklin was not at the table and she felt a surge of relief. Even that did not quell the stress on her nerves caused by her encounter with Logan.

Josephine sat glaring at her with her dark piercing eyes. Violet pulled her gaze over to her father. He gave his head a slow shake, one that told her whatever she was in for he had no power to prevent. Violet knew the look well. It was a conversation batted silently at their table like invisible ping-pong.

The dinner plates were put in front of each person around their table. All the while no one spoke. Violet looked to her friend and comrade for support. Ted gave a shrug and took a generous pull of his amber-colored beverage.

To top off the moment, Franklin arrived at his place and sat down with a plop. He snapped his napkin onto his lap with a tilt to his chin that looked to Violet distinctly like a childish pout.

When a waiter popped his head between them and asked if she'd like some chardonnay she said "Yes" so loudly that she startled the silence like a slap. Ted chuckled across the table.

"The salmon's wonderful," Aunt Marguerite exclaimed, with her fork in midair. A flake of the pink fish sat on the tines. "How's the cordon bleu?" she asked Ted beside her.

"Great. But you can take a slab of cardboard and jellyroll it with Swiss cheese and ham and I'd eat it."

Marguerite tittered behind the linen napkin she held at her lips. While Violet hadn't been looking, her sweet little aunt with the penchant for crochet had morphed into a school girl with a crush on the boy in the lunch room.

Violet gave a side-glance to Josephine whose dark narrow stare was now fixed on Marguerite. Violet cleared her throat to chase away the urge to laugh. She knew her mother was not above swatting at her, even in this setting.

Instead, Josephine turned to her daughter and leaned in close. "That Mr. Salami of yours is pretty funny."

"Solomon, Ma."

"My sister is certainly making her opinions known—" Josephine leaned even closer to Violet, her mouth close enough to kiss her on the cheek "—just like you've done with poor Franklin."

Violet took another bite of her salmon, trying to savor the essence of its preparation. But on her tongue, it was a flat tasteless substance that might as well have been Ted's cardboard.

She stole a glance of Franklin eating his dinner with his head down, his chin nearly to his chest. Suddenly she felt ashamed. *The poor guy is probably not even interested in me. He's most likely just trying to make his mother happy by doing her bidding. But, that's his problem to contend with. For just this one night I guess I can be pleasant to him, courteous, be a good guest at my sister's wedding.* She swallowed the morsel in her mouth and turned to Franklin. "How's yours, Franklin?"

Franklin turned to her, halting his jaw from chewing the food in his mouth. His lips glistened with the slick of rich sauce from the cordon bleu. His eyes studied her through thick lenses. Then they softened and his shiny lips curved up into a puffy, though wary smile. The dinner gave his mouth an

221

orange-y tinge. Although she willed her mind to stop, Violet could not help but think it looked like a pair of Cheese Doodles had been glued to his face.

"Delicious." He swallowed, his Adam's apple bobbing up then down like an express elevator. "And yours?"

"Wonderful. Have you tried the chardonnay?" she offered as she took a nice big sip from her glass. She noticed the still-full pour of golden liquid in front of him. As though in response to an order he jutted his hand to his glass and grabbed it with enough gusto to toss the wine and pitch it dangerously close to the brim.

A pang poked at Violet's insides. This poor guy had been trained to ask *how high* whenever a woman said to jump. What he needed was a backbone, not a girlfriend.

"It is good, isn't it?" he asked after taking a generous sip. The tension that pinched a crease along his forehead had disappeared. "I'm a bit of a wine enthusiast. I'd love for you to see my collection sometime."

"Oh, a wine enthusiast!" Josephine piped in. "That's right up Violet's alley, isn't it dear?"

The pianist returned to his keyboard. He now had a vocalist with him, a middle-aged woman in a dramatic bat-winged, beaded dress. She began to sing an old ballad.

Violet felt a panic rising inside her like the tide. *'Poor Franklin' will take my polite dinner conversation as a romantic interest. I just know it.* As if on cue, he dabbed at his mouth with his napkin and gave his dinner plate a tap of his thumb pushing it forward just a hair. But, Violet knew what that push meant and she braced herself for the offer to dance.

"Violet, I believe this is the dance you owe me," Ted said from across the table. His mouth was turned up on one side, a swashbuckler's smirk. "Come on. You promised."

Relieved, Violet stood, placing her napkin on her seat. She would remember to thank him once they were on the dance floor.

The vocalist sang with the deep, mature tone of someone who had experienced her songs. Violet savored the sounds. She closed her eyes as she and Ted danced among the cluster of couples on the dance floor.

"You owe me, Terhune."

"No argument there, Ted. Carte blanche at Durkins."

"Is that poor guy lovesick or what?"

"There seems to be a lot of that going around," Violet answered. She loved when an opportunity arose for her to be on the giving end of a good tease between her and Ted. Usually it was the other way around.

"Oh yeah?" Ted asked with a smirk on his lips, a laugh in his eyes. "For instance?"

"I think you know, Mr. Ted E. Bear."

She expected Ted to laugh out loud in protest to the absurdity of her suggestion. She did not expect him to look lovingly back toward their table.

"She's something," Ted said, appreciation coating his tone like glaze on a donut.

"Why, Ted! You surprise me."

"What's so surprising? Marguerite is a beautiful, smart, sassy lady and I'm having a great time talking with her."

"Really?" Violet said. *Is there be a punch line coming?*

"And, she gets my jokes. She thinks I'm funny."

"Does she now?"

"And, she says my eyes are dove-gray."

"Dove-gray?" Violet repeated to the man. *This is delicious. This grumpy old curmudgeon is besotted with my Aunt Marguerite.* Violet looked into his eyes, dove gray that they were.

"Speaking of doves...and birds..." Violet said. "I can't wait for you to take a look at my piece for the magazine. I think I really played up birding as the new vogue for the young urban professionals looking to commune with nature. With luck, Robert Matthews will see dollar signs with all the advertisers for binoculars, birding guides, and hiking boots coming his way."

Ted had his head tilted while Violet talked, his signature gesture for when he was really listening to her, reading her. When she was done he did not comment but rather just kept looking at her like that.

"You okay there Romeo?" she asked.

"Terhune, I'm going to look at your feature, and give you my best advice. But, kid, then I'm out."

"Out?"

"Ever since I told you about telling Robert that I'm done, the more I like the idea. I feel this renewed sense of anticipation. I don't want to be their consultant—which we know is just a courtesy bullshit appointment anyway."

"Ted, that's not true. *Today's Hearth* values your expertise."

"No it doesn't. They've got plenty of fresh *new* expertise. Besides, I can't wait to pursue new priorities." He looked back again to the table where Marguerite sat watching them.

Violet was speechless. This slightly stoop-shouldered bullet of a man looked like Ted, and sounded like Ted with the gruffness of a bear in need of lunch, but this was *not* the Ted she'd known all these years. She knew there was no punch line about to zing through the air like an arrow. This man was serious.

"You mean it," Violet said.

A full-sized grin broke out on his face. "It's time I did what matters to me. I'm going to snap pictures of the world around us. Now that I have my camera back. Oh, and I'm sorry about the, uh, whole thing."

"Yeah, Ted. I'm sorry, too."

"Hey, kid, no sweat. All's well, and all that. I did see your mother at the counter that day when I was waiting for someone to show up and store my bag. I only looked away for a minute to answer my cell phone and then she was gone. I didn't mention it because I figured she wasn't there long enough to have seen anyone swipe my equipment. I never figured her for the culprit. She's quick, I'll give her that. I'd be concerned about her, if I were you."

"We're all concerned about her, Ted."

"Yeah," he nodded somberly. "People change, things change."

"Speaking of change..." Violet said, desperate to restore the mood. "You're going off to shoot the world frame-by-frame kind of astonishes me."

"I astonish myself these days," he looked back toward their table. "I've invited your aunt to accompany me to Cape May when I go next month. Turns out she loves bed and breakfasts."

Violet thought for sure Rod Serling was about to appear on the dance floor and announce that they had arrived in the Twilight Zone. "There'd better be a heavy emphasis on the breakfast. That's my aunt you're talking about. Next thing I know you'll be telling me to call you Uncle Ted."

The bride and groom danced over towards them. Penny was still radiant, her groom a white-toothed knight at her side.

These were the shiny happy people that Violet knew Robert Matthews looked to snare into his magazine's readership. They were young and free to spend their hard-earned money on whatever suited them. She tried to imagine the two of them in cargo shorts and trendy zippered vests trudging through grassy pathways in search of a glimpse of some obscure species of bird through the lenses of their Swarovski Binoculars.

Violet tried to ignore the deflated feeling that came over her. *Do I really care about any of this? How many more years am I going to plug away at writing pieces on things that matter to others, but not to me?* Suddenly she felt absurd to be vying for the spot at the magazine.

I might be named Senior Feature Writer if Robert loves my story the way I think he will. I have no idea what Melanie Rosen's finished product will look like, but I know mine will be just what he wants. But, is this anything akin to what I want?

Suddenly everything blurred together in one big fat ball of nothing.

The music ended and all the guests in the room applauded as though in agreement with Violet's thoughts.

"Violet!" the bride said. "I feel like I haven't seen you all evening."

"Penny, Ben, it's a lovely wedding. Everyone is having a great time."

"I'm so happy my Benny thought of this." She looked to her groom and crooked her arm through his. "The Pines is the perfect place to have a wedding."

Ben beamed with his neon choppers fully exposed in a satisfied grin. If a man's true character was indicated by his teeth, Violet was sure her sister got the best of them.

"Yes, this has been a wonderful place to celebrate the beginning of our lives together." Ben looked down at his diminutive bride with her fancy hairdo still in impeccable order.

Violet touched her fingertips to the back of her head to see if her clip was even still there. It felt askew. Violet thought that perhaps a good way to judge a woman's state of mind would be on how well she kept her updo.

Because, certainly, she felt pretty askew herself.

Chapter Twenty-Six

After the bride and groom cut the cake, wait staff hustled like ants in black vests delivering cubes of cake to each guest.

By this time, Franklin had taken residence at his parents' table and Violet could see him being talked at by his mother. He really was *poor Franklin*, and he was doomed. Violet wondered what he would do if he suddenly had any guts. *Would he tell his mother to put a cork in it? Would he go find his own girlfriend and not badger women his mother aimed him toward? But, then again, what gives me the right to ponder on someone else's courage and what they'd do with it? What would I do, if I was gifted with some of my own?*

When the soloist began her next song, Violet immediately recognized the lyric and its melody, *Moon River*. She felt her heart squeeze itself like a well-wrung rag. Logan and his request, or rather his plea, for her to meet him at midnight scorched her thoughts, flooded her like a sudden blast of heat. Violet grabbed her evening bag and headed to the ladies' room. A splash of cool water to her brow would help.

As she made her way across the room, Penny sidled up beside Violet and hooked her arm through hers. "Where's the fire?" Penny asked. A giggle hovered over her words as if a feather had tickled her chin.

Funny, Violet thought. *The only fire going on is inside my own thoughts.* She looked to her sister and gave a full-sized grin so broad that no one could detect the quiver on her lips. "After seeing how perfect you look, little sister, I thought I'd find a mirror and assess my damages."

"I'll join you. You can help me with my hair. I feel like bobby pins are poking out all over the place. The photographer has a few more pictures to take. I saw Ted with his camera, too."

"I'll be anxious to see what he produces. He's a genius, you know."

"Well, he's been so busy entertaining Aunt Marguerite, don't be surprised if there are none," Penny said.

There was one waitress drying her hands on a hand towel as Violet held open the door for the bride. When she left, the two sisters stood before the mirror alone. "I think ol' Marguerite's got a boyfriend," Violet said as she rummaged for lipstick in her little satin bag.

"The two of them are thick as thieves," Penny agreed, touching her fingertips to the rolls of hair on her crown. "Violet, tell me something." Violet could sense that the subject was turning away from Marguerite and Ted. Penny's eyes were serious, filled with question.

"Okay." Violet leaned closer to the mirror and aimed the point of her lipstick to her lips. She pretended to concentrate on a new application of gloss as she braced herself for what Penny wanted to extract from her.

"You were gone for a while. I was watching for you. The photographer wanted to take a picture of the two of us with mom."

"I'm sorry, Penny. As soon as I do a little repair work we'll go find him and let him snap away."

Penny gently touched her hand to Violet's arm, stopping her before she could make both her lips shiny again. Violet let her hand fall away from its task and straightened her stance. She met Penny's gaze. "Violet, when you came back into the reception you looked like you had seen a ghost."

Although Violet was sure it was not her intent, Penny's words stung like salt water in her eyes. Violet tried to blink it away. "I don't know what you mean," she managed.

"Violet, I'm thinking that you did see a ghost and he's about six-two with a head of blond hair."

The stinging in her eyes got the better of her and Violet could not prevent the sudden brimming of tears that blurred her vision. She opened her mouth to speak, but closed it again.

"Oh, honey," Penny soothed. She reached for her sister and pulled Violet close.

For a moment Violet did not move. She savored the chance to avert her eyes from the truth she saw in Penny's gaze. *How can I explain to this bride, with all her hopes and dreams ahead of her, that I have indeed been visiting my own past? And that I desperately want to meet Logan tonight, even though I know in my heart that it is stupid?*

She straightened from Penny's embrace. She needed to dash the look of concern her sister wore. It was not fair for the girl to worry on her wedding day. "Penny, I'm okay. Really," Violet said. She was forcing cheer into her tone with as much effort as it would take to drive a nail into a wooden plank. "Ghosts don't scare me."

"What does Logan have to say? I've spotted you two together a few times this week, and it's just so obvious there's still that energy between you. I can almost feel it zipping in the air like an electrical current."

Violet looked down at her hands, searching her mind for a response. *Yes*, she wanted to shout. *Yes. That energy does still exist and it is a dangerous force. It has clouded my judgment and has almost made me believe I can throw all logic out the window and rendezvous at midnight—for just once.* "Logan wants me to meet him after the reception," Violet said. Just hearing the words jarred her like the touch of a flame.

"And?"

She gave a laugh. "And, nothing. I can't."

Penny tilted her head; let a sly smirk play over her mouth. She studied Violet for a moment. "And why not?"

"Why not?" Violet was incredulous. Surely, this conventional girl in lily-white was not suggesting she go along with a one-night stand. "Penny, be serious."

"I *am* serious. Look, come on, Violet be honest with yourself. Do you want to meet with him?"

The answer was a no-brainer. Every fiber of her being wanted it. She would continue to want it for the rest of her life. She was resigned to that miserable fact. But, acting on those feelings would only make it worse. "Yes."

"So, then?"

"As much as I'd love to meet Logan tonight I know I'd be setting myself up for heartache. It took me a long, long time to get over him the first time around."

"Why do you have to *get over* him? I mean, you're both single. Why can't this be the start of something?"

"Because I live in New York and he lives in Vermont. Because you can't go backwards. Because we're not kids anymore. Because what's done is done."

Penny reached out and pulled Violet's hands into her own. She gave her a gentle smile. "Violet, you don't seem *done*. You're acting pretty undone."

Violet held Penny's gaze. *When did this girl turn into an adult?* Suddenly, she realized that even though Penny stood before her as a grown woman, up until now Violet had still thought of her as the little kid that needed her encouragement and advice. *Well, isn't it funny how things change? Now I'm the one that could use some of what I've doled out to the kid throughout the years.*

And, interestingly, the new Mrs. Layne was doing just that. "I'm not used to you giving me guidance, kiddo," Violet said, her lips curved into a half-smile. "And I'm not sure I should listen to you."

"Well, don't then. Listen to your heart."

Chapter Twenty-Seven

It was just after eleven o'clock when the reception ended. Violet walked her parents to their room.

Aunt Marguerite and Ted had disappeared earlier. What they were up to was anybody's guess. Nothing shocked her any more.

She wasn't even shocked at her own decision to rendezvous with Logan at midnight. As soon as Penny had told her to listen to her heart, Violet knew her battle with herself had ended. She was choosing not to look beyond this one evening. She would dash into Logan's waiting arms, savor the experience, and let tomorrow be damned.

Her footsteps kept pace with the beating of her heart as she headed toward her own room. Each step took her closer to the moment when she would be with Logan. Now that she knew they would be getting together the time would not go fast enough.

The clock said it was eleven-fifteen. She took a deep breath. What to do now? She couldn't meet him in her maid of honor getup. She lifted the long-skirt to reveal her dyed-to-match peau de soie sandals. Violet kicked off the sandals, then fished for the zipper pull at the back of her neck. She shunned the garment like a snake sheds its unwanted skin.

In matching ivory panties and bra, Violet hurried to the closet, tugged a sweatshirt from a wire hanger and shrugged into it. She went to the dresser and pulled open its bottom drawer and snatched out her favorite pair of faded jeans. After stepping into her canvas deck shoes, Violet stood in front of the full-length mirror. Her body was ready, but her hair and face were not.

In the bathroom, Violet scrubbed off the remnants of the stylist's handwork. She applied a gentle layer of tinted moisturizer and a quick slick of lip gloss.

She unfastened the clip on her head and rooted through the strands for any stray bobby pins hidden inside her coiffure. She placed her finds in a row on the edge of the sink, a half dozen black pins discarded like spent matchsticks. Her brush fought against the heaviness of the mousse and hairspray and God knew what else Bethany had tortured her with.

It took minutes of diligent effort, but eventually her hair looked and felt pretty much like itself again. She pulled it back from her face in a nice neat ponytail. Violet put on small hoop earrings and dabbed a bit of Red Door behind each ear and onto one wrist. She rubbed her wrists together to have them share in the fragrance. Violet was ready.

The clock said quarter-to-twelve. If she walked at a normal pace she knew she would get to the lake at the appointed hour. It felt good to have a cushion of time. She would not set her heart to a frenzied beat in trying to hurry.

Violet made her way down the hallway past her parents' door. The carpeted floors made for a soundless passage. If she was going to sustain her courage, she needed nothing to be in her way. She wanted nothing to snap her back into rational thinking. She was confident that would return in its own good time.

Through the subdued lighting of the hallway she noticed a couple huddled on a loveseat near the fireplace in the lobby. For a second she thought it was Marguerite and Ted and felt her heart quicken at the notion.

She slipped along the front desk as inconspicuously as she could manage. When the man lifted his head, Violet froze. This was not the aging Romeo and Juliette. The couple on the sofa was her parents and they were not knotted in an embrace. She could see now that her mother was crying and her father was doing his best to console her.

Charlie met Violet's eyes with a worried gaze. The look rattled her. She had seen her father with fear in his eyes precious few times in her life. The last time she had seen that look was when he had learned that his mother had dropped dead of a massive stroke.

Somehow, Violet managed to command her frozen feet to move. Once they did, she flew to his side. "Daddy," Violet said, unsurprised at resorting to calling him by the name she had abandoned years ago. When it came down to it, she'd probably never be too old to call for daddy when fear gripped her like a vice.

"Violet's here, Josie," Charlie said to the woman in his arms trembling like a frail waif—something she totally was not. "Look, Josie. See? It's Violet."

Violet crouched in front of the sofa and reached for her mother's hand, knotted around a wad of tissues.

"Ma." Violet's eyes were not fixed on her mother, but on her father. She mouthed a sentence—"What is going on?"

Charlie did not respond to the question. He just looked at his wife with such sadness that Violet thought she herself might break in half. *Dear God,* Violet said inside her head, *what is going on?*

"Why are you crying, Ma?"

Finally Josephine raised her curly gray head. Her face was a mess, a Monet of colors running together as if in protest to the intricate makeup applied by the adept Bethany. It was garish, frightening like a scary clown. Violet heard her own breath suck in.

"Tell me," Violet urged. "Tell me what's wrong."

"I'm lost," Josephine whimpered like a child. "I mean I thought I was lost."

"You're not lost, Ma. You're here with us. Remember? We're at The Pines."

Josephine ran her crumpled tissues over her face messing it up even more. Grabbing her mother's little purse from the floor, Violet fished inside for more tissues. She gave three fast tugs to the little travel packet inside and took over the task of wiping Josephine's face. "Here, Ma, let me do it. You're making a mess."

"Well, if that crazy-haired hairdresser hadn't thought she was doing up a circus act, maybe I wouldn't look like this."

Violet and Charlie exchanged a look. That was definitely the Josephine they both knew and loved. Whatever had come over the woman was dissipating and the loveable old wisecracker was finding her way back to them. Charlie brightened, sitting up a little straighter beside his wife.

"You didn't look like a circus act at the wedding, Josie. You were beautiful."

Josephine turned her head slowly and studied Charlie's face. Violet could see the two of them locked in a stare.

"What's going on with me, Charlie?" Josephine's voice was haunted.

"I don't know, Josie." Charlie was nothing if not honest. Violet knew he was as baffled as the little woman next to him. "But, we'll find out. When we get home we'll make an appointment with the doctor. Maybe you need vitamins."

"Vitamins," Josephine spat. "Charlie, don't be ridiculous. How could I need vitamins when I cook the way I do? I make everything. I eat everything. I eat more colors than that quack could paint on my face."

Violet and Charlie laughed together, sharing a glance filled with relief. Josephine was definitely feeling like herself.

"Tell me what happened," Violet said to the both of them.

"I started to get changed," Charlie began. "I took off my jacket and tie. When I went into the bathroom I thought I heard the door to our room. I came out and found your mother gone.

"She was tired at the dinner, I could tell. We should have left earlier. This happens more when she's tired."

"So, where did she go?"

"Stop talking like I'm not here," Josephine said. "I was mixed up. I thought we were home in our house, and then I thought I was in my old house on Warren Street in Montclair."

Violet felt a stab at that. Montclair was where her mother had lived when she was a girl. She hadn't lived in Montclair for more than fifty years. Violet tried not to look the way she felt. She didn't want to scare her mother.

"So," Josephine continued, "I'm losing my mind."

"No you're not either," Charlie said with a conviction that sounded as much for his own ears as for hers. "You're just tired and…"

"Yeah, yeah, I know, Charlie, vitamins," Josephine said with a wave of her ball of tissues. "How many vitamins are in vodka? Because I could use some of that right now."

"Ma, how about if we get you upstairs and make us all some tea. You have tea bags in your room?"

"Of course I have tea bags. I have everything. I have Vienna Fingers, too. You like Vienna Fingers, Violet? They're Penny's favorite."

Violet put a hand under her mother's arm and

helped lift her from her seat. She felt as light as a feather. Josephine wobbled on her feet and Charlie put a steadying arm around her shoulders. She didn't bother to correct her mother about her cookie reference. Vienna Fingers were her favorite, not Penny's. Penny liked chocolate chip best.

"I do like Vienna Fingers. Let's go have some with our tea, Ma."

"That's a good idea," Josephine said, her voice absent of its gusto from a moment ago. Now, to Violet's ear, the woman sounded like a weary child needing her nap.

The three Terhunes walked in slow little steps as they made their way across the lobby and navigated the stairs to Josephine's room. No one spoke. But, thoughts careened around in Violet's mind. *What if this really is the beginning stage of Alzheimer's? What if we lose Ma to that dreaded disease? What will I do if she begins to disappear right before our eyes, one lost thought at a time?*

Is it worse to lose a parent in a flash, or in a slow and steady kind of vanishing, like a big pink eraser rubbing back and forth over all the things that make Ma the Josephine we all know? Violet watched her mother with her head down, concentrating on the steps she took one by one. She tightened her grip on Josephine's arm.

Violet knew when she got home she would see to it that her parents had her support in finding out what was happening to her mother. For now, all she could think was that she needed to help keep Josephine from losing her memory. She remembered how they had taken turns with Grandma Sophia, playing endless games of gin rummy, not bothering with keeping score, and ignoring the rules. The specialist had said to keep her mind stimulated and it had been wise advice.

"Ma, I have another good idea. How about when

we get home you come over to my place and show me how to make your meatballs and sauce?"

"Okay," Josephine said. "But, I'm not making any promises you'll get it. Last I remember, you have a tough enough time frying an egg."

Charlie started to chuckle. Instead of feeling the old familiar bristle, Violet felt relief.

Inside their room Charlie flopped on the chair near the TV and pushed the on button of the remote. The television screen sprang to life and Charlie proceeded to flip through the channels. Violet stood at the counter in the kitchenette watching two mugs of water spin around on the turntable inside the microwave.

The clock on the wall now reported that it was twelve-fifteen in the morning. Violet knew it would be at least another half hour before she could extricate herself from this situation and bid her parents good night. She withdrew the mugs of steaming water and submerged a tea bag into each. She held the little paper ends of the strings and bobbed a two-handed dip watching the bags bleed in brown swirls into the water.

She looked to the window at the far end of the room and could see nothing but the darkness outside. She wondered how long Logan would stand at the water's edge before he knew she was not coming. Violet could not decide if the foiled opportunity was a tragedy or a blessing in disguise. Either way she felt exhausted, spent.

Josephine emerged from the bathroom swimming inside a pair of sky-blue cotton pajamas with white puffy clouds strewn all over them. She shuffled over to Violet in her terry slippers and accepted one of the mugs of tea and took a sip.

Chapter Twenty-Eight

When the alarm blasted at eight in the morning Violet groaned and slapped the bedside clock radio as many times as it took for her hand to finally find the off button.

She had an hour to get her act together in time for the breakfast. She was anxious to see how her mother was this morning, and was equally happy that the bride and groom were not disturbed on their wedding night by last evening's scariness.

Violet went to the window and looked out to the sunny sky above the pine trees. Her heart ached for her missed opportunity. While trying to fall asleep she had decided it didn't pay to find Logan and explain about why she had stood him up. They were probably both better off for the thwarted chance.

She gave the view from her window one long last look before turning away to tackle the job of packing up her belongings. The wedding breakfast was at ten, but she was meeting Ted first to go over her article.

She jumped into the shower and put her face right up to the spray, allowing the fine jets to sting her skin. The water now swirled with the body wash she had applied generously and allowed to run down over her body in loose sudsy puffs. She rinsed herself clean, pirouetting under the warm stream. The remnants of soap bubbles whirled at her feet and disappeared into the drain, like lost dreams.

Dressed in neatly pressed chinos and a button-down white shirt, Violet grabbed her laptop and briefcase. She headed to the lobby to find Ted.

She passed by the big mirror at the landing of the staircase, saw her image, and stopped. She was wearing an almost identical outfit to what Melanie Rosen had worn on the day they met. Only, she was no Melanie Rosen.

Violet was in her forties, not a twenty-something gung-go over-achiever. And, now she wouldn't have Ted Solomon to lean on at *Today's Hearth*. She felt like an island, one surrounded by sharks wearing khakis.

"There she is," Ted said. He sat in a plaid armchair. His laptop was open on the rough-hewn coffee table in front of him with a mug of steeping hot coffee beside it.

"Where'd you get that?" Violet asked pointing to the beige ceramic mug. She placed her laptop on the table beside Ted's.

"Back over there," Ted said motioning toward the dining room. "The ladies are setting up the buffet and I begged them for a cup."

"Well, you do have a way with the ladies these days," Violet said with a crooked grin.

Ted flashed her a smirk and winked. "You look like shit, by the way." Ted stared at his screen, rolling his index finger over the mouse pad.

"Flatterer." She plopped down beside him. She picked up his mug of coffee and took a sip from it.

"Help yourself," he said without looking away from his screen.

Violet looked over at Ted's laptop and saw that he was reviewing images from the wedding. The picture on the screen was an appealing close-up of her Aunt Marguerite.

"Nice picture," Violet said.

"Nice lady."

"So, did you get any pictures of the bride or is this a pictorial of my Aunt Marguerite?"

Ted gave Violet a look that said, "Watch this."

He clicked around and a new image appeared on the screen. It was a lovely photo of Penny and Ben dancing together, perfectly centered under the wrought-iron chandelier above the dance floor.

"How lovely," Violet leaned in closer to the laptop. "What a couple, huh?"

Ted nodded, then clicked again. An image of Josephine being ushered to her seat at the ceremony came into view. Josephine looked stunning in her long, pretty dress holding her little beaded bag.

Violet felt a lump form in her throat. A picture of her mother sitting in this very room last evening, like a frightened child, popped into her head. If only she could use the delete key on Ted's keyboard to banish that image with a simple click.

The next picture was a close-up of Josephine, seated in her chair at the ceremony. Ted had managed to capture the woman's look of love and admiration as she gazed toward the entrance of the room.

"Oh, Ted," Violet said, putting a hand over her heart. "That look on my mother's face...she's radiant. That will make such a great memory for Penny to savor. That's when Penny was coming down the aisle, isn't it? Good job, Ted. You're amazing."

"Thanks," Ted said turning from the screen and looking into Violet's eyes. "But, your mom wasn't looking at the bride in this shot."

"She wasn't?"

Ted shook his head. "No, she was looking at you."

Violet felt movement inside her chest, like a fault line shifting the earth. A tiny change can do big things. "Me?"

"Yup. Look closer. The minister is standing alone at the lectern. You were the first one down the aisle."

"Yes. I was," Violet said, her mouth dry. "I was first."

****

While Ted read through Violet's article he made notes on where to insert photographs he had taken. He had pulled up his bird pictures and Violet clicked through the images as Ted read. They were amazing. Violet marveled at the great shots Ted had managed to get despite the camera having gone missing for a while.

"Your camera's magic, Ted."

"It's not the apparatus. It's the genius behind the lens." He gave her one of his wicked ear-to-ear smiles.

Violet groaned. "Okay, genius, let me see the photo of the Hermit Thrush. I have an idea I want to run by you."

The picture of the little brown bird with its speckled breast particularly appealed to her. The splash of red on its tail looked as if it had paused on a red fence having failed to read the "Wet Paint" sign. It was perched on a sprig of a young sugar maple, evidence of yellow appearing on the green leaves, hinting at the coming autumn.

"I really like this picture, Ted. Look at him. He's magnificent."

Ted eyed Violet over the tops of his reading glasses. "That's my favorite, too."

"One of my pamphlets had a whole piece on the Hermit Thrush. I'm going to dig it out and find a quote to use for the caption. I want this to be at the top of my piece...catches the eye immediately, you know?"

Violet reached into her canvas tote and withdrew the stack of pamphlets she had collected from the Audubon Society. She flipped through them until she found what she was looking for.

"Okay, good. I knew there was something poetic

in here." She had the tri-fold open in her hands. "Listen to this, Ted. Tell me what you think. It's by Walt Whitman:

In the swamp in secluded recesses,

A shy and hidden bird is warbling a song.

Over the breast of the spring, the land, amid cities

Amid lanes and through old woods

Where lately the violets peep'd from the ground."

Ted nodded his approval. "He even mentions violets. What better quote for the Head of the Feature Department who happens to be named Violet? I say use it. And, Terhune, this piece is terrific."

"You mean it, Ted?" Violet asked, excitement pricking her skin with a tingling sensation.

"You've got this in the bag, kid. I can't imagine that Melanie Rosen coming up with anything as good, let alone better. You'll have every yuppie along the Northeastern seaboard running to the woods to become birders."

"You're prejudiced." Violet beamed at her mentor and friend.

"Not so," Ted shook his head. "You know me, Terhune. I calls them as I sees them. If this was crap, you know I'd tell you it was crap."

"Ted, I don't know what I'm going to do without you at the magazine."

"You'll do just fine. Better than fine."

She fought the urge to throw her arms around the old softie. She did reach over and give his upper arm a gentle tap with her knuckles—a love tap. His mouth turned into a crooked smile.

Charlie Terhune appeared, carrying a mug of coffee, the morning paper folded under his arm. "Good morning." His tone was absent of any of the previous evening's distress. He looked a bit tired around the eyes, the lines on his forehead a bit more pronounced. But his eyes were bright and Violet knew that meant her mother must be back to her old self this morning.

"Where's Ma?"

"She's coming," Charlie said, sitting on the love seat opposite Violet and Ted. "She and her sister are preening like a couple of peacocks."

"Any idea why?" Violet teased, looking sideways to Ted.

Charlie nodded towards Ted as he opened the paper. "If I were you, buddy, I'd head for the hills. Your name was being batted around between the two of them like a ping-pong ball."

A quick snap of laughter popped out of Ted's mouth, and Violet imagined an arrow making a clean, fast bull's eye. She shook her head. This man was loving the attention from Marguerite and he was not about to head for any hills. Not by himself anyway. There was a bull's eye all right, and Cupid was the marksman.

Guests began to wander through the lobby on their way to the breakfast, offering greetings as if they hadn't seen each other for a long time instead of just having spent an entire week together at the lodge.

Violet watched her mother and Aunt Marguerite walk slowly down the staircase. They were arm-in-arm, shoulder-to-shoulder. Each step they descended seemed to dislodge a separate giggle from the *two school girls with a secret*. Violet felt her heart swell. Whatever was around the corner was anyone's guess. But, for now, Josephine was her old self. She had the devil in her eye and that eye was aimed right at Ted "Salami." Charlie saw it too.

"There's a back door to this place, in case you need one, Ted," Charlie quipped.

"He's not going anywhere, Dad. He's already a goner."

Ted said, "You're just glad your mom's laying off you and that Franklin dude."

Charlie laughed behind his open paper. Violet reached over and gave the taut newspaper a slap. Her eyes riveted to a black-and-white photo of long-necked swans. The familiar bird's image forced her attention to the bold headline of a two-column article. She read the words aloud, "Marshland at Risk from Development."

Charlie peeked over the edge of the paper in his hands. "What was that?" he asked.

"An article on the back page of that section you're reading. It's about the Marshland. When you're done with the paper, Dad, save it for me. I want to find out what that's about."

"Good morning, Violet," Josephine crooned, as she and her sister approached. "And good morning to you, too, Ted."

Violet was impressed. Her mother let slide an opportunity to refer to the man as a salami. *This* was serious now. She looked over to Marguerite, dressed in an ecru linen pant suit accented by an elaborate necklace of beads and chains that screamed "Chico's." Her sandals matched her outfit and her clutch matched her shoes. The woman was dressed for success.

"Good morning, ladies." Ted addressed the two women, but his eyes were solely on Marguerite.

"Good morning," she responded in a low, sexy tone that Violet had never, ever heard from her aunt before.

The milling guests applauded as the dynamic duo newlyweds descended the staircase. Violet marveled at the nearly palpable happiness that emanated from them. Suddenly she recalled what Penny had said about her and Logan having a visible electrical current between them.

She dismissed the thought, willing herself not to

dwell on a fleeting revisit. After breakfast she would hop in her Saab and head back to New York. And, while the bride and groom cruised their way through the Western Caribbean, Violet would resume her normal life.

Well, on second thought, there would be some abnormal aspects of her existence, unavoidable changes. There'd be no more Ted at the magazine, and she'd have to contend with the decision of the new boss man regarding her position.

Hell, she'd even asked her mother to show her how to cook. Now, *there* was something to look forward to.

The guests made their way into the dining room, set up now with a long line of stainless steel chafing dishes. Little folded place cards marked the contents of the dishes, including French toast, Eggs Benedict, and Canadian Ham. A line formed and slowly selections were made, tongs from each dish being handed to the person following, like a relay team passing a baton.

"Come here, you." Violet turned to the voice. Penny stood with two champagne flutes filled with mimosas.

"Good morning, Mrs. Layne," Violet said, accepting a glass from Penny.

"I want details."

"I didn't go."

"Why not?" Penny asked, her protest too loud for Violet's comfort. She grabbed Penny's elbow and ushered her from the dining room into the bar, empty with exception of the bartender who was busy pouring mimosas and Bloody Marys.

"For crying out loud, Penny, pipe down."

"I'm so disappointed," Penny pouted. "I imagined you having the time of your life last night."

"I might say the same for you there, bridey-poo."

That got Penny to laugh. A redness crept up her

face, but Violet was not fooled by the apparent blush. Penny loved the mention of her wedding night. The girl so enjoyed being the topic of conversation.

"Okay, so?"

"So, what?" Penny asked with a demure lift of one shoulder.

"What's it like being Mrs. Benjamin Layne?"

Penny closed her eyes, a rapturous smile bursting like the first daffodil at Easter.

"Oh, brother," Violet said with exaggerated appall. "Don't tell me. I don't *really* want to know."

At that moment Jessica strode into the bar with a large jar of maraschino cherries. She handed them over the wooden counter to the bartender and spoke softly. When she turned to leave she spotted the two sisters in the corner by the doorway to the dining room. "Oh." She gave a little nervous laugh. "I didn't see you there. Good morning."

"Good morning," Penny said.

Ben appeared in the doorway and called to his new wife. Violet found herself alone with Jessica. Awkwardness hung over them like Spanish moss.

"I was just out in the lobby and your friend showed me a few shots he took at the reception. He's quite a photographer. I'm so glad he got his camera back."

"Yes, that was fortunate." Violet said. "He's taken so many great pictures of birds for my magazine article. I'm going to have a tough time choosing which ones to use. Oh, and by the way, we made sure we kept The Pines out of the shots, as you requested."

Jessica gave a little snort, her face clouding with a veil of discontent. "That wasn't *my* request," Jessica said, her words turning into icicles in the air. "That was my father trying to keep us in a bubble. We don't see eye-to-eye on The Pines, or anything else these days."

Violet had no response. She fought the urge to tell her that Logan's motivation was his love for her, his need to protect her feelings. None of that was her place or her right to say.

"Well, you and The Pines have been gracious hosts, and my sister and her new husband could not be more thrilled with their choice to come here."

"Thank you."

"If you'll excuse me," Violet smiled, "there are some Eggs Benedict with my name on them."

****

After breakfast, Violet felt a heaviness in her belly that was more than her buffet choices. It was time to leave. Time to leave The Pines and every memory it held. It was time to put Logan Monroe behind her once-and-for-all.

She kissed her sister and new brother-in-law, said goodbye to everyone else, the sullen Franklin included. She found her parents and was relieved to see that her mother was her sharp self.

"Ah," Josephine said when Violet approached her. "Back to the city?"

"Duty calls, Ma." Violet turned to her father and linked her arm through his. They shared a smile, one that said they appreciated that Josephine was okay today.

"So, when's the cooking class?" her mother asked.

Violet pursed her lips. *No memory loss on that topic*, she thought. What had she been thinking when she asked her mother to give her a lesson on tomato sauce and meatballs? Everyone in the whole world knew nobody could exactly reproduce the woman's magic meal. There was no recipe to copy. It was a quest doomed to fail.

"Whenever you want, Ma," Violet said with the enthusiasm of a goldfish floating belly up.

"You listening to that tone?" Josephine asked, conjuring a put-off lilt to her voice, but her eyes danced with playfulness. She turned to her husband. "Charlie, does that sound like a girl who *wants* to learn to cook?"

"Got to admit, Violet, you don't seem too thrilled," Charlie laughed.

"You'll see," Violet said with an attempt to sound convincing. "I'll surprise you with my culinary abilities."

"I've got to see this one," Charlie said.

"I can't wait," Josephine added.

Violet left them, went back to her room, and retrieved her things so she could get on the road as soon as possible.

She loaded the trunk of the Saab and set up her Blue Tooth for the ride home. She had a water bottle in the cup holder, her Dad's newspaper from the morning on the passenger seat and a granola bar in the console. She started the engine, backed out of the parking space, put the transmission into drive, and headed away from The Pines.

She had not seen a sign of Logan all morning. He had not shown up at the breakfast. It was as though he had vanished. And, to Violet, that's just how it felt. Logan was there one minute, arms open, and the next he was gone.

She knew that he did not know what had kept her from meeting him last night, but that was all the better, really. What good would it have done either of them to be together? Her thoughts were clearer in the light of day, especially without Logan's nearness. So, his vanishing was good, too.

Violet wasn't even to Route 87 when she needed a pit stop. She admonished herself for drinking that third cup of coffee. And maybe she could blame the coffee on the way her insides jittered as if she'd swallowed a handful of Mexican jumping beans. She pulled into the parking lot of a cute little ice cream shop. Maybe a soft serve cone would coat her tummy and still the acrobats within. A legitimate purchase would gain her access to the "Customers Only" restroom. It was a win-win.

Violet chose a vanilla-chocolate swirl cone, grabbed a wad of napkins from the holder, and went back to her car. She opened the windows and a rush of cool air came in from the driver's side and blew across her to seek its escape through the passenger side. The breeze ruffled the morning newspaper that sat beside her like a flat traveling companion. She remembered the article she had glimpsed, reached a hand over to the paper, and flipped the top section over to find the article about the marshlands.

It turned out that the marshland in the area of West Rutland was in jeopardy. Although the area surrounding the marsh was primarily privately owned, there was speculation that a large developer was inquiring about purchase for a proposed luxury townhouse community. An activist group sponsored by the Wildlife Habitat Incentive urged citizens to contact their local politicians to protest new construction to the area.

Violet dabbed her tongue into the hollow cone when the ice cream dwindled. Then she began to take tiny bites around and around the perimeter until it was gone. She wiped her sticky fingers with a napkin and studied the paper in her hand.

The article went on to say that urbanites' increasing interest in nature made the marshland a desirable location for luxurious living for those seeking a woodland retreat. Landowners might be faced with exorbitant offers from builders that would sway them to sell.

Violet laid her head back onto the black leather headrest. She closed her eyes and enjoyed the breeze blowing in one window and out the other. She pictured her spread in *Today's Hearth*. She agreed with Ted, the article was good, *really good*. Surely, Matthews would make her the head of the feature department as a result of the article.

Robert would see just what she brilliantly portrayed—getting back to nature, birding specifically, was the new vogue. And, realistically she knew that any of those phantom builders seeking to make big bucks at the marshland's mercy would jump for joy if they read what she had written. She thought then of Walt Whitman's words, picturing his poem's shy bird in a marshland that could possibly change from a wooded lane to a paved street.

She opened her eyes and let them scan the newspaper article one more time, and once again took in the photo of the mute swans. How easy it would be to be mute, too. Ignore the implication her article might fuel in the quest of these building interlopers.

Violet took a deep breath and looked at her watch. If she got back on the road right now she could make it home by the dinner hour. But, Violet knew that wouldn't be happening now. She started the car and pulled out from the ice cream store's lot and made a left heading back north. With any luck she'd get to the Audubon office she and Ted had visited, and that little self-professed ornithologist with the thick glasses and nasal tones would be on duty to talk with her.

Chapter Twenty-Nine

It was nearly 10:00 p.m. when Violet finally made it home. Exhausted and achy, she grabbed her necessary toiletry bag from the trunk. She snatched her laptop and briefcase, now filled with notes she had taken from today's talk with Jacob Anders at the Audubon office.

She was way too tired to work tonight, but first thing in the morning she would get cracking. She knew the revisions would take her all week.

A fire burned inside her to write the new article—a desire she hadn't felt in years. She had something important to tell the readers, something that served a greater purpose than anything she'd ever produced for *Today's Hearth*. The feeling was nearly heady. If she hadn't been so completely worn out she might even jump for joy.

She went through her bedtime routine in a zombie-like state, fell onto her mattress, and relished the cool sheets. Violet thought for sure she would fall fast asleep. She did not.

She stared at the ceiling. Visions of the week's events paraded through her mind with Logan Monroe leading the marching band. She saw his face clearly. He had the same handsome face of his youth only with more character, more definition, and, admittedly, more appeal. Forgetting him again would take work.

She groaned. She had *real* work to do—work that would save her job. *What if Matthews doesn't like my new twist on the birding spread? What if environmentalism isn't part of his mindset for the new format?*

Yet, how can I—in good conscience—hand in my original story? Especially after talking with Jake Anders. I can really feel his passion for the preservation of the natural habitats.

Violet felt so off kilter that sleep just would not come. She flipped on her bedside lamp and tugged open the drawer in her nightstand. She fished around for a book to read, something easy and light, something that would lull her to sleep.

Violet knew the hard volume that her fingers found was her diary. *No,* she thought. *There's no way the contents of that book will help me sleep. I'd have a better chance of slumber with a Stephen King novel.* But her hands did not listen. She pulled it out and cracked it open.

Tucked in the very back, adhered with a yellowed strip of Scotch tape was *the card.* She had done her best to avoid looking at it. She was reminded of when she had first seen the envelope addressed to her in Logan's elegant script.

She was too tired to fight with herself and figured she was on a runaway train anyway. *So why not? Why not take a look at Logan's last greeting card from the Christmas after his decision to marry the pregnant Bonnie Creswick?*

Violet pulled the card from the envelope. She recognized the red border on the front of the card and the black background surrounding the swan in the center. A wreath of holly ringed the swan's long, elegant white neck. Gold lettering offered "Season's Greetings" in a fancy old-world script. Violet let her fingers trace the letters, and then trace the outline of the swan.

If she had any sense she would put the card back in its envelope and go to sleep. But she had neither sense nor ability to sleep. So she took a breath and let it expel from her lungs like a sad little breeze too powerless to squelch even the tiniest of flames.

December 21, 1982

"May you know all the joys of this holiday season."
Dear Violet,

I have not stopped thinking about you, and our last moments together. My heart has cracked into a million pieces and it will never be whole again. I wish this were not happening, but there is nothing I can do to change it.

I don't expect you to respond to this message and I promise to leave you alone from now on, but I wanted you to know that the duty of my obligation has forced my hand. Perhaps someday you will understand what it has meant to me to give up what I want most, for the love of a child on the way. This baby is my family.

I'm so sorry, Violet.

I will never forget you...just like the cob knows his one mate in a sea of swans...

Logan

Chapter Thirty

When Violet woke at six a.m. the card was still in bed with her, face up, the swan on the cover staring at her with one intelligent eye. Violet felt like she had run a marathon uphill carrying a bag of bricks. Two bags of bricks.

She sat up and fished in her bedclothes for the envelope, found it, and snatched the card up into her hand. Delicately so as not to pop open the old, dried glue that held the envelope together, Violet slid the card back in and tucked it into the back of the diary. She shoved the volume back into her nightstand and shut the drawer with a heavy hand. Now she needed to make sure that she herself did not become unglued.

She kicked free of her covers and pushed herself up and out of the bed. There was work to do—work that had nothing to do with her past and her memories of Logan Monroe. Maybe her remembrances of the mute swans had sparked her interest in the newspaper article, but it was a renewed sense of purpose that fueled her desire to inform others of nature's preservation. As soon as she sunk her teeth into the task the better she'd feel, and the further away she could push all thoughts of the wedding week.

After her shower, Violet made a full pot of coffee, toasted an English muffin, and slathered it with her favorite blackberry jam. Her laptop was open at her kitchen counter, her notes stacked in front of her.

Her mind buzzed. Her fingers flew over the

keyboard. The article nearly wrote itself. She was amazed at how quickly and smoothly the words tumbled from her fingers onto the screen. It was as though they were pouring out from her heart and not her head.

She wrote about the importance of keeping the preserved areas, not just for their beauty but for the key they held to the condition of our world. *Birds in their natural habitats are barometers to environmental health,* she wrote. *Learning about birds and their behaviors is not just an awesome observation of nature's beauty; it is a treasure that citizens should rally to maintain.*

By the time Violet had finished her article she felt like she had run another marathon, just not uphill with the bag of bricks this time. This time it felt like she had flown on gossamer wings.

She called Ted. Her words were still up on her computer screen.

"Hey, Terhune."

"Ted, we have to talk."

"Now what?"

"I changed my article and I want you to see it before Monday's meeting. Can I email it to you?"

"Sure, but, it was shaping up pretty good. What'd you change?"

"I just sent it to you. Read it and call me back."

"Hold on, stay on the line, I'll go over it now."

Violet waited. In the silence she scrolled through the article on her screen, her heart filled with anticipation. Finally, she heard his voice "Terhune? You there?"

"What'd you think?" she breathed.

"When did you decide on 'Our Bird Calling: Safeguarding Nature's Elegance?' "

"I saw a newspaper article on how a developer is threatening the marshland in the Rutland area. It got me thinking. Actually, I got really charged up. It made me want to get the word out to people that we can enjoy our countryside, really learn things about our environment, *and* that we are all called to preserve it. So I went back to talk with the guy at the Audubon office, Jake Anders."

After an agonizingly long pause, Ted finally spoke. "I don't know if this magazine's going to appreciate it, Terhune. But, I sure as hell do. And, if these new X-generation execs don't go for it, I'll go with you to the ends of the earth until we find somebody that does."

Tears sprang to her eyes, and a lump lodged itself in her throat. She feebly attempted to swallow it. "Thank you."

"Good job kid. I'll play with the pictures, give you my expert advice on placement and send it back. If this damn computer fails to cooperate with me, I'll call you."

"Thanks for doing this, Ted. It…"

"All right, all right. Come on, you're holding me up. I've got work to do here."

When the call ended, Violet held the phone for a long moment. She startled when the ringtone sounded. She thought it was Ted calling back to say he had been kidding her and that the changes were total crap. She answered breathlessly.

"Why are you breathing like that?"

It was Josephine. Just the sound of her voice dashed Violet's thoughts about her article

"Hi, Ma I, uh, ran for the phone. You okay? Where's Dad?"

"He's here bugging me about bringing me into the City to see you. So when do you want us to come?"

"I'm not bugging her, Violet," Charlie shouted from the background.

"Hush, Charlie, I'm on the phone," Josephine scolded him.

Violet felt her hand release its fervent grasp of the handset. Josephine was acting like her usual self and the relief of that made Violet smile against the mouthpiece.

"I don't know, Ma, let me think. I have a meeting at the office on Friday. I need to get that out of the way first." Violet didn't want to let her mother, or either of her parents for that matter, know how crucial this meeting was. Why give them any added stress? "How's Saturday?"

"Charlie," Josephine called out to her husband. "She says Saturday. Can you take me in on Saturday?"

"What time?"

"I don't know what time. Why? You have a date with Raquel Welch on Saturday?"

"I just wanted to know. You know, in case there's a ballgame on."

"Oh for crying out loud," she said. Josephine spoke into the mouthpiece of the phone, "Saturday's fine. He's worried about the Mets game. Big deal."

"It is a big deal," Charlie called from the background again. "They're playing Philly."

"Oh so what," Josephine answered him. "Charlie, *this* is an emergency."

An emergency? Violet almost laughed into the phone. She enjoyed the familiar bickering between her two parents and had learned these jabs spelled love in their own crazy language. However, Violet needed to nip this three-way conversation now before it went on all day.

"Ma," Violet said. "Ma, listen."

"Your father's being difficult."

"Dad can always watch the game here. I have a TV."

"She says she has a TV you know, you can watch it over her house," Josephine said to Charlie. "And besides, the sooner she learns how to cook the sooner she'll find a husband. Don't you want your other daughter to find happiness?"

Violet sat down on one of the kitchen chairs and propped her elbow on the table, the phone still at her ear. She shook her head when her eyes fell onto her still open laptop. Just when she felt some satisfaction—happiness even—in the quality of her writing and a possible new direction in her career, she remembered that she was her mother's failure in the realm of domesticity. And the spry little woman was determined to fix Violet's flaw.

Josephine and Charlie were coming to her place on Saturday to rectify the situation and there was nothing Violet could do about it. After all, this was a *meatball emergency*.

Chapter Thirty-One

On Friday at quarter-past-noon Violet sat in her cubicle with her microwaved cup of Healthy Choice Chicken Noodle soup steaming her face. She stirred her plastic spoon around in the yellow liquid, periodically scooping a carrot or a chunk of celery into its bowl. It was too hot to eat. *Two minutes in the microwave was too long. One-and-a-half would have been perfect.*

She consulted the clock on her desk. The baseball-sized brass globe of the world with a timepiece wedged into its surface looked like a space alien with sweeping arms had taken over Europe.

It had been a Christmas gift from Martin, the man she had dated on and off for the last five years. She hadn't heard from him in a couple of months, but she was unfazed. He might resurface or he might not. The gift, he had said, was to remind Violet that they had all the time in the world. Well, not today she didn't.

She read and re-read her article, fretted and re-fretted.

It was half an hour until *show time*, and Ted was nowhere in sight. He knew the meeting with Robert Matthews and the golden Melanie Rosen was scheduled for one o'clock.

"Another gourmet lunch I see." Ted peeked his head into the opening of her cubicle. "What'd you do, nuke it too long?"

Violet looked down at her hand. She hadn't realized she was stirring the soup with such a frantic motion. She withdrew the spoon but the soup still moved in a chicken noodle eddy.

"No Ted, it's just nerves. I might be a total wreck."

Ted plopped into her one chrome-framed, brown vinyl guest chair. He held his ratty old briefcase on his lap.

"No, you're not." he said. "Eat your soup, and just relax."

"What if they hate it?"

He looked up at Violet sitting with her spoon frozen at her lips. "This'll wow them. Go in there like a superstar."

She wanted to hug the man, but knew enough not to. They had maintained a comfortable distance over the years. Their mutual affection had become so apparent to her over these past few weeks that she could not stop the tears that brimmed in her eyes.

"You mean it?" she asked.

"You have parsley on your tooth."

Violet smiled at the stoic bear who had stopped fooling her with his façade long ago. After all how many bears named Teddy, as Aunt Marguerite had started calling him, were anything but huggable?

Violet's intercom light flashed on and the string of beeps that followed confirmed that she was being summoned. Ted motioned his head toward the black phone on her desk. "Show time!"

****

Robert Matthews sat in Armani pinstripes at the head of the long glossy mahogany conference table. Melanie Rosen strode in with a long-legged assuredness, making a swift path to the chair at Robert's right. Melanie's assistant, a young Asian girl in dark-framed glasses, sat beside her and proceeded to pull folders out from her leather portfolio. Violet took note of the nod exchanged between Melanie and Robert as she took her seat.

Ted pulled out the chair next to Violet and sat

with a flourish. He reached across the table and grabbed a stainless steel water carafe. He filled a glass half way, slid it over to Violet and leaned in to whisper into her ear. "Pretend it's Grey Goose."

She gave him a grateful look and took a swig.

"Thank you, everyone, for joining me today. This is another important step we take in the rebirth of our magazine. *Today's Hearth* is confident that we are moving in the right direction with competent, dedicated people."

Nods around the table gave Violet the distinct feeling she was in a roomful of bobble-head dolls. She recognized most of them: Terrance Osborne, the CFO; Allen Davies, marketing guru, with his gung-ho team; Henry Shepherd, the newly-hired head of the Art Department; and his assistant, Claudia, an ever-zealous marionette.

Violet straightened in her chair and wet her lips. She passed out the packets she had prepared, sliding them along the smooth table's surface. Robert and Melanie immediately opened the cover page and dug into her work.

She watched as Robert read her story. She didn't know his body language, hadn't spent enough time in his company. His mouth was turned down at both corners nearly forming a lower case "n" and his lower lip protruded forward, pink and wet. He was either in deep concentration or he needed a Tums to quell a pocket of gas. Violet took a deep breath in an attempt to loosen the mortar that had taken residence in her lungs.

Melanie's assistant got up from her chair and personally handed each attendee a copy of Melanie's piece like a good little paper monitor chosen by a discerning teacher. The only noise heard during the silent reading was the rustling of pages as they turned.

Violet periodically shared a glance with Ted as

they read Melanie's article, titled *Rejuvenation in Our Midst*. Violet had to admit that the piece was good. Not just good, it was clever, succinct and a perfect depiction of what Robert's projected target audience would buy hook, line, and sinker. If this were a baseball diamond and not a conference table, Violet knew this would be a homerun.

Finally, Robert lifted his gaze. He looked to Melanie and offered a wide smile. He turned toward Violet and gave her the same. Violet made a mental note never to play poker with this guy.

"Violet, let's start with your article." Everyone placed Violet's piece in front of themselves, holding open the covers, as though ready to read along.

"You've done an extensive job here, Violet, and I commend your effort," Robert said. From his bland smile Violet was getting the message that her idea meant nothing to him.

"It's relevant and interesting," Melanie offered, surprising Violet.

"My problem is that I don't feel this is in line with the pulse of *Today's Hearth*. If we were, I don't know, *Today's Earth*, perhaps. But..." Robert let his words trail off, letting everyone around the table end the sentence for themselves.

Violet knew exactly what this meant. This was what Ted Solomon would have said was "Close, but no cigar."

"Robert," Ted spoke up. "I've been in this business a long time. Your target audience is much savvier than when *Today's Hearth* first came on the scene. We all know that. People like to think they're contributing to the good of the land—that kind of thing. Violet's article pulls the reader into enjoying nature, which is just what your *pulse* aims for, but with an individual's conscience in mind. Your readership will eat it with a spoon, and a recyclable spoon, at that."

Robert kept his head tilted at an angle that indicated he measured Ted's words with care. Without response, however, he turned to Melanie Rosen, sitting pert and straight in her chair.

"Melanie, congratulations. I feel what you have presented is the exact embodiment of the new *Today's Hearth*. It's smart, it's sexy, and it gives the greater yuppie majority perfect direction for their time for pleasure, to say nothing about where to spend their fun money."

"Thank you," Melanie said. Her face, with all its smooth youthfulness, was a beacon of glory.

Robert turned back to Violet. His hands came up onto the table and clasped in front of him. He tapped his fused hands lightly making it appear as though what he would say was going to be tough. Violet sensed it was more for effect rather than sincerity. To her, Robert Matthews was suddenly turning into a cardboard cutout.

"Violet, you are a talented asset to this magazine. I am sure that we will continue to benefit from your contributions, but this article does not meet our needs. I have decided that Melanie will take the lead on all features as new head of the department. It makes sense, I'm sure you'll agree."

Violet, although she saw this coming from the moment the man opened his mouth, was speechless. Her lips parted but she remained mute. At her side, Ted leaned forward in his chair, poised and ready for further debate.

It was that gesture that jumpstarted Violet's vocal chords. She reached to Ted and put her hand on his arm. She gave her head a nearly indiscernible yet emphatic shake. Ted got the message and sat back, remaining quiet.

"Thank you, Robert," Violet said. "I'd like nothing more than to be a contributor to *Today's Hearth*. And, as I'm sure *you'll agree*, I will continue to pursue avenues where work such as this will be welcomed. Will that be a problem?"

"Well—" Robert began.

Melanie interrupted him with a lift of her delicate hand. "Robert, may I?"

A grin broke out over his face as though he were a piano teacher and his protégé was about to play a concerto. "Yes, please. As the new Feature Editor, please, the floor is yours."

Melanie leaned forward in her chair. "Violet, I'm not totally in agreement with Robert on this. I think your article does have a place in our magazine and I agree wholeheartedly that our target audience *is* developing a green consciousness. I'd like to use your piece as an adjunct to my centerfold. How do you feel about that?"

Robert sat back in his chair, folding his arms over his chest. It appeared to Violet that the man had not seen this coming, nor had she. Violet knew an olive branch when she saw one extended her way, and she also knew a golden opportunity.

"Thank you, Melanie, I'd be more than happy to work with you on this. For future projects, how do you feel about my outsourcing? I'm thinking that I could be a regular contributor to *Today's Hearth* while testing other waters."

"What other projects are you considering? Any ideas?"

"Well," Violet said, turning to Ted with a flash of anticipation in her indigo eyes. "I've been thinking lately about the importance of family traditions and keeping them alive from one generation to the next. I thought I'd do a piece on that subject."

"Sounds ideal for our Christmas issue," Melanie said, looking toward Robert. "I think Violet's onto something here. I feel our new magazine format definitely seeks to encourage preservation of all kinds, be it the world around us or the worlds within our own homes."

Robert Matthews continued to smile, but its fraudulent curve had begun to wane. *Perhaps,* Violet thought, *it was because his newly-named Feature Editor was stealing his thunder.*

Silence blanketed the room, but Violet could almost hear the wheels turning in everyone's heads. For her, the wheels were spinning with anticipation of writing from her heart. Maybe she would include her experiences in the upcoming cooking lesson with her mother, if she wanted a little comic relief in her story. Surely tomorrow's event would prove to be laughable. A flock of ideas flew around her brain.

"Robert..." Melanie said.

Robert had unfolded his arms and had placed his hands on the tabletop in front of him. "I'm listening, Melanie," he said.

"I'd like for Violet to be happy enough with her creative license at *Today's Hearth* so that she won't want to pursue other venues. What steps do we need to take to make this happen?"

"I have every confidence in your vision, Melanie," he said, with his meaningless smile plastered back onto his face. "We can work on the details when we finalize both your contracts. I trust your instincts. That's why I named you head of the department."

"Violet," Melanie said, turning toward her. "You in?"

"Melanie, thank you. And congratulations, I think you'll be a great department leader. I'd like to make an appointment with you to discuss our ideas."

Violet gathered her papers and tucked them into her portfolio. She zippered it closed, and looked over to the silent Robert Matthews. She gave a try at her own plastered grin; one that she hoped said nothing *and everything* in its Mona Lisa ambiguity. Her heart danced in her chest as she stood. Ted rose from his chair as well.

"I'll have Coral email you with a meeting time so we can continue this and work on the spread for the issue."

"Thank you, I look forward to it." Violet extended her hand over the width of the table to shake Melanie's. Her handshake was firm, assured, and genuine. Violet shook Robert Matthew's hand and then exchanged a nod with Melanie's assistant, Coral.

Ted thanked everyone as he pushed in their chairs. Violet could tell by his tone that the man was just shy of slapping his own knee and laughing out loud.

Outside the conference room, Ted hooked his arm into Violet's and steered her away from the direction of her cubicle. "Come on, Terhune. This calls for a martini at Durkins."

"Ted, it's not even three o'clock."

"It's five o'clock somewhere, kid. Besides, I need to toast that look that on Dapper Dan's mug. That was priceless."

****

Apparently, Violet and Ted were not the only two people in the city with the notion that an early Happy Hour was a good idea. Durkins was crowded with the business set, a sea of Brooks Brothers suits and career separates from Ann Taylor's Loft.

Ted made his way across the room, pushing Violet ahead of him as though she was in a boat and Ted was the rudder. "Today's luck just doesn't end," Ted said, remarking on finding available seats at the coveted bar. "Maybe we should go to the track."

"What can I get you two?" Kevin, the bartender, placed two compressed cardboard coasters in front of them. "This is early for you guys, isn't it?"

"Yes it is," Ted said. "We're celebrating."

"Great I'm in. What are we celebrating?"

Violet turned to Ted with a question in her eyes. What words explained what had just happened? Emancipation came to her mind. She'd lost the title of Head of the Feature Department, but in the process had gained a chance to try new things—things that gave her a sense of renewal. Is that what they were drinking to? Renewal?

"We're celebrating life," Violet said suddenly. "And how it takes some of us a while to figure out what we're doing with it."

"Well, that's definitely worth celebrating," Kevin said. "First round's on me."

Violet sipped her martini, and even ate one of the olives off the toothpick, something she didn't usually do. Ted drew in a long sip of beer. Before the drinks arrived, he had ordered a burger for the two of them to share with *extra crispy* fries. Kevin placed paper placemats in front of them and stuck a bottle of catsup on the counter.

"That's a good way to put it, Terhune. Celebrating life. Good for you."

"Not just me, though, Ted. You, too. You're doing the same thing. You're going out on your own. You're taking that camera of yours and hitting the horizons."

"True. By the way, we're going to Island Beach State Park next weekend. We're taking a tour of the natural preserve and I'm hoping to get a shot of some wildlife, ospreys if I'm lucky. And, the Barnegat Lighthouse, of course."

"And, by 'we' I'm assuming you are referring to my Aunt Marguerite as your travelling companion."

Ted gave her his roguish grin and shrugged a shoulder, a gesture that Violet knew meant, "Yeah, so what?"

Just then Kevin brought their food, already separated onto two white ceramic dishes. "Eat your burger," Ted said, changing the subject.

"I had lunch, remember?"

"All you had was soup, for crying out loud, Terhune. If you're going to go out there and conquer the world you're going to need a little meat on those bones."

"You're talking like an uncle. Uncle Teddy," Violet said, teasing and trying the name on for size.

Ted waved a french fry at her. "I think that deserves another round, and you're paying."

"No second martini for me, Ted. Can't do it."

"Why not?"

Violet picked up her half of the burger and took a bite. She dreaded the reality of what she was about to say. It suddenly occurred to her that if they were celebrating life then she had to celebrate *all of it*, even tomorrow's cooking lesson with the legendary guru of Italian meatballs and tomato sauce.

"I have to go food shopping for tomorrow. My mother is coming to my place to teach me how to make her famous meatballs and sauce."

Ted gave out a guffaw and slapped his knee the way Violet knew he had wanted to do in the conference room when Melanie had stunned Robert into silence. She couldn't help but chuckle, too. After all, this would be nothing, if not a joke.

Chapter Thirty-Two

Saturday morning Violet was as ready as she'd ever be. She had purchased all the food items her mother had told her to get.

Because her kitchen lacked many of the staples that Josephine kept on hand—things like oregano, basil, and tomato paste—the grocery bill had been a small fortune. She hoped what she created with the ingredients would at least be salvageable. It would be a shame to have to toss it, but she didn't have high hopes for her efforts.

When the doorbell rang, Violet consulted the clock above her kitchen sink. It was too early, her parents were supposed to arrive at noon. That Josephine was compelled to get this party started two hours early only added to Violet's apprehension.

Does Mom really think she needs two extra hours to train me in the art of cooking? Is she that desperate to give me what she believes are the tools necessary to snare a husband? Wouldn't it be easier for her to go to a witch's den and conjure a spell in her cauldron?

Violet slid from the counter stool and padded to the front door, taking a deep breath. She exhaled and opened the door.

Jessica Monroe stood looking wary. The red rims of her crystal blue eyes indicated to Violet that she had been crying.

"Jessica," Violet said, the name breathed out like the exhale of smoke from a drag of a cigarette.

"I should have called, I know," the girl said, averting her troubled eyes.

"Come in," Violet said. She stepped aside for Jessica to enter. The girl looked around briefly, her eyes darting around the living room as though checking to make sure the two were alone.

"Am I interrupting anything?"

"Not at all. Can I get you something? A cup of tea, maybe?"

"No, that's okay. I'm sorry to just show up like this."

"Come on, let's go into the kitchen. Have a seat and I'll make us some tea." Violet motioned to a stool and Jessica sat on it, raking her fingers through her long silky locks.

Violet filled the kettle—a gift from her mother—set it on the stove, and turned the flame up high. She had decided just this morning to dig it out of the closet and give it a new home on her stove's burner.

Searching a cupboard for something to serve, she found a bag of plain vanilla cookies. She put a few of them on a salad plate, carried it over to the small island, and then sat opposite Jessica.

"You know the truth about my mother, don't you, Violet?"

Her heart stalled in her chest, but there was no sense it pretending she didn't understand the words. "Yes."

"And I know about you now, too."

"Me?"

"Well..." Jessica smiled now, which only confused Violet more. "I know that it was you my father was wrapped around up at the lake that night."

"Jess, I..."

"It's okay." She put up a hand. "Really, I'm not mad or anything. Not anymore. That's what I came here to tell you."

The kettle whistled. Violet was glad for the chance to take her eyes off the girl, happy for a moment to breathe. She poured the hot water into two tea-bagged mugs, returned to the kitchen island, and offered one to Jessica.

"Thanks," Jessica said and began to dip the bag up and down in the cup.

"Have a cookie," Violet said, reaching to the plate and retrieving one for herself. She bit into it thinking with any luck maybe Josephine had been right all these years. Perhaps food might solve everything.

"I confronted my father regarding the rumors buzzing around about him and some guest at the lodge. I was already pissed at him for lying to me all this time about my mother. And then the thought of him out there in the moonlight having a grand old time made me really nuts."

Violet nodded and took a sip of her tea to loosen the clench of her jaw. "I'm sorry, Jessica.

"Do you take sugar or milk?"

The girl shook her head then continued. "Turns out it was the best thing I could have done. We talked it out. He told me that it was you by the lake. And, he told me all about what you two had meant to each other."

Violet was speechless. She made an effort to pull off a Mona Lisa smile—not likely to happen when there was mention of her and Logan Monroe. Jessica reached, grabbed a cookie, and took a generous bite. Her stance loosened. She offered a small smile.

"It's crazy. You think you know someone. Then you find out there's so much you don't know."

"Yes." Violet breathed. She had managed a word. *One down...*

"I'm not just talking about my birth mother. I'm talking about my dad. I always thought he *loved* running The Pines." Jessica laughed then.

"He's got this sign that he keeps in his office. He told me he made it when he was a kid. I always thought it meant 'I love Vermont.' Well, now I know that it means 'I love Violet Terhune.'"

"He still has it?" Violet asked, too shocked to hide her reaction.

Jessica nodded, her eyes smiling as she sipped her tea. "Our talk made me realize that I'm not the only wounded one in this. My dad gave up a lot. And I know you did, too."

Now it was Violet's turn to nod.

"I had no idea the man had wanted to be a writer. I never knew he used to write. Can you believe that? I was totally in the dark."

"I'm glad he told you, Jessica. He did love to write. It was almost all he ever talked about."

"Well, now he is."

"He's writing?"

Jessica put her cup down and folded her arms onto the countertop. "Yes, he's here in New York."

Violet felt the world spin. The floor and ceiling of her little kitchen traded places. What had been up was down, and down up. She placed her hands onto the cool stone surface of the center island, waiting for the dizziness to dissipate. She stared at Jessica, her eyes feeling like saucers in her head.

"He's enrolled himself in a course at the Writing Institute," Jessica continued. "He's subletting a place in the Village."

"Wow!" Violet said. Her mind buzzed as if a family of bumblebees had gone in one ear and couldn't find their way out the other. *Logan's in New York. He's here.*

"He's going to come up to The Pines periodically, of course—but he's trusting me to be in charge."

"I'm sure you've got it in you, Jessica. I've seen the way you operate. You're already running it, really."

Jessica smiled. "I know. It's what I've always wanted. The Pines *is* in my blood."

Violet smiled back at her. Happiness flashed in the girl's blue Topaz eyes.

"Dad and I are in a better place now. I'm not sure what I'm going to do about my mother...whether I'll ever try to locate her. There's plenty of time to mull that idea. There's, you know, no hurry. I want to know for sure before I take a big step like that."

"That sounds like a wise decision, Jessica. I'm so glad that you and your father are on the mend and that he is able now to pursue his writing," Violet said. She then added, "Honestly, it's really nice of you to come here and tell me all this. So, thank you."

"I'm not just here to update you on my life," Jessica said. "I came to tell you something else."

"Okay," Violet said. She didn't know how much more information she could take being on overload already.

"I wanted you to know how to find Dad. I want you to have this..." She withdrew a slip of paper from her jeans pocket and gave it to Violet. On it was written Logan's New York address.

Violet's mouth felt as if it was filled with cotton, packed so tightly that swallowing was impossible. She grabbed her mug of tea and took a tentative sip, forcing the now tepid liquid down her arid throat.

The night that Logan had carved her initials into the wall of the hunter's cabin with the tip of his penknife came to her mind. She saw his hand diligently cutting into the wood, saw his full, sensual mouth pursed as he blew into the crevices ridding them of crumbs from his effort.

Violet met Jessica's gaze. Father and daughter had faced their truths. She knew now was the time for truth. But first Violet had to find her own before she shared it with anyone else. She remained silent.

"My father is a good, honest man who has set aside the desires of his heart because of his love for me." Tears filled the girl's eyes again. She reached up and dabbed at the corners of her eyes with the pad of her index finger. "So, I owe it to him to do these two things—to take care of The Pines and to come here and tell you this: He has never stopped loving you, Violet. His devotion to his family—to me, specifically—is what has kept him away."

Now Violet's eyes filled with tears. Violet knew what devotion to family felt like, even more so these days with her concerns for Josephine. "Thank you, Jessica," she managed.

Jessica stood from her stool and shoved her hands into the pockets of her faded jeans. She gave Violet a little smile. "Well...I have a train to catch."

"Can I give you a ride to the station?"

"No thanks, Violet. I've got to learn how to navigate this city. Looks like I'm going to be visiting here a lot."

Together they walked to the front door. Hesitantly, the two women embraced.

Violet closed her eyes and wondered what she would do with the knowledge she had just received. Would she do anything but store it away in the back of her mind?

She thought of the clock on her desk at the magazine, and the words Martin had said about "having all the time in the world."

Was that true?

Did anyone really have any guarantee about all the time they had? An image of Libby's face crept into her mind.

She couldn't sort through all her thoughts now. Feelings, memories, pain, regret—and yes—longing, swirled inside her like a funnel cloud about to uproot her from her foundation. Violet pulled out of Jessica's embrace.

"Have a good trip home, Jessica. Thank you again for coming."

After her unexpected guest had gone, Violet leaned against the closed door.

She curled her shaking fingers around the little card in her palm.

Chapter Thirty-Three

By the time Charlie and Josephine Terhune arrived at Violet's apartment she had set her counter up with what few utensils she had: a cutting board, knives and mixing bowls. She was grateful for the myriad of preparations, anything to keep her mind busy. Today, anticipating the chef aficionado's appearance, Violet had readied her kitchen enough to rival Rachel Ray's. None of it was enough to keep Logan from her thoughts even as the doorbell rang for the second time that day.

"Well, will you look at this, Charlie?" Josephine carried a grocery bag in her arms and placed it on Violet's countertop. Charlie, trailing behind her, carried a smaller bag. "Little Miss New York means business, don't you think?"

"Ma, what's in the bag? I bought everything you told me to. You didn't need to raid your kitchen."

"Oh, I didn't." Josephine peered into the bag, rummaging around in it, making things clink like a mad scientist. "These are just some of my tools. I didn't know what you'd have around here. I didn't want to take any chances."

Violet screwed her mouth to the side and narrowed her eyes. Well, if nothing else, this event would chase away any thoughts that didn't include garlic and parmesan cheese. For that, she was glad. She turned to her father. "Okay, Daddy-o, what's in your bag?"

"Heineken. What else?"

"No more than two today, Mister," Josephine said. She withdrew items from her paper version of

Mary Poppins' bag of tricks. "You need to drive home."

Violet watched her mother pull an old dented ladle from the bag, examine it with pride, then place it on the counter. Next came a cheese grater—not the fancy kind with the crank that her misguided daughter had purchased from a trendy magazine—this one was a stainless emery board-looking device with a faded red-lacquered handle. Violet felt like she was watching a doctor prepare for surgery.

"Ma, I have all this stuff. You didn't have to do this."

"How was I supposed to know what you have? I know to come to you if I need to use a computer or a blueberry…"

"Blackberry."

"Blackberry, whatever. You know what I mean. But, kitchen necessities? I had my doubts."

Charlie stuck his six-pack in the refrigerator and saluted the two women that stood on either side of the little square island in the center of the room.

Violet suddenly had an image of two gunfighters in an old western ready for the sheriff to give the go-ahead to duel. The sheriff had just put his beer on ice and was exiting the room before he got caught in the crossfire.

"Chicken," Violet called after her father. She heard him chuckle as he snapped on her TV.

Josephine examined the food items that Violet had carefully lined up on the counter. She lifted the cans of tomatoes, the bottle of olive oil, and all the other ingredients ready for use. By the look on her mother's face, Violet could tell she had done a good job in making her purchases.

"Okay, Violet, let's get started. Is this the pot we're going to use for the sauce?" Josephine asked, stepping over to the cook top and putting her hand to the pot's handle. She lifted its lid.

"Yes, why?"

"It's kind of small, don't you think?"

"It's the biggest one I have, Ma."

Josephine shrugged. She gave her head a little shake that appeared laced with pity, as if Violet couldn't help her inadequacy.

Is a woman measured by the size of her sauce pot?

The two women stood side-by-side and mixed the meatballs as Josephine directed. Violet's hands were in the gooey mixture because Josephine said she needed to "feel" the consistency.

"See that? It's too loose. You need to add some more bread crumbs."

"Okay, how much?"

"*How much*," Josephine said with a snort. "Shake some in and let's see."

So, Violet shook the cylindrical cardboard container over the meat, dusting it with crumbs. She then submerged her fingers again and worked the breadcrumbs into the mixture.

"How's it feel now?"

"Disgusting," Violet said, hating the pulpy feel on her hands.

"Does it feel too wet? Too dry?"

"Ma, honestly, I don't know. You feel."

"Violet, you're the one that has to know. What have I always told you and your sister? When you cook you have to know in here—" Josephine tapped her temple with her index finger. Then she touched it to the center of her chest. "—But you also have to know in here. It's like anything you love. What your head says is important, but what your heart says is the trick."

Violet looked down at her fingers in the bowl, covered with red gloppy meat mixture. What came to her mind and what throbbed in her heart had nothing to do with Josephine's theory on preparing food.

Josephine came back from washing her hands at the sink and stuck one hand into the bowl. She fiddled around, touching Violet's fingers as she tested the preparation.

"It's just right, Violet. Take a good feel. See? Not too sticky, not too dry. Remember the way this feels."

Violet would remember. But it was not just the appropriate consistency of this bowl of goo that would lodge into her memory. She would remember Josephine and her happy eyes at the sight of it.

"Come on. Now we have to form them." Josephine pulled a hunk into her palms, rubbing around and around.

"You know, Ma. I have an ice cream scoop. What if I use that to make them? Wouldn't that save time?"

Josephine's hands stopped their movement. "Are you kidding me? You use your hands. No scoop."

Violet sighed, tugged a glob of meat into her hands, and rolled it around between her palms. When she was done with it she noticed her mother had already lined four perfectly matched spheres onto the cookie sheet, all the same neat size. Violet's attempt was the size of a baseball.

"You going bowling?"

"Too big?" Violet asked, holding the red ball in her hand.

"Unless you're feeding King Kong," Josephine said. She took the ball from Violet's hand, ripped a wad off, and tossed the remaining lump back into the bowl. She reformed the ball to match the proper size of her creations. "Like this." Josephine held it like a prize. "You see? Now come on, do it."

When the trays were full they slid them into the oven to bake, Violet was glad to be done with having to mess with the sticky mass.

"I used to fry my meatballs, but they're too fattening. The doctor said your father's cholesterol has to come down or else they're putting him on medication. Over my dead body will a husband of mine have to take pills. Huh! I can fix him with the right food."

"Yeah, Ma. I know. Food is life."

Charlie appeared in the room and went to the refrigerator to retrieve another beer.

"You have anything to snack on, Violet?"

"Pretzels." Violet went over to a cabinet and opened the door. She pulled a bag of her father's favorite pretzel rods from a shelf. The look on his face said she had pleased him. His little smile warmed her. Violet walked with her father to the doorway of the living room, leaned in kissing the side of his head near his temple, and whispered softly. "How's Ma doing?"

"She's got a doctor's appointment on Tuesday. I'll let you know what they say."

"Can I come?"

His eyes showed surprise, then knowing. "Sure, honey."

"Don't leave today without giving me the info."

"Sure."

"Any new episodes?"

"Last night she got up in the middle of the night and put her clothes on. I heard her rummaging in the kitchen for all that stuff she brought with her today. She thought it was daytime."

"Oh boy," Violet said. Her heart sunk like a stone.

"Sometimes she gets her days and nights a little mixed up," Charlie said, sadness appearing in his deep blue eyes. She knew his sadness like she knew her own. She kissed his temple again.

"Her episodes at The Pines really threw me."

"I know, but at least nothing bad happened."

The man shrugged. "I mean, we found her when she got lost. But, don't worry, my girl. We'll get to the bottom of this."

"I know, Dad,"

"Hey," Josephine called from the stove. "We need to start the sauce. Come on. Pay attention."

She gave her father a quick hug, feeling his warm cheek against hers. They would get through this, *all of them*. But, right now, she had a task to learn and memorize. Josephine's tone told Violet that her teacher was losing patience.

The pupil watched as Professor Josephine added olive oil to the bottom of the sauce pan, sans measurement. She lifted the pot by its handles and swirled the thick liquid around, coating the bottom. Violet watched her mother's eyes. The dark orbs emitted wisdom for her craft. There was assuredness in her movements, strength in her hands. This little tiger *had* to be okay. Violet felt a pull in her chest.

"So, how do you know how much oil to put in, Ma? I mean, you just pour it in and make sure it covers the bottom?"

"Now you're getting it," she said. "Open the cans of tomatoes."

Violet squeezed the handle of the can opener and turned the knob as its blade cut into the first tin.

"He's a good man."

"What?" Violet looked up from her little project.

"Your father," Josephine said.

Violet just looked at her mother, not knowing where this came from or where it was going.

"He's a pain in the ass most of the time—don't get me wrong," Josephine added, looking away from Violet's glance. "He plays that Irish music of his too loud and he sneaks Twinkies when he's not supposed to. But you know...I'll keep him."

"I think that's a good idea, Ma."

"You know, I knew it from the beginning. Some things you just know, like I was saying before. There's not too much difference between loving what you make and loving a man."

Violet felt her throat tightened. This was not a good time to hear about "loving a man." She put greater effort into her twisting action of the can opener's knob. The can separated from the opener's hold and tipped away. Crushed plum tomatoes spilled onto the counter.

"Oh, boy, now look what I've done," Violet said. Flustered, she wished there was something she could do to banish the feeling. Her mother was her usual sharp observer today, and Violet did not want the woman to sense that she was experiencing anything beyond kitchen clumsiness. Violet grabbed a fistful of paper towels and mopped up the spill.

"I had a phone call this morning," Josephine said, her tone casual. Violet was not fooled. The cock of her mother's curly gray head said a bomb was coming.

"Who called?"

"Jessica Monroe from The Pines," Josephine said.

"Wh...why did she call you?"

"Because she wanted your address. She only had *our* information from the reservation at The Pines. She called to ask how to get in touch with you."

"Oh," Violet said flatly. She tossed the soiled paper towels into the garbage, and then turned to the sink to rinse her hands. When she reached for the dishtowel she saw that Josephine had it in her hand, extended toward her. Violet took it.

"Is everything okay with you?" Josephine asked.

"Yes," Violet said, walking over to the oven and snapping on its interior light. "How do we know when they're done?"

"Sometimes the only way to know is to test one.

Take a fork and split it open, see for yourself."

"Should we do that now?"

"Yes, do it now."

Josephine did not bring up the subject of Jessica again. The two worked cutting onions and garlic and continued in their quest to have one Terhune woman teach the other.

Finally, while their aromatic masterpiece simmered on the stove, Violet and Josephine sat at the center island. Violet got up and pulled a half bottle of cold chardonnay from the refrigerator.

"Booze during the day?" Josephine asked.

"Ma, it's almost four o'clock. Besides we worked hard, we deserve it."

"You city people."

Violet poured the golden liquid into two wine glasses she retrieved from a cabinet. She cut up a chunk of Colby cheese, then arranged it on a plate with some wheat crackers.

Violet lifted her glass. "To my first attempt at your famous sauce and meatballs. Thanks, Ma."

Josephine clinked her glass against Violet's and took a sip of her wine. She nodded approval. "You did good."

"Well, it sure smells good," Violet said.

"So, did she come here about her father?"

The unexpected question startled Violet. She thought she had gotten away with leaving that subject alone. She should have known better. This woman was not about keeping quiet, and notorious for going after an answer. As annoying as that fact had been over the years, suddenly the threat of her mother's *keen knowing* beginning to diminish made Violet want to savor it.

"Yes."

"What about him?"

"I don't know, Ma. It's a long story, I guess," Violet said with a sigh. There was no way to begin, especially since she hadn't allowed herself time to process what Jessica had said to her.

"I wondered how it would be when you two saw each other again. Even though so much time has gone by. I know how it used to be for you and him. That's no secret."

"It was a long time ago, Ma. So long ago."

"Look, Violet. I'm going to tell you something and I'm only going to say it once. So, listen. Okay?"

"I'm listening," Violet said, taking an extra large sip of her chardonnay.

"You said 'food is life' before. It's true, that's how I feel. Food *is* life. But, more important than that is *life is food*. You understand? Life is the food that cures the hunger inside you. You've been so busy with your career, and whatnot, you've forgotten that you're starving."

Violet blinked her eyes against the sting of tears that itched to fill her eyes. Josephine reached across the table and touched her hand to her eldest daughter's fingertips. "When are you going to take a big bite out of life? Huh? When?"

"I—" Violet began.

Just then Charlie Terhune came into the room, a welcome relief to the heaviness that hung in the air over their heads. Luckily, the man appeared too happy to notice.

"They're killing them," he said. "It's the bottom of the ninth."

"Go Mets!" Violet said, forcing some enthusiasm.

"Boy it sure smells good in here," Charlie said. "When do we eat?"

Violet slid off her stool and headed toward the stove. She stirred her concoction, savoring the rich, pungent sauce.

"I got torpedo rolls from the Italian bakery down the block," Violet said.

"Yeah," Charlie said. "I could go for a meatball

sub."

Soon the three Terhunes indulged in sandwiches brimming with meatballs that tasted amazingly good, drenched in sauce that was close enough to her mother's fare to rival it.

"Ma, this is so good, I can't believe it."

"See? Look what you can do if you put your mind to it."

"Yeah, well, let's see how I do next time I try, when you're not with me."

"Ah," Josephine said with a wave of her hand. "You're a pro now."

Violet smiled, her mouth closing over a big bite of her sandwich. She would always remember this day. The familiar and comforting aroma filled the air of her kitchen for the first time. Lingering here was the magnificent scent borrowed from its master creator. She would remember that from now on it belonged to her, too.

When her parents were leaving Violet gave her father a hug and then turned to her mother. "Thanks, again, Ma. We did it."

"Wasn't so hard, right?"

"Not when you're taught by the master."

"Remember what I told you, Violet," Josephine said, pointing first to her temple then to her heart. "Don't forget."

"I won't, Ma."

"Make sure you're not hungry."

"Hungry?" Charlie asked. "How could she be hungry? She just ate a huge meatball sub."

"She knows what I mean," Josephine said, nodding at Violet. "And, one more thing."

"Okay, Ma."

"No ice cream scooper. You use your hands. You got that?"

Violet laughed. "Got it."

Violet pulled her mother into her arms and gave

her a tender squeeze. She smelled of oregano and basil. Or was it Violet, herself, that carried the scent?

After they left, Violet checked the pot on the stove, placing her palm along the side. It was still warm. She would wait a little longer for it to cool enough to divide it into smaller portions for freezing in plastic containers. She would have food for a week.

She poured the rest of the wine into her glass and went into the living room. The television was still on from when her father had watched the game. She sat down. A couple of guys at a desk bantered back and forth about the teams. Violet picked up the remote and hit the off button, and the screen went black.

With nothing in her hands to stir or cut or chop or mix, her mind did all those things with the fragments of what had transpired since her waking this morning.

She relived Jessica's visit. The girl had been pained when she arrived. Violet had been surprised to learn that Jessica's distress was for her father's regrets and what she perceived as her part in them. She was a good kid and she loved Logan very much. Violet could see that.

Next Violet stirred around the thought that Logan was in New York. She all but floated into her bedroom unable to stop her hell-bent urge to read the last entry in her diary.

****

May 26, 1984
Dear Diary,

This is it, Diary. The end of the road for you and me. I haven't touched you in so long I almost forgot you were shoved in the back of my closet with my high school yearbooks. After today, I'm going to put you in the attic and, with any luck, forget about you—no offense. You'll be a 'closed book' for more reasons than one.

I just graduated from Montclair State with my BA.

My parents hosted a little backyard barbecue in my honor yesterday afternoon. My Aunt Marguerite and Uncle Bob came, as well as a few of my friends, Libby of course. Paul was there. I'm not sure how I feel about Paul so I just take it day-by-day. Penny and her insufferable best friend, Corinne, were in attendance, blasting their music. If I hear the Thriller album one more time I might have to hit somebody.

Libby graduated from Farleigh Dickinson and has a job as an assistant manager for a marketing research firm in Florham Park. She's ready to jump right into her life. Me? Not so sure. I know I want to write. I want to write things that matter, things that have a purpose, things that offer hope or encouragement in some small way.

I have an appointment with a head hunter next week in the city. That's what I know I want—to live in New York, eventually anyway. For now, if I get a job there, I'll commute until I can afford a place.

Tonight Libby and I had our own celebration. Since the New Year we've been planning on how to celebrate our graduations. We thought about going to L.A. and seeing some of the Olympic Games. We thought of going to New Orleans to see the World's Fair. But, Libby has a job already and it just isn't feasible. So, what did we do? We went to see Indiana Jones and the Temple of Doom then went to Rod's Ranch House for a great dinner. We sat in one of the train cars and drank a whole bottle of wine. Then we went into the lounge and listened to the piano player and sipped coffee until we felt our buzz subside.

It was then that the subject of Logan came up and that is why I'm writing this now. I figure it's a fine last chapter in this diary. Because, I began the first page with Logan Monroe and now I will put his name to rest once and for all.

Libby started it. She had more wine in her than I and that meant she'd be talkative. Chardonnay is truth serum to that girl.

"So, let's talk about you and Paul," she said, her voice thick like her tongue was swollen.

"Let's not," I said.

"You're not into him at all, are you?"

"I don't know," I shrugged, tracing the rim of my cup with my index finger, round and round.

"If you were, you'd know it."

"Then I guess I'm not."

Libby made that grimace, the one that contorts her face like a sudden whiff of dirty socks meeting her nostrils.

"Violet, you know I love you," she said. "I'm not harping. You've got your mother for that." We both laughed then. It's no surprise that good old Josephine is always looking to have me settled with a guy, a nice rock on my left hand, a big fat wedding for her to plan.

"Libby, I know where this is going. If you say his name I'm going to jump up on the piano and dance like a freak just to embarrass you. Is that what you want?"

She gave me one of her sly sloe-eyed looks, challenge in its shininess, like firelight. She said his name slowly, savored each letter like they were chocolates on her tongue.

"Logan Monroe."

I looked up at the ceiling over the bar, closed my eyes. "You're lucky I'm too tired to dance or I'd jump on that baby grand and make a scene," I said.

The man at the keyboard, as though in cahoots with my dearest friend started to play Lionel Richie's latest tune, "Hello." The lyrics swirled in the air, then *wrapped themselves around my torso like vines choking a tree.*

"You need to love again, really love," Libby said. "That mushy, lovey-dovey way you felt about Logan."

I shook my head, giving up the pretense of thinking this conversation would cease. So, I let the words that were trapped in my heart break free and I uttered them.

"I don't think I'll ever love anyone the way I loved Logan," I said. "I do hope to love again, Libby, so don't worry. It just won't be the same as Logan."

"When the time comes you better promise to go for it."

"Okay, okay."

"Hey," Libby said, raising her coffee cup to initiate a toast. "Always keep your alma mater's motto in the back of your mind."

The words of Montclair State's motto, carved in stone near the school's library, now were etched in my head. "Carpe Diem." Seize the day.

Good bye, Diary...It is time for me to seize the day...

Chapter Thirty-Four

The apartment was a walk-up in the meat packing district on Fourteenth. Violet reached the door, her hands tightly gripping the plastic container she held. The meatballs and sauce were still warm. She stood staring at the little black doorbell affixed to the molding.

The thought occurred to her that it all came down to that little button, seemingly so innocent in its place on the well-painted white door jam. *Push or not? Stay or go?*

Just then the door opened and a young woman appeared, wide-eyed, startled to see Violet standing on the flagstone landing. The woman recovered, offered a benign smile, and allowed Violet to enter the building as though she belonged. Violet slipped into the semi-dark vestibule.

Apartment six was upstairs. Violet climbed the long flight, a hand gliding along the smooth surface of the varnished mahogany banister. At the top of the flight, number six was directly in front of her. From within its depths Violet could hear soft music, something with brass and violins. That was definitely Logan. She remembered that he loved jazz.

A brass knocker was set at the center of the dark maroon door. Her alma mater's motto thundered in her chest. She lifted the bar gingerly with two fingers then pressed it firmly onto its base. The knock was loud enough for him to hear over the music playing. Logan's voice called out a casual, "Coming."

The door swung open. In his half-buttoned, pinstriped Oxford with the sleeves rolled up to the elbow, he stood there wide-eyed, mouth agape. His jeans hung on his hips, beltless. She could not keep her gaze off him.

His eyes were a kaleidoscope of feelings she tried to read—shock, surprise, sad, happy, wary. All of them flashing at her, all of them soaring to her heart.

"How?" he asked, frozen like a doorman statue. "How did you know?"

"Jessica," Violet said with a shy smile.

"Well, come in, come in." He stepped aside, raking a hand through his messy, yet attractive locks. "I was expecting a delivery. Pizza."

Violet wet her lips. She entered the apartment and Logan closed the door behind her. The place was small, but filled with charm. The wall on the right side of the living room was made of old, quaint bricks. The floors were hardwood, stained dark. As they walked, their footsteps echoed.

"Watch out for the boxes," Logan said, sidestepping a cardboard carton in the center of the room. It was filled with books. "I'm still unpacking."

Violet didn't move. She looked down at the small plastic container in her hands. On impulse, she thrust it toward Logan. "I brought you some, um, meatballs and sauce. Homemade. You know, in case you're hungry."

Logan took the container from her, their fingers touching. Violet could see Logan's chest rise with a deep breath.

"Wow," he said, exhaling with a little laugh. "You cook?"

She laughed, too. The man remembered many things about her and her inability to cook, apparently, was one of them.

"It's never too late to learn, I guess," she said.

Their eyes locked.

"Well, I'm impressed."

"I had a cooking lesson from my mother today."

"Hey, how is your mom?"

Violet shrugged a shoulder, felt emotion building inside her like a volcano that rumbled below its rocky surface.

"She's got a doctor's appointment this coming week. Hopefully, we'll get some answers. She's scared us a couple of times."

"Yeah," Logan said, his voice smooth and soothing like a sip of brandy. "I, uh, I hope she'll be okay." He placed the plastic container in the refrigerator. He shoved his hands into the pockets of his jeans revealing a glimpse of his plaid boxers along the denim waistband.

"Logan," Violet said softly. It was time to say what she came to tell him. She had come this far and there was no stopping, not anymore. Truth, and feelings, and hope, bubbled up from her depths, spilling out in the form of tears in her eyes. "I…"

Logan swiftly pulled his hands from his pockets and pulled her to him. He held her tight, as tightly as she held him. He smelled of pine like the backdrop to their past, and he smelled of cinnamon from the lit candle on the glass coffee table of his new home, his new life.

"Logan," Violet began again, pulling from his embrace, needing to look into his eyes. "I wanted to tell you that, the night of the wedding, I was coming to meet you."

"You were?"

"I didn't stand you up. My mother needed me, she was confused again. I had no choice. But, I was going to come. I was."

Tears glistened in Logan's eyes. Behind the tears was a look of tenderness and gladness. He smiled, gifting her with his dimple. He touched his finger to her mouth, catching an errant tear that had made its way to her upper lip.

"It doesn't matter, Violet," he said. "You're here now."

A word about the author...

M. Kate Quinn draws on her quirky sense of humor, hopelessly romantic nature, highly developed sense of family and friendship, and her love for a good story while writing her novels. She is particularly proud of her Perennials Series that began with *Summer Iris* (released by The Wild Rose Press in July, 2010) and the heroines that she says possess the same hopes, fears, and ultimately the courage that lives in all of us.

Ms. Quinn, a life-long native of New Jersey, makes her home near the beach in Ocean County. She and her husband (the man she attributes to her belief in soul mates) have a combined total of six—yes, that's six—children and two beautiful granddaughters. The king of their castle is a magnificent, apricot-colored Siberian cat named Sammy.

CPSIA information can be obtained
at www.ICGtesting.com
Printed in the USA
BVHW041247271221
624890BV00018B/152

9 781601 548900